Tasty Love

TN Jones

Urban Divergent Pen
TN JONES

Acknowledgment

First, thanks most definitely go to my Pretty Prin; you mean the world to me. Without you, I wouldn't be anything. Mommy loves you, yes, I do!

Second, to Big Jones.

Third, to Mona.

Fourth, to my lovely readers and supporters.

Dear Gorgeous Reader,

This standalone novel includes possible triggers.
- A grieving mother
- Mention of death
- Husband abandonment
- Infidelity
- Vulgar language
- Explicit sex scenes

I apologize if I've created something within this story that triggered you. I have no intention of causing any past hurts to return.

TN Jones

Chapter I
Solomon "Hussein" Hampton

"Every great love starts with a story."-Nicholas Sparks, The Notebook

Saturday, July 4, 2015

I came from a loving two-parent household. My parents came from a loving two-parent home. Love and marriage were essential to me, and they always would be. I adored my parents, grandparents, and brothers' relationships.

Every time I saw them, they showed me why love and marriage would go together. One had to be willing to give their spouse utter happiness, honesty, respect, time, openness, excellent communication, including listening, and be ready to compromise.

Among those small factors, more elements contributed to a sacred union to produce and maintain a healthy marriage, which many people didn't know or simply didn't give a damn about. A healthy marriage wasn't about paying the mortgage and bills, maintaining the house and the property, or monetary gains. Marriage meant unconditionally loving and constantly needing to be with the one person who made you a better person.

Love and marriage didn't mean much to some men but meant the world to me. In my eyes, love was the most splendid thing to feel and experience. I didn't play around with the word love. If I said it, I meant it. I would never tell someone I loved them for the fuck of it; 'I love you' were powerful words.

The word love should be used wisely; that's what my father and grandfather taught my brothers and me. Marrying someone should be the same way. After all, it's a beautiful union tying two souls together. One should never marry if they had no intention of faithfully spending the rest of their lives with said person.

I couldn't imagine meeting a woman, dropping down on one knee, and abandoning her. I couldn't imagine making promises that I didn't intend to keep or bring a life into this world with a woman I wedded and left every chance I got. That's not how marriage was supposed to work.

As I sat on my grandparents' porch, watching their lonely, beautiful neighbor stare into the clear sky while slowly sipping from a wineglass, I thought, *one day, you will be mine. You will never worry 'bout where I'm at because you'll know I'm comin' home to you. You'll never have to sit on the porch, lonely an' drinkin' wine while wonderin' where yo' life headed' an' why. You'll never have to sit alone again in yo' life because I'll always be here fo' you, rain, sleet, hail, an' snow. I will never leave you because you were created fo' me, an' I was made fo' you, Ava Morris.*

"What are you still doing, Solomon?" my grandmother snickered, tearing my eyes from her lonely neighbor.

I placed my brown eyes on her and replied, "Avoidin' going home, Grams."

"I bet you are. Your mother is itching to tear into your ass. So, how can your lovely grandmother help you out of the jam you've seemed to find yourself in?" she softly asked, walking from the expensive screen door.

Clearing my throat, I sighed deeply before saying, "To say that the weed was yours an' that I was hidin' it fo' you since Pop Pop dislikes you smokin'."

Taking a seat in her favorite brown rocking chair, Grams balled her lips tightly before smacking me upside the head. "Now, I know damn well you ain't running around here selling weed and ain't brought me a gram or two every three days. I oughta beat your ass myself, Solomon. Boy, call your mother with your ugly ass self."

Busting out laughing and dialing my mother's number, I asked, "Grams, you be chiefin'?"

"I have been for years. Now, shut up while I get your stupid ass out of trouble," she sternly spoke, grabbing my phone.

After I handed my phone to Grams, she placed it to her ear. Meanwhile, my eyes fell on the most captivating female I'd ever seen.

"No, ma'am, this is not Solomon," Grams giggled as I watched Ava wipe underneath her mesmerizing eyes.

What kind of man will leave his beautiful wife, an amazin' mother, home alone on the fourth of July? What kind of man acts as if he doesn't have a great woman an' child in his life? What kind of man wants his woman to sit on the porch 'til the wee hours of the morning waitin' an' worried 'bout him? He doesn't deserve yo' tears, Ava. Truthfully, he doesn't deserve you or Mica, I thought as Ava stood on wobbly legs, pushing her naturally long, jet-black hair out of her face.

As Ava stepped towards her front door, I hopped off my grandparents' porch, running into the lonely beauty's yard while saying, "Shouldn't you be sleep, woman?"

I caught her off guard; she stumbled and quickly placed a fake smile on her gorgeous face. Even in despair, Ava was a stunning woman. Her round, brown eyes sparkled. Her smile was alluring. The soft, feminine tone that escaped her juicy mouth was music to my ears, and it always would be.

"Hey, Hussein, what's up?" she asked as I gazed at her.

"Nothin'. Just wanted to say goodnight before I head home," I voiced, itching to comfort the sad woman.

"Oh," she lowly responded, observing my eyes. "Goodnight. Drive safely."

The expression in her peepers informed me she didn't want me to leave; thus, I said, "Care to talk fo' a while."

After exhaling heavily, she smiled. "Sure. Tell me, what have you done now?"

Chuckling, I sat on the steps of her porch and voiced, "You have to sit down fo' this one."

"Oh Lord, will Pastor Hampton give an entire sermon dedicated to you tomorrow?" she questioned, smiling while sitting beside me.

"I hope not." I laughed as my grandmother walked into Ava's yard, greeting her before sternly calling my name.

"Ma'am?" I responded, planting my eyes on the woman who'd saved me from quite a few ass-whoopings.

As she extended my phone, Grams stared into my eyes and said, "Tomorrow, preferably before we go to church, I need *my* six grams of weed. In addition, I need a joint rolled, and the weed pre-rolled better not be from *my* six grams. Understood?"

"Oop." Ava chortled unexpectedly.

At the same time, I laughed. "I gotcha. So, I'm in the clear?"

"Yes, ugly ass boy, you are in the clear. Your father has your plants in the trunk of his car. Solomon, I will only tell you this once, so you better listen up. Do not get too big for your breeches. Meaning you better know what the hell you are doing and why you are doing it. Understood?"

Nodding, I responded, "Yes, ma'am."

"Good because after church, your ugly ass is going to tell me all about it while you clean my floorboards … all of them," she giggled, backing away.

"Oh, come on, Grams. Are you serious?" I asked, disappointed as hell.

Nodding, the heavyset, light-skinned woman announced, "Oh yeah, I'm serious. What, you thought the weed was my fee for lying for you? Oh hell no, my floorboards being cleaned is the fee. The weed is a bonus. Now, goodnight, because your mother has one hell of a sermon prepared, and it's dedicated to me … thanks to your ugly ass."

"Man, I should've taken Momma's punishment," I sighed, shaking my head.

As the women giggled, Grams blew me a kiss before walking away.

Nudging me, Ava said, "So, church will be very entertaining tomorrow, huh?"

"Indeed," I voiced, eyeing the not-too-sad woman.

Ava bit her bottom lip, and it took everything in me not to pull her close and taste her favorite wine on her tongue. Staring into her peepers, I saw our lives flash before my eyes. I saw her smiling, laughing, and genuinely happy every day because I made her happy.

"Hussein," Ava softly voiced.

Clearing my throat, I said, "Yes."

Her lips moved, but nothing came out of her mouth. Those medium-beaded, brown eyes searched mine as she tried to speak. Seeing she couldn't form words, I inquired, "How was your day, Ava?"

A sigh of relief escaped her gorgeous mouth before she said, "It was okay. I guess."

"I know Mica enjoyed the firework show since he was beside me, but did you enjoy it?"

"Of course I did. It was the highlight of the night. A beautiful scene while watching my son's eyes light up like a Christmas tree was what the doctor prescribed," she softly yet sadly uttered, looking at her hands.

Grabbing and shaking them, I forced her to look at me as I articulated, "Ava, you are worthy of the world an' nothin' less. *You* will always be mo' than enough because you are special, kind, an' sweet. Don't let life's bullshit get you down an' make you feel less than. You an' you alone is enough. Never forget that."

Eyes becoming teary, Ava struggled to speak. There was much for her to say, and I knew it wasn't best that she said anything. Her body language had been screaming for me to touch and kiss her. It yelled for me to love on her greatly and shout from the mountains.

Feeling the urge to do so, I released her hands and stood. Meanwhile, I calmly said, "Have another glass of wine. Go lay beside Mica and whisper that Hussein will see him after church tomorrow. Go to sleep wit' a peaceful mind knowin' you are mo' than enough because I, Solomon Hussein Hampton, told you so. Goodnight, Ava. Sleep well."

"Goodnight, Solomon. Drive home safely," she stated, voice breaking.

There was a specific time Ava called me Solomon—when she didn't want to be alone. Like the other times, tonight would be no different; I would sit my ass down and be with the woman abandoned by her husband.

Gazing at the woman, begging to be loved and held, I asked, "On second thought, would you like to help me out wit' a small problem?"

Patting my previous sitting spot, Ava happily replied, "I'll be happy to aid you in your small problem, Solomon."

"Cool," I replied, taking a seat next to her.

"So, what's the small problem?" she inquired, biting her bottom lip.

Shit, Ava, don't do that lip bitin' thing, or you'll know my real problem. You'll know I've been assaultin' my male organ badly because I want him inside of you. You'll learn how badly I want to slowly take off yo' clothes, place you on the sofa, an' sluggishly spread those slender, cinnamon brown legs. As I have you spread eagle, my eyes will drink in the sight no man other than yo' husband has seen. I'll kneel before you like the queen that you really are; then, I will watch you watch me move closer to the one place I know is fantastic. Yo' breathin' will be erratic while mine is steady. With my nose ticklin' that pink bud hidden underneath its hood, I'll inhale yo' sweetness before the tip of my tongue grace yo' prized possession. In a matter of seconds, I'm very sure I'll become lost in tastin' an' fingerin' you. Six orgasms are what I'll give you before I climb out of my clothes an' shoes; then, I'll crawl on top of you, placin' delicate kisses all over yo' body. Indeed, our hearts will be racin' Yours from being nervous an' anxious; mine because I'll be eager an' excited to please you. As I grip my dick, gently rubbin' the head against the pretty pink monster I'd been suckin' on, you will be cooin' my name. Upon enterin' you, I'll be starin' into those allurin' brown eyes; you'll gasp an' moan my name. Once I have a nice amount of my dick inside of you, I'll groan yo' name before tellin' you how much I love you.

"Hussein!" Ava loudly called as she waved her hands in front of my face.

"Huh?" I asked, snapping into reality.

"I'm waiting for you to tell me what the small problem is so that I can try to help you out," she voiced, eyeing me.

"Oh, um, um, um," I stammered.

Giggling, she said, "There is no small problem, is it?"

"It's not really small; it's more like a big problem. How 'bout we forget 'bout my problem, an' talk 'bout something else. Say, Mica?" I inquired, feeling my dick waking up.

"If that's what you like, we can. But, before we do, I need to run inside and grab another bottle of wine," she breathed while running her slender fingers through her hair, ogling me.

"Okay."

Standing, she asked, "Would you like anything to drink?"

That pussy juice, I thought, shaking my head and saying, "No thanks, I'm good."

As I watched Ava walk away, I fought the urge to walk behind her. Some really nasty shit would pop off, and I didn't want to deal with the aftermath. I didn't want to destroy our friendship; I couldn't afford for Ava to lose her mind. Most importantly, I wanted to look into the mirror and not see someone who had slept with another man's wife.

While Ava took her time returning to the porch, the urge to step inside and check on her was at an all-time high. Once again, I had to battle not to stand and slip inside the large house. One attractive look from Ava and I would disrespect her marriage.

I was thankful yet agitated when the porch light was no longer shining. I was grateful because Ava was close; I was disturbed because I knew I had to fight the demon inside me to keep my hands to myself. After all, everything

I experienced with Ava wasn't just a few months type of interaction. For close to two years, we've been sitting on her porch. It started three months into them living beside my grandparents.

"Finally, I'm back. I hope I didn't take too long," she softly voiced, stepping onto the porch wearing an oversized, off-the-shoulder white T-shirt and a pair of black ankle socks.

"Nawl, you didn't," I replied as my dick was out of control and my mouth watered.

Planting her back on the column, Ava placed her slightly open legs in my lap and said, "Okay, Solomon, what shall we talk about first?"

My God, she ain't got on no pannies. There's no hair on that pussy. I want it. No, fuck that, I need it, I thought, struggling to keep my eyes off Ava's fat pussy.

Clearing my throat several times, I closed my eyes and shook my head. After I had gotten myself together, I looked into her eyes. I asked, "What do you think 'bout us takin' Mica to a waterpark next weekend? Allie an' her kids can come along. I'll fund it all."

"*Or* it can be just you, me, and Mica," she voiced before taking a gulp of the wine straight from the bottle.

That would be great, but you are a married woman, Ava. I'm just tryin' to be yo' friend, no sex or anything like that, I thought, shaking my head and replying, "Nawl, I think Allie an' the kids should come. That way, Mica will have someone to go down the slides wit' beside me."

"Okay," she voiced disappointedly.

I don't want to disappoint you. If you weren't married, I promise you, it would be just you, Mica, an' me, I thought as I retrieved my phone.

Upon unlocking it, I handed Ava my device and said, "Let's plan a weekend Mica will enjoy."

"Okay." She smiled, ensuring her hand touched mine.

Jesus, help a brother out. I don't know how much longer Satan gon' to breathe on my neck. I need this woman, but she doesn't need me; she wants me. Give me the strength not to take this woman into a house she half

12

shares wit' her nothing of a husband. Because if I go inside wit' my mouth attached to hers, our friendship will be in jeopardy, an' that's not what I need, I thought while watching Ava's slender fingers glide across my phone's screen.

Chapter II

Ava Morris

"You'll stop hurting when you stop hoping." — Guillaume
Musso, Seras-tu là?

My life was far from the fairytale I thought it would be.
Yet, I had some benefits of a fairytale ending: the beautiful
house, a handsomely paid husband, and a smart and
handsome son. At nineteen, I married a man a year older
than me, Jak Morris. I knew my love life would be just like
the romance movies I loved to watch. I would be a happily
married and well-loved wife to a professional basketball
athlete while being a human resource manager. Instead, I
was lonely and extremely sad, married woman to a pilot
of a well-known airline who blew out his ACL while in
college. However, I was a human resource manager at
Bigco Distribution Center.

Whatever my heart desired, I received either from Jak
or myself. Mica and I never wanted anything except Jak's
presence more than he'd been giving us. I didn't know
when I realized I was a lonely wife and mother. Maybe it
was the late-night hours of Jak being in his man cave or
being gone for days. It could've been when we were on
vacation, but he wasn't mentally there. I didn't know
which hurt me the most, hoping my husband of eight
years would recognize that I was slipping from him or
that my husband made so many promises to us that he
didn't keep.

I was drowning in misery, pain, lack of love, and
unhappiness to the point I became self-conscious. I
wondered if I was pretty, smart, or worthy enough for my
husband. Doubt seeped in, causing me to rethink
everything I had done before becoming Jak's wife and

after we had wed. I was at a crossroads with my life and the future.

Constantly, I pondered how to fix our marriage. I didn't know how to make Jak be more in my and our son's lives. Most importantly, I didn't know how much praying I could do to give myself the happy ending I deserved. What I bestowed upon my husband, I didn't receive, and I surely didn't deserve that.

Talking to Jak about our marriage issues went into one ear and out of the other. He would be present for two weeks before the bullshit about his job started sounding off in our three-bedroom, two-and-a-half bathroom, high-rise ceiling home. Just like that, the pilot would be off in the night with minimal contact. Upon his return, it was as if we hadn't discussed the downfalls of our marriage. I would be in a house with our son, thinking, praying, and hoping my husband would realize what he had at home—a great, loving wife and son.

I'd been waiting for the man I married to mentally return to me for nearly two years. For a year, I patiently waited to see Jak slide through the front door and apologize for leaving me with a handsome, well-mannered guy to fill the void that sunk deep into my heart. Little did my husband know that the hole he left me with was slowly being filled by someone else—Solomon Hussein Hampton.

The nineteen-year-old being was a great friend with pure intentions. He was beyond sweet, compassionate, protective, and thoughtful. Whomever he would spend the rest of his life with would have a great man by their side. There was no doubt in my mind that Hussein wouldn't make a great husband. He possessed all the qualities of a man raised to respect love and marriage.

Hussein had plenty of times to come on to me, but he didn't. When the tension became too strong for us, he would always stand and try to send me off with goodnight wishes. I stopped him from leaving because of the things I didn't want to do. I didn't want to go inside a huge house meant for three people, but only two occupied it. I didn't want to face that my husband found a better place than the one I wanted to create with him. I didn't want to observe the house I had to have with Jak and Mica before having more children. I didn't want to cry myself to sleep as I'd been doing every time after Hussein left my property. I didn't want to feel unworthy, undeserving, and unhappy.

Therefore, I had drunk myself into a happy state while sitting on my porch with Hussein. While he observed me and shook my hand or held it in a friendly way, he didn't know how much joy and temptation he brought into my world.

No matter the day or time, Hussein was beside me, informing me that I was more than enough. He breathed life into a tired body from pondering if I wasn't enough or what I could do to become enough. The young man was at my son's beck and call, ensuring Mica had a great day and weekend. He loved my child as if Mica was his; sometimes, I wished Mica was his. Hussein had become one of the most critical people in my life, which frightened me. At the end of the day, I was a lonely married woman who wanted to put her marriage back on track because I had made a vow in front of God and our family.

When I'd have my fair share of Merlot wine, I would cross a line that caused Hussein to carry me in the house and place me into the bed I was supposed to have rumpled around with my husband. After placing a throw blanket over my body, Hussein would kiss the back of my hand and tell me to get some rest. Before I could call his name and ask him to lay with me, he was at my bedroom door, hand hovering over the light switch. As he flipped it into the off position, he would lovingly tell me goodnight and sleep well before dashing out the door.

As usual, I would lie in bed, staring at the ceiling as Hussein did his routine check-through of the house. He would check on Mica before exiting my son's room, laughing about how much of a horrible sleeper he was.

Mica's head would be on the bed, but his legs would dangle.

Shortly afterward, Hussein would check the backdoor before grabbing the trash and carrying it out of the house. Hussein ensured we were safe before he started the engine on his 1990's something truck and listened to music in the front of his grandparents' yard. He didn't care about disturbing the peace, which I appreciated, yet I never told him.

Tonight was no different, except Hussein started the engine on his custom-painted 2015 Dodge Challenger and his choice of music, The Gap Band's "Yearning for Your Love".

Smiling, I shook my head and yawned, "And you know just how to put me to sleep with a peaceful mind and my morals intact. Thanks, friend. Be safe on your way home."

Hussein's car speakers became louder, indicating he was leaving. The void in my heart appeared tenfold, making me drunkenly hop from my bed. Bending the blinds, I saw the burnt orange vehicle slowly cruise from his grandparents' home. Tears welled as I badly wanted him to come back and hold me. My heart sank knowing that I, a married woman, lusted after a nineteen-year-old guy. Or it could've been my heart dropped because I, a married woman, was in love with the nineteen-year-old male. Who had never missed a day out of Mica's and my life since we moved into Grove Land.

Chapter III

Hussein

"Those sweet lips. My, oh my, I could kiss those lips all night long. Good things come to those who wait."-Jess. C. Scott, The Intern

Wednesday, July 8th, 2020

If I didn't have mad clientele fo' this weed shit, I wouldn't be wastin' my first night on vacation sittin' here breakin' this shit down, I thought, bobbing my head to August Alsina's "Fuck Me Like You Love Me".

My brothers and our homeboy, Jerrard, always wondered why I had a legit full-time job with great pay and benefits and still chose to sell weed. Every time, I would explain to them that all sources of money were good. I had an incredible connection for the quality marijuana.

Thanks to Ava, I was hired as a full-time material handler five years ago. My clientele increased during my first week at one of the city's largest household goods distribution centers. It was only suitable for me to receive some of their paychecks while on the White man's wealthy business clock.

To work a legit job and hustle weed was a win-win for me. Of course, those semi-do-right niggas, my brothers and Jerrard, didn't understand my thinking. Thus, I ceased trying to make them comprehend that I was a greedy nigga for money. Unlike them, they didn't know that it was never my goal to work for someone else longer than I had to. I was destined to have a business, even though I didn't know what it would be.

Without a clue as to what I wanted to own, that didn't stop me from stashing my profits into a shoebox inside my closet; I had been doing that since I was fifteen. Upon turning eighteen, I opened a savings account, dumping my entire weed profit inside without any intention of touching it until the time had arrived for me to do so. To this day, I continued stashing my weed earnings into that account and didn't touch a penny.

A few months ago, I started analyzing the types of businesses in the city. I was satisfied with my observation but wasn't impressed with said business's products. I didn't want a restaurant, furniture store, etc. I wanted to invest my time and money into an organization I could be proud of while smoking a blunt and saying, "All mine."

I talked to agents and completed tours of those buildings to get a general idea of commercial real estate prices in Montgomery, Alabama. A few agents told me to chat with someone at my bank to discuss being financially equipped to become a business owner. After I had done so, I sat on the knowledge given to me. It was the best thing for me to do since I didn't know what I wanted to own, the name of my company, or had a logo in mind.

Ava would've usually been my go-to person, but I didn't bother her about my goals and dreams. The exceptional woman's life changed drastically, as did her view on life, love, career, and relationships. Three years ago, the day came when Ava's world was no longer her world. Thus, it crushed me.

To this day, I hated it, yet I was thankful that I was present. I disliked witnessing a mother unable to save her child from a fall, even though she ran as fast as she could. I hated seeing the right side of Mica's head slamming onto the driveway's curb. I loathed how Ava screamed for her sorry-ass husband to call 911 while she was afraid to touch their son.

I hated hearing that peculiar scream that sent chills running wildly through my body as tears welled. I knew what that scream meant. My grandmother and mother yelped the same way the night my younger cousin was murdered. He was live streaming on a social media platform. I disliked witnessing Ava crumble as the coroner placed Mica's thin yet long body into a black bag. Seeing them place him into a coroner's van, an indescribable noise escaped her mouth; without a doubt, Ava was hurt to the depths of her soul, just as I was.

Throughout the sadness, I was very thankful I was present because her fuck ass husband humiliated her in front of the entire neighborhood. He blamed Ava for their son's death, knowing damn well she loved Mica more than anything. I had to pay attention to the aggressive nigga as he was too close to Ava, clenching and unclenching his fists.

One too many times, he acted like he wanted to hit the grieving woman. I couldn't let him lay a single finger on her or act as if he would. Tired of his ways towards her, I was in his face, shoving him from her. I became so engrossed in her hurt and his madness towards her that I repeatedly popped him in the face while telling him he had no right to blame his wife. If it wasn't for the police restraining me, I was sure the fuck nigga would've been in a body bag as well.

That horrible day was the first time I held Ava until she cried herself to sleep on the sofa. When the night fell, her nothing-ass husband packed his things and left without speaking to his pained wife. That incredibly disastrous night, I refused to leave Ava's side; thus, I lay on her bedroom floor and didn't sleep. I, too, had lost a special someone.

Upon the sun rising, I gracefully lifted off the floor, stood over a sleeping, tear-stained-faced Ava, and kissed her forehead before making breakfast. While I did so, I vowed I would be the only man in her life because she needed a real man, not a fuck ass character. To this day, I kept that promise and all the others I made to myself.

"Do you need some help?" Lakin Letterson asked, walking into the living room, interrupting my thinking.

Not looking at her, I shook my head and replied, "Nawl, I'm almost done now."

"But you have three more duffel bags to take care of," she said, sitting beside me.

"The contents in those bags are already accounted fo', as is."

"Are you serious?" she inquired, shocked.

"Yep," I voiced as my cell phone rang.

"Wow. So, you will need to re-up soon, huh?"

"No, I doubled the order. I should be good fo' another two weeks."

Snatching my cell phone off the arm of the sofa, I stared at Jerrard's name. On the fourth ring, I answered, "Talk to me, ugly ass nigga."

"Dude, fuck you." He laughed. "It's this jazz spot we are going to hit up. Are you in?"

"Y'all finna head out like right now?" I inquired, looking at the clock.

"Um, yeah. That jazz spot gets pretty packed by eight-thirty."

"I can't leave right now. I have a few mo' things I need to take care of. I'll slide through when I'm done."

"A'ight, we'll see you when you pull up."

"A'ight."

After ending the call, I placed my phone on the sofa and continued my business. Deeply exhaling, Lakin glared at me. Not planting my eyes on the beautiful woman, I asked, "What's wrong wit' you?"

"I'm going to assume you will not invite me out with you, huh?"

"No, their old ladies ain't going."

"I don't care if their bitches ain't going. That has nothing to do with me," she stated nastily.

"Lakin, I don't feel like arguin' wit' you. Damn. It's the same shit wit' you every fuckin' time I step out wit' my brothers an' Jerrard. I don't understand why because I swear we are not in a relationship. So, why act an ass when you know what it is an' why you are here?"

"Don't worry about it," she announced with much attitude as she hopped her petite, light-skinned behind from the sofa, stumping towards my bedroom.

"Oh, trust, I ain't worried," I replied, rushing to finish my task.

Three weeks ago, the worst day for Lakin arrived. She was saddened by the pregnancy loss, whereas I was one happy, nonchalant motherfucker. Of course, I didn't show her that side, but I celebrated once I was away from her. Indeed, I would be celebrating heavily when the next three weeks arrived. She would officially receive the boot.

Thirty minutes later, I was done breaking down the weed and on the phone with Moxley Anderson, aka Mo. Mo was an associate from high school. The three duffel bags filled with weed were for him. I zipped into the bedroom after informing him when and where he could pick up his product.

As soon as I walked in, I saw Lakin dressed sexily as she applied makeup to her round face. As usual, she wanted me to say something about her attire. Like always, I didn't say anything about her short outfit because I didn't give a fuck. She wasn't nor would ever be my girl.

While strolling toward the closet, I knew exactly what I would wear—a collared shirt, khaki shorts, and casual low-cut shoes. Most men had to iron their clothes before putting them on, not me. Faithfully, everything I owned made a visit to the dry cleaners. I hated doing laundry. My preacher of a mother was hell-bent on making my brother and I clean our clothes upon us reaching the age of fourteen. Oh, the number of clothes I fucked up. When I started working at a fast-food restaurant, I placed my clothes in the cleaners. Momma learned of it and nipped that shit in the bud. I hated she dictated what I shouldn't do because she knew I could complete the tasks myself.

Growing up, Momma was obsessed with us learning to manage money and take care of ourselves. She did her job well because my money didn't burn a hole into my pocket, and I was very independent.

"So, you ain't going to say anything about what I have on?" Lakin inquired as I placed my well-pressed clothes and shoes on the dresser.

I wasn't going to fall into her madness. As usual, the spoiled broad was trying to get my attention, and I didn't want her to have it.

"Nope," I voiced, taking off my shirt while walking by her.

"And why not?"

Strolling into the bathroom, I sighed, "You are seekin' a reaction out of me, an' I'll be damned if I give it to you. You know where we stood months ago; we still stand the same. You are only here because of one reason, Lakin. You miscarried our child. Once yo' six weeks are up, which will be in three weeks, you will be movin' back into yo' spot as we agreed."

I knew I would hear her mouth when she took several deep breaths. Thus, I zoned out while turning on the water knobs. I was fully dressed when I came to, strutting into the living room to retrieve the needed items.

"So, you are ignoring me, huh?" she loudly voiced, walking behind me.

"Yep. Have fun an' be safe," I responded, opening the door.

"You have some fucking nerves, Solomon!"

Walking out the door, I replied, "So do you, Lakin."

While hopping down the stairs two at a time, I couldn't wait until I delivered the product to Mo. I was eager to enjoy my first night on vacation without thinking about Lakin's antics. I understood she was vulnerable, but she didn't have to carry on the way she did. Within the ten months of being friends with benefits, there was no nagging, constantly checking up on me, or the need to be underneath me twenty-four-seven. Thanks to the condom breaking, resulting in an unwanted pregnancy, my world became chaotic and drama-filled. I was miserable because I didn't see a future with her. I didn't want to have a child with her; my sperm was pre-destined for the one woman who had my heart and always would have it.

Ring. Ring. Ring.

Grabbing my phone from my pocket, I looked at the screen. I slid my hand across the answer option and unlocked the doors on my whip.

"Where your ass at, lil' nigga?" the eldest of Pastor and First Gentleman Hampton's son, Thaddeus, asked.

"Finna leave the crib."

"A'ight. The usual jazz spot we didn't feel, so we came to the other joint, The Gem."

Sitting in the driver's seat, I nodded and voiced, "A'ight, gimme 'bout twenty-five minutes, an' I'll be there."

"Okay," he replied before we ended the call.

Dropping my phone into my lap, I didn't waste any time sticking the key into the ignition and turning it over. My recently painted midnight blue Dodge Challenger roared to life before I sped off, eager to have a fun night with the fellas.

According to my brothers and Jerrard, The Gem was the place to be on a Wednesday night. Since I worked Monday through Thursday, I had to settle for the weekend side of The Gem. The juke joint spot was extremely laid back; the shit-starters weren't anywhere near the building.

The first time I allowed my brothers and Jerrard to drag me to a place that didn't play rap music, I vowed I would never return. That's until I stepped inside and fell in love with the atmosphere. As great-smelling food wafted through the air, soul music pumped through the speakers. There were plenty of old heads talking shit while playing pool. There were classily dressed women, but I didn't pay them attention. My eyes were already accounted for.

Ring. Ring. Ring.

Gliding through a yellow traffic light, I glanced at my phone before answering Mo's call.

"Talk to me," I voiced, racing down the most traveled street in the city.

"Yo, the Jazz club isn't the lick to drop an' collect. So, I pulled up at The Gem," Mo's deep-voiced stated calmly.

Pressing further on the gas pedal, I smiled. "Even better. I'm ten minutes out."

"A'ight. Ay, you don't have me on speakerphone, do you?" the calm-talking character inquired.

"Hell nawl. Plus, I'm ridin' solo. What's up?" I questioned, hopping into the right lane, bypassing a smoking older model Ford Explorer.

24

"Shid, the lil' chocolate bunny you be scopin' out fell off in The Gem wit' her lil' friend. Shawty lookin' good as fuck wit' that blonde hair. She cut her hair into a bob-like style. Them old niggas was houndin' her soon as she stepped out the car," he breathed, exhaling.

She's makin' a lil' progress, I see, I thought, smiling and mashing on the pedal.

"Word?" I happily exclaimed.

"Yep. Ay, bruh?" Mo quizzed.

"What's up?"

"How well do you know lil' chocolate bunny's friend?"

"Very well. Why?"

"I been seein' her ass 'round town, but I didn't have the courage to approach her. I want that lil' no titties minimal ass having motherfucka," he chuckled.

Shaking my head, I laughed. "Step to her."

"I might just do that."

"Bet. Ay, bruh, I'mma be there before you know it," I rapidly spoke, sitting upright and pressing further on the pedal.

As I bobbed in and out of traffic, Mo chuckled, "A'ight. Be safe, lil' homie."

"No doubt," I replied before we ended the call.

Oou shit, Ava out. Now, I can start implementin' my plan fo' her to be my woman before I ask her to marry me.

The further I arrived at my destination, the more my heart pumped and my grin became wider. The thought of seeing Ava Langston dressed to be fucked until the sun came up had my fellow eager to engage in a few rounds of raunchy, ear-splitting sex. Ava could have her way with me no matter the day or time.

That time was approaching sooner than later because my Ava had been through enough. It was time for her to be treated like the queen she truly was. There was no doubt that once a confident Ava was in my arms, she wouldn't regret being there while smiling as joy soared through her perfectly crafted body.

Turning onto the rocky gravel of The Gem, I observed the parking area while saying, "Damn, this motherfucka packed tonight."

Immediately, I located Mo's white Dodge Charger sitting on 23-inch black rims. Parking beside him, I quickly shut off the engine as we opened the driver's doors. After we dapped, he gave me my money; in return, I handed him his products. Discreetly and quickly, Mo placed the three duffel bags of weed into the back seat.

Usually, the six-foot-five, dark-skinned, bulky character would leave, but this time, Mo locked his whip and said, "Let me see what this joint talkin' 'bout."

"So, you just gon' leave yo' shit in the car like that?" I asked, shocked.

"I wish a nigga would break into my whip an' take what don't belong to him. His motherfuckin' ass gon' be dead before he sold anything. I have cameras installed in my shits. I don't trust a soul in this ratchet ass city," the calm, talking man voiced as we walked towards the front door.

"I feel ya' on that tip, woe," I replied, nodding.

Upon being searched by the security guards, we entered an unusually filled place. Tucka's "Back to the Sweet Shop" had me bobbing my head and jigging to the beat as we walked to the bar. Along our way toward the liquor keepers, I noticed Ava and Allie standing on the far-left side of the bar. There was never a time they didn't step out looking absolutely stunning.

Immediately, I made my way towards them. Near them, I observed the seductively yet classily dressed Ava Langston. She wore an olive green, tight, knee-length dress, gold jewelry, and sandals. Her medium-length nails were polished in a sparkling white color. Her pretty toes were polished white, and two designs were on her big toes. The blonde-dyed, bob-styled hairdo fit her to the T. The blonde set off Ava's eyes, causing one to stare into her peepers.

As always, she has my eyes open an' my nose wide, I thought, quickly observing Allie's attire.

26

Before I greeted the best friends, Mo tugged on my arm. Looking back at him, he motioned for me to come to him. After doing so, he said, "Bruh, I know you finna say something to them. Tell her friend that I want her."

"I gotcha," I replied before placing my eyes on the women, seductively swaying from side to side.

My goodness. This woman here will drive me insane if I don't make a move on her, I thought as Allie retrieved her cell phone.

As they positioned their bodies to take a picture, I tapped Mo on the wrist and pointed in front of me.

"Picture time, huh?" He laughed.

"Yep." I nodded.

A few seconds later, we hopped in the lovely ladies' photo. The expression on their faces was priceless. Turning around to face us, the ladies shook their heads and laughed. Shortly after doing so, Ava and Allie waved at me. While I greeted them, I stepped closer to Ava. The sweet-smelling scent that ran off the kindest and sweetest woman had me wanting to nibble on her.

Wrapping my arm around her waist, I placed my mouth to her ear and kissed it before asking, "I ain't seen you in a few days. How you been? How's the nail services going?"

"I've been doing okay, I think. Being a nail technician is getting boring. I'm not into it as I once was," she stated sweetly. "Thank you for asking about my day and my little career. Have things been going well for you?"

"Ava, you know you can get yo' old job back at Bigco. Just say the words, an' I'll make som' things shake."

She shook her head and replied, "Nope, don't want the old life back."

Seeing that her mood was changing, I quickly changed the subject. "You asked me was things going well fo' me. In a way, yes."

"That's good," she voiced, eyeing me.

"Did I put you in a sour mood?"

"No," she lied.

"What I told you 'bout lyin' to me, Ava?" I voiced, searching her eyes.

"No, Hussein, you didn't put me in a sour mood. I'm okay. I promise," she replied, eyes informing me she was not okay.

As I studied the woman, I could tell she wanted to slip out of The Gem. Knowing I didn't want her to, I asked, "May I buy you a drink?"

"Sure. I'll have a Crown Apple with Sprite. More liquor than Sprite, please."

Smiling, I said, "As you wish. Place the order fo' two."

"Okay," she voiced as I grabbed a wad of cash out of my front pocket and handed her a crisp twenty-dollar bill.

Biting her juicy, glossy bottom lip, Ava faced the bar. Out of my peripheral, I saw Allie blushing as Mo was in her personal space.

Ah, he found the courage to step to her after all, I thought, analyzing Allie's body language. She was feeling him.

Shortly after he whispered something into her ear, she nodded and faced the bartender. While she chatted with the heavy-set woman, Ava extended my drink to me.

As we stepped a few feet from the bar, the DJ played Ronnie Bell's "Cotton Candy". At that precise moment, I saw a different side of Mo. That foolish smooth-talking nigga and Allie held onto the plastic cups and danced toward the semi-cluttered dancing area. While I chuckled, Ava giggled and followed suit behind her best friend and Mo. Feeling the jam, I danced behind Ava while singing the song. Once on the dance floor, I nestled my dick on Ava's jiggly bottom.

Good Jesus, that thang soft, I thought, gulping a nice amount of my drink.

"Well, shit, brother, it's like that?" the familiar goofy person, my second oldest brother, Gideon, chuckled.

As the song ended, the ladies linked and greeted my brothers and Jerrard before sashaying to a vacant table. While my brothers and Jerrard questioned what Mo and I had going on, I couldn't tear my eyes from Ava. The more shit talk flew out of Gideon's mouth, the harder it was for me to focus on the ragging they bestowed upon Mo and me.

"Let's play a round of pool," Gideon commanded, staring into our faces.

"Sounds good to me. Set it up, an' I'll be that way shortly," I told Gideon.

Thaddeus did what he did best: joked about his little brother in love with an older woman. Before Mo and I dipped off with my day ones, we strolled towards the ladies who were chair dancing and chatting.

Upon arriving in Ava's presence, I whispered in her ear, "Before I leave this joint, you owe me two …nawl, fuck that …you owe me three dances. Non-negotiable."

Giggling, she nodded. Standing upright, I needed to suck Ava's lips off her beautiful, serene face. Lowly growling, I walked from the tipsy woman; however, I noticed Mo winking and blowing a kiss at Allie. A hearty laugh consumed me as I strolled toward the other end of the juke joint.

Arriving before my day ones, Sir Charles' "Just Can't Let Go" played. I didn't know why that song set us on fire, but we were so into the music that we didn't play pool immediately. As we jigged, Mo found his place beside me. Just like us, he jammed to the melody.

"I ain't finna let go! No … no … no!" I hollered passionately.

My head-bobbing brother, Thaddeus, had to kick the game off. If it was left up to Gideon, Mo, Jerrard, and me, we weren't going to do shit but sing and cut a rug. We focused on the game because it was time to get with the program. After each of us had a turn, Jerrard asked what we were drinking before visiting the bar. The first game wasn't complete, yet we visited the bar six times. A brother was beyond lit and horny. In need of being from the stiff legs, Mo and I found ourselves in the company of Ava and Allie.

Before we sat, we gave them money to get them a drink or two. While we massively grinned, our eyes were on the woman we were interested in.

Licking my lips, I thought, *oh, Ava. Oh Ava, wit' yo' permission, to-fuckin'-night, I'm gon' lift that sexy ass dress an' pull that G-string off before kissin' every inch of yo' body. I'm tired of waitin' to do so. You deserve everything I'm gon' bless you wit'. Tonight is the night I begin to make yo' world so much better than it has been. I promise.*

Chapter IV

Ava Langston

"C'mon good girl, be bad."-Nicki Elson

I was thankful my female best friend dragged me out of the house. Tonight was the best night I had in a long time. I had never smiled and enjoyed the company of an unknown male sitting close to Allie and me. If it wasn't for Hussein being present, I was sure Mo wouldn't have stood a chance with us. Allie and I had enough of life throwing bullshit in our faces. We, best friends, had been through it!

While partying with my friend, clearly before Hussein had arrived, I had hoped he would fall off in the place. Yet, I knew he wouldn't. The Gem wasn't his style. It was more laid back and filled with blues and old twerking jams. I needed him present for a few reasons. The main was so I could smile into his handsome face, and the second one was to keep random men from sliding into my space, inquiring about my name, and if I was available to date. I was beyond done with males, except for one person—the only man I loved chatting with and had been for five years. The one I shared a great friendship with, and his behavior towards me never changed.

The one who subliminally told me, two years ago, who and what he needed. The same one, in return, I subliminally dismissed. In my destroyed mind, it was the best thing to do, given what I had and still was going through. The timing wasn't right for us, or it could've been that I wasn't mentally suitable for him. Either way, I didn't want him caught up in my cyclone. I treasured him too much for that.

Tonight, when my hopes of having Hussein close to me turned into a reality, I couldn't stop smiling at the handsome male who had been my rock ever since I moved beside his grandparents. Even though I was tipsy and going through my own personal hell, there was no doubt I harbored feelings for Hussein. If anything, they increased over the past three years.

Unlike the other times, his presence was more potent, and I couldn't lie as if I wasn't feeling what he was trying to serve. In the past, I fantasized many times about participating in a few nasty things with my neighbors' grandson. I stared at him often to see what he was working with or ogled his juicy lips. The light-skinned, six-foot even, well-groomed male was fine as hell. However, his age was a big issue for me, thus causing me to chastise my thoughts when it came to him. Now, I was drunk, lonely, and didn't give a single fuck about him being eight years younger than me.

Surely, I didn't give two fucks when he carried me to his car after he noticed I was good and wasted. Indeed, I was hoping he would kiss me upon gently placing me into the passenger seat of his vehicle. When he closed the door, my heart hurt, and my eyes became teary. I was hoping he would do what I was too scared to do.

"You alright?" Hussein handsomely inquired.

"Yes, just extremely tipsy, that's all," I slurred, opening my eyes to look at him.

Upon planting his hand on top of mine, which rested on my thigh, he gently stroked it and softly said, "Okay."

The different shapes he drew on the back of my hand caused butterflies to float in the pit of my stomach. The sensual touch of his soft and long fingers set my body ablaze, as it had done many times before. Several times, I had to tell myself to think with a level head. The more I tried to chastise my body's reaction and thoughts of Hussein and me, the more I craved him.

As Carl Marshall's "Good Loving Will Make You Cry" sounded at a reasonable listening volume, he said, "Ava, can I ask you a question?"

"Yes," I responded, giving him my undivided attention.

Turning into my neighborhood, the sultry, baritone voice male asked, "Can I lift yo' dress an' pull down yo' G-string before I spread yo' legs an' taste you? While my tongue is deep in yo' mouth an' my hands are caressin' yo' body, can I fill you up? I promise you, I won't rush. I'll take my time an' cater to yo' needs."

Shocked at how he asked to have sex with me, I cleared my throat and shyly announced, "Yes."

"Okay," he sexily replied, interlocking our fingers before placing a kiss on the back of my hand.

He finally asked! He finally asked! I thought, feeling elated and nervous.

Silence overcame us as a sex jam played. My heart raced as I silently thanked myself for regularly upkeeping my private area, which hadn't been used in years. Then, my thoughts turned on me. I started to curse myself out at the chance of jumping to have sex with him.

Hussein wasn't just any ordinary guy; he was a preacher's kid. The same pastor had given my mother the word every Sunday for five years. The same preacher that was heavily in my life since it crashed three years ago. It would be extremely awkward to step inside her church, which I did once a month, knowing I had fornicated with her son.

Just so happen to be, this upcoming Sunday was the day I'd be at Hussein's mother's church. I would feel highly uncomfortable stepping to the altar as Pastor Hampton preached and prayed, knowing her son had spread my legs.

As he pulled into my driveway, I cleared my throat several times. Apparently, Hussein knew I was getting ready to recant my answer. Thus, he chuckled as his hand slipped between my thighs, aiming for my pretty untouched coochie. As if they had a mind of their own, my legs spread.

After sliding my thong to the side, two of Hussein's slender, long fingers graced my famished pussy. Instantly, my body relaxed against the passenger seat as my breathing became erratic.

Take your ass in the house, Ava Jane Langston, I thought and moaned, "Hussein."

Working my middle just as he promised, Hussein thuggishly yet slowly voiced, "Open the garage doors, Ava."

Poorly, I did what he commanded. Removing his foot off the braking system, Hussein pulled his vehicle into my clean garage that held many precious items and memories.

Rapidly finger fucking me, he shoved the gearshift into the park position before shutting off the engine. While moaning and enjoying the familiar but not-so-familiar sensations, my body did several things it had never done: tremble violently, squirt, and lock.

"Husseinnn," I passionately cried, tears running from my pretty eyes.

"Close the garage door an' come here," he erotically growled while motioning inside my pussy for me to come to him.

"Oouu," I whined as my legs shook uncontrollably. At the same time, I pressed the close button on the garage controller.

"Come to me, Ava," he begged, gripping my waist and giving my pretty pussy a run for her money.

As I weakly climbed onto his waiting lap, Hussein parted my lips with his alcohol and weed-filled, thick tongue. Planting me on his lap, Hussein squeezed my right butt cheek while finger fucking me intensely. Shaking like I was having a seizure, our tongues seductively and perfectly clashed, driving me into a land I had never been to—even with my ex-husband.

Lovingly, I wrapped my arms around his neck and indulged in the fiery kiss that had my full attention as I welcomed every tongue connection. It was the most powerful and loving kiss I'd ever had. I wanted more of it, yet, with the excessive heat consuming my body and a gut-wrenching feeling, I hurried to break the intense smooch,

Gazing into his lustful eyes, I erotically screamed, "Solomon Hussein!"

As Marvin Gaye's "I Want You" played, Hussein whimpered, "Fuck, Ava. Wet me up. Shit wet me up. I've been waitin' on this moment fo' a long time."

For God knows how long, I squatted over Hussein as he fingered me wonderfully. The massive wetness that fled my pussy, dropping onto his shorts, had me thrilled and eager for more. He breathed life into me through his fingers, and I loved it. I admired his ability to cause my body to saturate his clothes. In fact, I welcomed the euphoric feelings every time he rapidly tapped against my G-Spot.

"Damn, Ava, it's like that?" Hussein handsomely asked, increasing the speed of his fingers while gazing into my eyes.

Stuck in place, unable to speak and move, I stared at him with lazy eyes. Eyes that were fixated on a man who had given me the world just by being the most solid person in my life. My eyes became crossed like my legs when I wore a short dress.

My back arched massively as I felt a wave rock and roll through me. I started sweating, gasping for air, and jolting. My eyelids had a mind of their own as my body grew weaker but hotter. Unable to hold onto the exhilarating sensation longer, my body released much of my sweet goodness as I gripped his neck and howled, "Husseinnnnn!"

"It's time to get out of this car. What do you say?" he voiced, nibbling on my nipple through my dress.

Rapidly, I nodded. "Mhm."

Digging inside of the driver's door compartment, he observed me and inquired, "How you been sleepin' lately?"

"Some nights, okay, and other nights horribly," I poorly articulated.

After retrieving the condom, Hussein opened the door. Calmly, he responded, "Well, I'mma make sure you sleep fuckin' fantastic tonight 'til late tomorrow. That you can bet on. Hold on."

"Okay," I cooed as he stepped out of his vehicle.

While walking towards the back of his car, Hussein's fingers continued bringing me to pleasing and soaking me for all I had to offer. Before placing me on the trunk, the amazing man removed my clothes. Shortly afterward, he eyed me while slowly stripping out of his clothes and shoes.

Standing before me in black boxers, I dropped my head to focus on the dick print. It seemed big, but looks could be deceiving, especially with certain kinds of male underwear. Eager to know what he had after all these years, I held my breath as he took off his underwear. Rapidly, I dropped my head and rapidly blinked. I couldn't utter a word as Hussein laughed. He had a beautiful, crafted light-skinned dick. A beauty mark rested on the right side of the mushroom-shaped head. Hussein had a dick for centuries; I would've never guessed he was holding that much lengthy and chunky meat between his legs. He was bigger than Jak, width and length.

"Gotdamn! Where did all that come from? Or am I imagining things because I'm drunk?" I screeched as he made his dick jump.

"In dem drawls, woman," Hussein handsomely responded.

"My goodness," I spoke in awe, still fixated on a dick I couldn't house in my cobwebby pussy, let alone fuck it.

Stepping into my face, he lifted my head, so my eyes were on him. Satisfied that I was looking into his face instead of his dick, Hussein softly said, "You okay?"

Quickly, I shook my head and said, "No, I'm not. I can't go through with this. You are entirely too damn big, Hussein."

"Yes, you can go through with it. I told you I'm going to take my time. I won't hurt you; I promise," he implored while gently rubbing his knuckles across my cheek.

"Hussein, *that* isn't an average-sized dick. That's too much. I won't be able to enjoy you, nor will you enjoy me.

Let's be real," I sighed, placing my hands on his chest, indicating him to step back.

Gripping my waist, he gently pushed me backward. I tried to resist, but the second I saw his head traveling toward my hairless pussy, I laid back and opened my legs wider. I had oral sex performed on me a few times; those times, I could count on both hands. When his face found my goodness, I cooed as my back arched. At the same time, Hussein moaned, "Mhm."

Slowly and passionately, Hussein licked me from my perineum to my clit, causing me to moan his name as my legs shook. The handsome being took my pussy on a journey it had never been on. In the years I was sexually active, I had never experienced the euphoria Hussein bestowed upon me with his mouth and fingers.

The back-breaking arch, hair pulling, squealing, running, begging for him to stop, and squirting were things I had longed to experience. He gave them to me incredibly with no shame. Spread eagle on the back of his trunk, my mind was silent as my body craved more of his intoxicating loving. That's until he had me sounding and acting as if I was possessed.

"Hussein, please. I can't take anymore," I cried as my body shook violently, more fluids gushing out of me.

"Do you really want me to stop?" he inquired, finger fucking me.

I shook my head and replied, "I don't even know."

Chuckling, he shook his head and continued what he had been doing—beautifully destroying my body and mind. Solomon Hussein Hampton didn't stop the foreplay until I was limp like a noodle. I was one tired being, yet I was ready to feel him inside me.

"You good?" he asked, gazing at me.

Licking my lips, I nodded.

"Can I slide him inside you, Ava?" he sweetly asked, searching my eyes.

I nodded as my breathing was all over the place.

"I need to hear you say yes or no. So, I'mma ask you again, can I slide him inside you?"

"Yes," I whimpered, eager to be filled to capacity.

"Okay," he voiced, looking at me while putting the condom onto the organ he called a dick.

Afterward, he pulled me further towards the edge of the trunk. Hussein's eyes never left mine. I surely couldn't stop looking into eyes that reflected much respect, adoration, admiration, and love for me. Seeing that in his eyes caused me to see forever with him.

"Oou," I cooed, feeling pressure from the fat mushroom-shaped head entering my tight palace.

Immediately, I started to pray. Hussein had a little trouble bypassing the gatekeeper of my pretty kitty. Indeed, she was wet; however, my pretty kitty was a force to be reckoned with since she had been operable for many moons.

"I'm sorry," I sincerely voiced as his dick and my pussy played cat and mouse.

Cuffing the right side of my face, he breathed, "Why you apologizin'? You have no reason to do so. I wasn't expectin' you to be able to receive him. I am expectin' you to enjoy what you can. This is the part when I said I will take my time."

In love with how he catered to me, I nodded. "Okay."

The second Hussein's head and a few inches of the shaft graced my pussy, I rose off the back of his trunk. Loudly, I hissed, "Good Jesus!"

"What He got to do wit' this, Ava?" Hussein inquired, loving while slowly thrusting.

Stunned at his comment, I couldn't say a thing. I ogled the man, slowly stretching out my pretty girl—making her feel again. In those eyes, I saw that he was elated to give me what I needed. The lustful look in his eyes was no longer present; it was replaced with a loving expression. His handsome peepers and body language showed he wanted to love on me forever—which he'd referenced many times subliminally.

"You okay?" he asked, rubbing the tip of his nose against mine.

38

"Yesss," I moaned, gripping his arm and meeting his thrusts.

While wonderfully and passionately exploring my loveliness through precise hip movements, Hussein sweetly whispered, "All those nights you slept horribly, why you didn't call me? It's not like you don't have my number. I thought I made myself clear when I told you no matter what you need, I would provide it whenever, wherever, an' however. Bringin' you ultimate pleasure was at the top of the list, Ava. Don't act like you ain't noticed how I hug or look at you. Please don't act like you ain't caught my subliminal messages. I gave you the ammunition to a gun you been had. So, tell me why you ain't bust that motherfucka?"

"Husseinnnn, I'm cumming!" I squealed as my chest met his, and my toes curled to the point they popped.

"Oooh, I know, Ava Langston. I know," he sexily growled, touching my neck.

While gently pushing me back onto the car, he leaned slightly backward. He fed my starving pussy some disrespectful, raunchy dick. Every spot with a cobweb attached to it was knocked down. He left nothing inside me untouched.

"Answer my damn question, Ava Langston. Why you ain't bust that damn gun all those sleepless nights you encountered?" he questioned, gripping my waist before snatching me off the trunk—still, he was feeding me dick.

Thrusting slowly yet deeply into my exclusive cookie-nookie, Hussein gripped my newly cut hair and pushed my head towards his. Before I could blink, he sucked my bottom lip into his mouth. Upon getting ahold of my tongue, another round of my sweet pussy juices drenched him. In return, he dug further into my treasure trove, causing me to moan into his mouth.

"Ava, you know I ain't going home tonight, right?" he moaned, making love to me.

"Yes, I know," I cooed.

"Good," he replied, slowly stroking my undernourished kitty and walking towards the white, six-foot table that housed my gardening tools.

My mind was blown at his ability to still sex me as he held firmly to my body while walking. Undoubtedly, he would leave one hell of an impression and challenge me whenever we saw each other.

Upon planting my naked body on the table, Hussein lifted my face and kissed my lips intensely. After the delicate, heartfelt smooch, he called. "Ava?"

"Yes," I whimpered, feeling his dick pulsating.

"You do know I have an ulterior motive, right?"

"Elaborate, please," I poorly spoke, analyzing his eyes.

"When I'm done wit' you, whatever I say or want, you gon' give it to me wit' no problems."

Oh, hell no. Hold up, wait. This can't be the same Hussein that has stood by me through all these years? I thought, rising off the table. My mouth was eager to curse him out.

I was a few milliseconds short of doing so when the good-looking dick slinger gently shoved me on my back. As he did that, he carefully drove his dick in and out of my clenching coochie. Eyeing me, Hussein genuinely said, "I'm done speakin' to you in subliminal messages. It's time fo' you to hear exactly what I'm thinkin'; shid, what I've always thought. Can't a soul love you like I do. Can't a livin' person cater to you like I'm gon' do, like I've been doing. I'm gonna build you a motherfuckin' house. *We* gon' create a life together, an' *not* exclude the one we had taken from us. I ... am ... yo' ... rock, an' I'll always be. Don't just let my dick in you; let me, Solomon Hussein Hampton, further inside you, Ava Jane Langston. Put me further inside yo' heart now, Ava, an' keep me there always. You were destined to be mine, an' I'll be damn if I wait any longer hoppin' on the path of claimin' who was made to be my other half. Wit' that being said, I got som' shit I have to take care of. Trust me, the second it's over ... I'm gunnin' fo' you an' our life together."

Unable to hold my emotions together, I wrapped my arms around his neck and cried while cumming on his dick. I heard everything he said, but only one thing had gotten to me—the root of my life being turned upside down.

Removing my face from his neck, Hussein observed my eyes and said, "I'll never leave you, Ava. Never. I'm still here. There ain't enough reasons fo' me to look fo' anyone or anything elsewhere. I must have a life wit' you, an' you must get back to livin' life but wit' me. You gon' give us that. Do you understand?"

Slowly, I nodded. "I think so."

Digging deeper inside me, Hussein tilted his head to the left and said, "You think so? Nawl, Ava, I don't like that answer. Either you understand, or you don't. So, which one is it, baby?"

"I ... I...." I stammered, trembling.

Rotating his hips while shoving dick in every corner of my wet pussy, Hussein loudly asked, "Do you understand what I need from us, Ava?"

As I felt an enormous amount of heat consume my body, I involuntarily gripped my hair as I struggled to speak.

"Answer me, Ava!" Hussein bellowed, continuing to beautifully destroy the one place no man had ever demolished.

While a gush of fluids erupted my precious volcano, I erotically hollered, "I understand, Solomon! I understand!"

Removing his dick from my pink walls, Hussein calmly said, "Good. Now, lay back, put yo' legs an' arms behind yo' head. Enjoy me suckin' every ounce of yo' cum out of you before I give you this splendid dick that's been messin' out of yo' life. I swear you deserve everything I'm gon' give you tonight an' every day after."

Oh, Jesus, I thought, placing my limbs where he needed them. Meanwhile, happy tears cascaded into my quivering lips.

Chapter V

Hussein

"Love all, trust a few, do wrong to none,"-William Shakespeare,
All's Well that Ends Well

The Next Day

I knew I would be in the hot seat when I arrived at my apartment. I hadn't planned on staying at Ava's house past noon, yet I couldn't tear my body from hers. She was home to me. Our union, bodies, bond, and chemistry couldn't let me shower and leave. I had longed to be with Ava the way I was. Nothing or anyone would get in the way, especially the situationship with my weed connection's daughter.

"All motherfucking night until well in the next day's afternoon hours, Solomon Hampton! Really? You didn't answer a call or respond to a text! You think you can stroll into an apartment *we* live in together as if you don't have anyone to answer to! Who gave you the damn right to do that? You are not a single man!" Lakin hollered before I could step across the threshold of the door.

"Shid, guh, I am a single man. Yo' housin' in *my* apartment was temporary. You know this. Don't start this shit as if we are a couple, Lakin. We had a solid understandin' when I told you you could come to live here after you miscarried. Don't think fo' a second I wanted a relationship wit' you because I told you I didn't. You've gotten beside yo'self, an' you need to know yo' damn place," I replied, sauntering towards the bedroom.

Pushing me, she screamed, "You got me all the way fucked up, Solomon Hussein!"

42

Spinning on my heels, I pointed my finger at the angry woman and said, "Keep yo' hands to yo'self, Lakin. I heard you, but it seems you didn't hear me. When we started fuckin' 'round, I told you I wasn't lookin' fo' a companion. You said you wasn't either. The condom broke, an' you got pregnant. That still didn't change what I wanted from us. The pregnancy ain't no longer, an' you want mo' than I'm willin' to give. Thus, we are done; the fuckship is over! Fuck waitin' on three weeks to arrive, gather yo' stuff an' leave."

The beautiful creature in front of me trembled massively. She wasn't hurt; she was angry. It soared through her petite body. I saw emotions that shouldn't have been there in her almond-shaped, teary eyes—hurt, frustration, and confusion. As her body shook uncontrollably, the clear liquids rapidly cascaded from her eyes.

Lakin clenched and unclenched her hand multiple times while sobbing, "Why don't you want more from me, us? I've done everything to make you see that I'm a great fit for you. I love you, Hussein, and want us to grow into something beautiful. What have I done to you? I miscarried your child, and this is how you are punishing me. I did everything in the book to cease miscarrying. I really did. So, tell me, Hussein, why are you punishing me like this?"

Sighing deeply, I sincerely announced, "The moment I realized you fell in love wit' me, I should've let you go. That was my fuck up, an' I apologize. Yeah, I care 'bout you, but I don't love you. I ain't punishin' you, Lakin. I promise. I don't want mo' from us because I never saw a future fo' us. You are gorgeous, no doubt. Thankful, most definitely. You have all the qualities of makin' a great girlfriend or wife, but you ain't not fo' me. I need an exceptional woman. Please don't take this wrong, but you are not exceptional fo' me. What you seekin' from me, you'll never get. I'm freein' myself from you; most importantly, I'm freein' you from me, a person who will never love you the way you deserve. You are miserable;

I'm miserable. After losing the pregnancy, I thought you would sink into depression. You never did. Therefore, I know you are mo' than capable of takin' care of yo'self. So, please don't make things harder than it has to be. I'm done fuckin' on you. So, can we please respectfully go our separate ways?"

Silence overcame us as she glared at me. Balling her lips and unclenching her hands, Lakin nastily replied, "I let my apartment go, Hussein."

Shocked, I replied, "What?"

"I didn't see the need to pay the rent there if I lived here."

Angry, I responded, "Lakin, you knew you would be livin' here temporarily. You knew our situation status wasn't gon' change. I told you this. So, why you ain't continue payin' rent on yo' spot? That was the dumbest thing to do."

Loudly, she said, "I thoug—"

"Yo' ass thought we would slip into a relationship, huh?" I asked, upset as three knocks sounded at the door.

"Are you expecting company?" she asked, pointing at the rectangular object.

"Nope. Are you?"

"No," she voiced, walking towards the door.

Man, this bitch stupid as fuck! I thought as my cell phone vibrated. At the same time, Lakin announced it was her mother.

Ignoring her, I retrieved my phone. Upon seeing Mo's name on the text notification bar, I read his message as Nanette and I greeted each other. While continuing to read Mo's message, I tuned out the conversation between my supplier of quality, exotic weed and her dumb-ass daughter.

Pleased with Mo's message, I agreed to tonight's double date event. Apparently, Mo reached out to Allie to inquire about a date night. Knowing Allie, she suggested Ava and I come along. Like Ava, Allie struggled to understand life a few years ago. As she wanted to return to the land of the living, I was confident Allie wanted the same for her best friend. Thus, Mo stepped in to do his part, as I was sure Allie had done hers—notify Ava.

Smiling at the thought of taking Ava on our first date, I shoved my phone into my pocket and strolled towards the closet. A few steps away, my phone vibrated. As the mother and daughter casually conversed, I retrieved my device and stared at a text message notification from Ava. My heart raced as a massive smile appeared. Quickly, I opened the text.

My Heartbeat: *It seems that our presence is highly recommended for a double date with your friend Mo and my bestie Allie. Are you available to attend this dating thing?*

Shortly afterward, I responded with: *Of course I am. From my understandin', we leavin' out in two hours, an' I'll be pickin' y'all up from yo' house before pickin' him up.*

A few seconds later, my phone vibrated, and my eyes were glued to Ava's text.

My Heartbeat: *You nailed it. Well, I shall get ready. Allie just arrived with a million damn outfits.*

As if my hands were on a computer's keyboard, they swiftly moved across my phone's keyboard.

Me: *How do you feel 'bout stayin' overnight in whatever city we land in?*

Please say yes. Please say yes, I thought while waiting for her response.

With my eyes glued to my phone, it vibrated. My heart was close to jumping out of my chest as I read her message.

My Heartbeat: *I'm okay with it. Now, I really have to go, or we will not be ready when you arrive.*

Fuckin' right, I smiled, sending a bunch of heart and smiling emojis before replying with: *Okay. See you in two hours, woman.*

"Bye, Solomon," Nanette spoke from the front room.

As my phone vibrated, I seriously replied, "Nanette, I need to holla at cha fo' a minute."

"Okay," she voiced.

Skipping out of the room, I looked at Lakin before focusing on her elegantly dressed mother.

"Shall we go outside and talk?" Nanette inquired curiously.

"No, ma'am. It's really a personal matter," I quickly voiced, searching her eyes. "Um, I really don't know how to say this, but I'm gon' spit it out as is. I ain't the man fo' yo' daughter. I care fo' her, but I ain't in love wit' her. I respectfully want out of this situation; however, I feel she will make things hard. I don't need unwanted drama, Nanette."

"And what do you propose I do, Solomon?" Nanette probed as Lakin ranted and raved.

"To see yo' daughter leave wit' her belongings as you lead the way out of this apartment," I calmly voiced.

"Solomon, you do know once Lakin leaves this apartment, the discount disappears, right?"

Nodding, I replied, "I'm fine wit' that."

"Very well. Lakin, grab your things and give Solomon his key," Nanette ordered.

Now, my real life can start without a single problem. Ava is all mine an' mine alone.

"Momma, Hussein's been playing me this entire time to get to you. Cease your business with him. He doesn't deserve to come up off my back," Lakin angrily cried as I strolled towards my room.

This girl here, I thought, shaking my head.

"First of all, Hussein wasn't using you to get to me; we were already in cahoots with each other. You just aided him in receiving a discount, which you clearly heard me say it's off the table. For me to dismiss Hussein's hustling abilities would be the dumbest thing ever, Lakin. Hussein is too gotdamn valuable to me. You see, honey, what he doesn't venture into others that he knows do. So, there is no way in hell I'm cutting Hussein loose. Now, he's spoken his peace about y'all's relationship. Gather your things so you can take your ass to your apartment. I won't go back and forth with you about parking your ass where it's not wanted. Now, hurry along; I have another stop I need to make."

"I terminated the lease on my apartment, Mother," she whined.

Stunned, Nanette looked at me and asked, "Did you know this before you ended things between the two of you?"

I shook my head and replied, "No. Nanette, we was never in a relationship. We … I … was cautious, but the condom broke; thus, she became pregnant."

Holding up her hand, Nanette casually said, "Hold the fuck up. So, y'all weren't even dating Solomon? Y'all were just fucking around?"

"Yes, ma'am." I nodded, staring at the woman, who seemed as if she was about to lose her mind.

Zit. Zit. Zit.

"So, this entire time, I thought you and my daughter were dating, y'all were not?" Nanette questioned.

"Yes, ma'am."

"Did you and my daughter talk about y'all's situation beforehand?"

Nodding, I responded, "I was frank wit' Lakin from the beginnin'. Everything I wanted, she agreed that's what she wanted as well. Sex wit' no strings attached."

Shaking her head, Nanette voiced, "She caught feelings, and you never did. My God, Lakin, go get your things at once. You will come to my house until we get your living quarters squared away. Trust and believe I will not pay your rent when your six weeks are up. You will be on someone's job, carefully thinking about your choices concerning men. Furthermore, what in the fuck have you been doing with the rent money I gave you?"

"I put it in my savings account," Lakin softly voiced as I walked into my room, aiming for the closet.

"Girl, get your silly ass out of my presence so I can properly curse your ass out once we arrive at my house!" Nanette angrily breathed to her daughter.

"Yes, ma'am," Lakin cried before storming inside my room.

Remembering my phone had vibrated many times, I retrieved my device and ignored the smart remarks from the angry bird. Seeing Ava's pet name on the text notification bar resulted in my heart leaping. Like earlier, my smile was huge as I quickly opened her text.

My Heartbeat: Um, where exactly are we going? The reason I ask is because I need to know how I should dress.

After I read her message, I rapidly replied.

Me: Whatever you put on determines where we go. Will that work better fo' you?"

"So, who are you conversing with while standing starkly still in front of the closet, smiling?" Lakin nastily interrogated from behind me.

"Now, that is not any of your concern. You should be focused on packing," I voiced, turning to face her.

She spat, "You are an asshole, Solomon!"

"Lakin Letterson, get your shit because I have something important to do besides cursing your ass out! Do not make me come in there because it won't be fucking pretty. My patience has run thin with your ass!" Nanette's smooth and classy voice boomed through my one-bedroom apartment.

Scurrying about, Lakin retreated to gather her things out of the bathroom. While she did so, I received a text from Ava, replying to my latest message. Seeing she was okay with her dress attire determining where we would go, I grabbed my black Adidas duffel bag from underneath the bed.

Afterward, I strolled towards the dresser that housed my undergarments; Lakin stormed past me, bumping me with all her might.

This chick is wild, I thought, laughing and grabbing my undergarments.

"You think this shit is funny, huh?" she loudly spat.

I ignored the broad while throwing the items into the duffel bag. I returned to the closet and retrieved many matched outfits and three pairs of shoes. Upon planting them inside the duffel bag, Lakin stepped to me and slowly voiced through her straight teeth. "You ain't nothing but a simple ass nigga that works a nine-to-five gig."

"Then, tell me why you are pressed 'bout my' simple ass'?" I laughed, moving towards the bathroom.

Before she could further talk shit, Nanette yelled, "Lakin, let's go now!"

Knowing not to further irritate her mother, Lakin skipped towards the door and said, "I wish you much misery, bitch ass nigga!"

While I brushed my teeth, Nanette said, "Solomon, we are gone. I've placed your apartment key on the kitchen table. Remember to have my full payment for all pickups."

"Roger that." I smiled before resuming to clean my mouth.

Upon hearing the front door close, I was one elated nigga as I rinsed my mouth, followed by flossing. Upon completion, I grabbed my hygiene items and ran into my room. After dropping the items inside the bag, I retrieved the outfit, undergarments, and shoes I had picked out to wear. Since I had showered right before leaving Ava's house, there was no need for me to do so again. Once dressed, I grabbed my duffel bag and skipped to the kitchen.

Seeing the silver key on the kitchen table, a massive grin appeared. Snatching it up, I placed it on my key ring as I walked towards the front door. Opening the rectangular object, I couldn't cease smiling as joy overwhelmed me. Finally, the time had arrived for Ava and me to grow as a couple, creating beautiful memories together.

A strange feeling overcame me as I climbed the stairs, two at a time. I willed it away, only for it to come back again. Arriving at my vehicle, I unlocked the doors on my car before aggressively opening the driver's door. Flinging the duffel bag into the backseat with glee, I hopped into the driver's seat.

"I finally got the girl," I happily stated, starting the engine.

While I reversed, my cell phone rang. Quickly, I retrieved my device and answered Ava's call.

"What's up, beautiful lady?" I sang, dropping the gearshift into the drive position.

As I skirted away, Ava nastily voiced, "Um, when were you planning on telling me you are in a relationship, Hussein? As a matter of fact, why haven't I seen said girlfriend of ten months with you at your grandparents' house or at your mother's church? Oh, that's right, you will not bring the main course anywhere near the appetizer's house. That would make it hard to place the appetizer on the side menu, huh? I've been through a lot of shit, which you know because your ass was in the middle. So, I tell you what … the shit that happened between us was simple and much needed. Thanks for that. A sister truly needed it. Have a great day; just in case you haven't caught the drift … I will not attend the double date thing."

Before I could say a word, she ended the call.

"Fuck!" I shouted, mashing the gas pedal while calling her.

Exiting my apartment complex, I tried my best to get Ava to answer the phone. Twenty calls later and a call from Mo, I pulled into her driveway, eager to let her know that I was a single man and had been.

Hopping out of my whip, I ran to her door and pressed the doorbell repeatedly. The door went unanswered; thus, I ran to her bedroom window, knocked on it, and called her name. There weren't any sounds coming from her room. Therefore, I called her phone again. Thankfully, that time, she answered on the fourth ring.

"What, Hussein?"

"I was never in a relationship, Ava. The chick an' I was messin' 'round fo' ten months; that's it. The condom broke; she became pregnant. Three weeks ago, she lost the baby. She was fo' months pregnant. She was temporarily stayin' wit' me because I felt she would sink into depression badly. I saw how depression did you, an' I didn't want Lakin to go through it alone. Granted, I was

50

the person responsible fo' her gettin' pregnant. My plan, which she knew, was to care fo' her fo' six weeks before she was due to see the doctor. The goal was fo' her to leave my apartment within three weeks because her six weeks would be up. She is no longer stayin' at my crib; she left wit' her mother while I was textin' you. I am done wit' her; I never loved her. Remember last night, I told you I had som' shit to take care of? She was 'the shit I had to take care of'. It's you that I need, not anyone else. I told you I would never hurt you, an' I meant that. Ava, baby, please tell me where you at so I can discuss this wit' you … face-to-face so you know I ain't lyin' to you. I could never lie to you."

"You could never lie to me, yet you withheld information. That mess you are spitting sounds good. I'm not at home; that's all you need to know. Look, Hussein, what we did was just that. I'm not angry at you, nor do I dislike you. We fucked, from the time you pulled into my garage until you left. Harmless sex, now you can go on about your business, and I can go on about mine. It's just that simple, Hussein," she calmly voiced as the wind blew wildly in her background before she ended the call.

"Ain't this 'bout a whole bitch!" I angrily shouted, walking towards the driveway, eager to find her.

She think I'm finna leave her alone. She's out of her fuckin' mind. Ava has no fuckin' idea how serious I am 'bout us being together. She don' opened the damn door an' allowed me to slide my ass right on in. I ain't walkin' out that fuckin' door, I thought, dialing Mo's number while jogging towards my car.

As I slid into the driver's seat on the second ring, he answered. "Nigga, what the fuck is going on? You have slaughtered our plans fo' the night."

Backing out of Ava's yard, I shook my head and said, "I know, but I'm determined to make things right. Have you spoken to Allie recently?"

"Yeah."

"What did she say?"

"That the plans fo' tonight canceled."

"Did she say if they were going anywhere?"

"Nope, but Ava was in the background statin' that she needed to breathe freely because you said something that had her thinkin' heavily."

Sitting upright as I sped down the street, I said, "I know where they are. Head to Morley's Cemetery."

"Nigga, what?" Mo laughed.

"That's not a laughin' matter, Mo. Ava's at her seven-year-old son's grave. Instead of sayin' she wants to visit, or she just left from Mica's grave, she says, 'I need to breathe freely' or 'I had to breathe freely'. Now, head that way."

Remorseful, Mo said, "Damn. Sorry, partna, I didn't know. I'm headed that way now."

"A'ight," I responded, ending the call. Pressing the hazard lights, I had to arrive at the cemetery on the north side of town fairly quickly.

I'm not lettin' you go, Ava. I will never let you an' Mica go. I didn't before, an' I sure as hell ain't finna do it now. I've told you that on mo' than one occasion.

Chapter VI

Ava

"Happiness is a risk. If you're not a little scared, then you're not doing it right."-Sarah Addison Allen, The Peach Keeper

Four years ago, Allie's fiancé passed away in a horrible accident. Michael Langley was the love of her life; thus, she shut the doors on love. If a man wasn't providing dick and mouth only, Allie didn't want anything to do with him. To my surprise, I received a call from my best friend, a mother of three, stating that my presence was required because she had a date with Mo.

I was proud of Allie for stepping into the dating world; meanwhile, I was ecstatic about being around Hussein on an intimate level. One thing I knew for sure: if Hussein had anything planned, he would cancel in the name of Ava Langston. Therefore, I contacted seven clients seeking my nail technician services over the weekend. After we agreed on a rescheduled date, I skipped around my bedroom feeling like a love-stricken female, all in the name of Solomon Hampton.

After Mo and Hussein confirmed everything, Allie dropped a bomb into my lap. Once again, I felt like a damn fool for entertaining a man. I had never lain with another woman's man. I had too much respect for myself. Firsthand, I knew what it felt like to know the person you loved wasn't faithful to you. It's not a great feeling, and I would never want another woman to experience the pain and humiliation I had.

Therefore, I informed Hussein that I knew about his relationship. In addition, I mentioned what happened between us was just that. I couldn't lie as if I wasn't disappointed or hurt. Hussein has always held a special place in my heart. I was comfortable and content around him. Seeing his light-skinned behind brought joy to my soul even though I didn't show it.

Upon ending the call with Hussein, it would've been wise to inform my clients that I recant rescheduling their appointment. However, the most critical words Hussein had spoken to me in the wee hours of the morning caused one of my feet to slip into the dark hole. In a flash, I knew I couldn't be around anyone this weekend, monetary gains or not. To halfway keep me from sliding down the dark hole's tunnel, I knew where I needed to be. I knew what I needed to do—find the one place I could breathe easily, my son's grave.

Even though Mica's small body was deep in the ground, somehow, I felt a little better whenever I was at his final resting place. Maybe I felt that way because I cried until my throat and stomach hurt, or I could've believed the lies that came out of my mouth that this would be the last time I visited his grave and shed tears until I couldn't.

Deeply inhaling, I stared at my son's headstone before sitting beside it. As I rubbed it like I had done his head before he fell asleep, I felt Allie's eyes on me from the car. Turning towards her vehicle, I stared into her worried face.

Planting my eyes on my son's grave, I softly said, "Hey, Momma's big guy. Today started off great, and now it's not going so well. A lot of emotions overcame me from a small conversation. Baby, I miss you, and I'm so so sorry I didn't take the time to make you put on your helmet. Every day, I pray I can return to force you to wear it. This thing called life is hard without you. I really hate life without yo—"

"Whew, big boy, Mica!" Hussein happily spoke from behind me. "Remember when we hid behind Gram's car, our hands held tightly to the Nerf water guns? Throughout the ordeal, yo' momma was screamin' yo' name an' lookin' worried?"

I smiled while rehashing the particular scene of that day.

Kneeling behind me, Hussein chuckled, "Buddy, she wasn't prepared fo' us. We came out like Batman an' Robin. That day was one of the best days I had wit' you. We had so many good ones, huh?"

While Hussein rehashed, I rested my head on his firm chest and listened to the man who spent more time with my precious child than his sorry-ass father had.

Thirty minutes later, Hussein cleared his throat and said, "Mica, do you remember me tellin' you that I'll always have you an' yo' Momma's backs? I meant that. I know you don't want to be excluded or forgotten, an' honestly, I can't have that. Always, I'll make sure you ain't, an' I still got yo' back even though you are not physically here. Of course, you know that because I bring you toy trucks every week before work. Yo' momma will always be looked after; you know I got her like I've always had her. Buddy, I need you to do us a favor. I need you to come to visit us in our dreams. When you come into mine, bring me a bag of sweet an' sour patch candies. Don't think I forgot you still owe me a bag."

And he's still doing fatherly things, I thought as tears spilled down my face.

As Hussein wrapped his arms around my waist, he kissed my neck and said, "I know I'm the reason you are here. I said som' things to you last night. You learned something today. I have never lied to you 'bout anything, an' I won't start now. Ava, I need you to do something fo' me."

"What's that?" I voiced, feeling the floodgates open.

"One, I need you to cease whatever you are thinkin'. Two, I need you to stop torturin' yo'self 'bout Mica's death. Ava, you ain't at fault."

"Yes, I am," I stated, voice trembling.

Hussein calmly voiced, "I'm going to be honest wit' you as I have been from day one. Ava, I never wanted to tell you this, but now you need to know. A few days after Mica had died, you had given me the authorization to talk to the medical examiner on yo' behalf. The information you wanted to know, I told you, he died instantly.

However, I didn't tell you that I took his helmet to her. I asked her if it would've made a difference if he had worn it. Her response was that Mica would've still died. The fit of the helmet would've resulted in him not dying immediately. He would've been suffering. So, baby, either way, Mica would've left us that day. I took an' still take comfort in knowin' that he didn't suffer. So, baby, Mica's death does not lie wit' you. It was his time to go peacefully."

Hearing the ugly truth and seeing the images of my son's head smashed on the right side as blood leaked, I hollered and clasped my hands over my face. The same emotions I felt the day he fell off his bike overcame me. To know my son would've died either way tore another hole into my body. I felt my heart shredding into pieces as Hussein held me tightly while planting kisses on the top of my head.

"I will continue to get you through this heartache, Ava. You have to trust me like you've always done," he softly stated, rubbing his face against my neck.

As I dropped my head into his left arm, I cried while hoping I could repair my broken life. I sat beside my son's grave, trying to let go of the pain his father brought into my life before losing him. I wailed at the thought of knowing I could never save Mica, no matter how much Jak hollered that I was stupid for not putting a helmet on my child's head.

"Let that shit out, baby, please let it out," Hussein spoke comfortingly as my sobs didn't cease; they increased.

Since my son's death, Hussein had been by my side, holding, comforting, and issuing sweet kisses. I didn't receive that care from my 'then-husband. Instead, Jak gave me cold stares and yells before acting like he never knew me. From that horrible day, Hussein was there to openly provide me the love I desperately needed from Jak.

Interlocking our hands, Hussein kissed my neck several times before whispering, "You be punishin' yo'self too much an' often. I don't like that, Ava. You deserve to be happy all the time, not som' of the time. Baby, let the pain go."

Little did Hussein know, I punished myself more when I realized I was super happy when he was with me. I felt tremendous guilt for smiling, laughing, and enjoying his company. In my mind, I believed I shouldn't have an ounce of happiness because my son wasn't alive.

"Ava, it's been three years since we lost Mica. I think you should talk to someone professionally. You need to forgive Jak so you can move on. You need to heal properly, Ava; you are not doing that. You are stuck. I promise I'll be right by yo' side as I've always been. If you don't want to see anyone professionally, we can join a support group filled wit' people who'd experience an' still go through what you do. Ava, you can't continue to be okay one day an' spiral the next day. It's time fo' you to start livin'. Like I said a million times, that doesn't mean you have to forget Mica. If you keep on spiralin' the way you, do all types of shit will go wrong wit' yo' health. Baby, live fo' Mica. Live, Ava Langston. I promise you; I will never let you forget him," Hussein gently breathed against my neck as he rubbed my stomach.

After I was cried out and Hussein breathed life back into me as he'd always done, we said our goodbyes. Along the way towards Allie's car, Hussein held tightly to my hand while explaining his relationship status. In need of analyzing his eyes while he spoke, I ceased walking and yanking his arm.

Once he turned to face me, Hussein stepped closer to me. While gazing into my peepers, he sincerely spoke, "She was simply a chick I was havin' sex wit'. She knew I didn't want a relationship wit' her. I didn't lie 'bout my intentions or lead her on. Every word I've said to you, I meant it. You are mo' than enough fo' me, an' I'm willin' an' able to show it every day of my life. Ava, give me another chance, please. Let me be in yo' life the way I'm meant to be."

In the depths of my soul, I knew Hussein wasn't lying. However, dealing with a lying and cheating Jak, I wasn't sure about anything I felt or witnessed. Knowing to tread lightly with my heart and trust, I shook my head while looking into Hussein's eyes.

"You know I hate drama. My life is chaotic enough. So, let's forget about what happened between us and keep things nice and breezy. I do not want to lose our friendship. Outside of Allie, our friendship means a lot to me," I voiced, observing his body language.

Placing his hands on the sides of my face, Hussein dropped his lips on mine and said, "I can't go back to the way we were, Ava. I will never forget our first time, let alone act like it never happened. You've given me something so precious that's a part of you. You are not a casual sex type of woman. If you allowed me to please you, you saw long-term like I've been seein' it."

Before I could respond, Hussein's thick, wet tongue parted my lips. Involuntarily, I stood on my tiptoes as my hands found their way to his neck. With a rapidly beating heart and butterflies floating in my stomach, we were engrossed in a sloppy, heated kiss. Instantly, the deprived sexual side of me awakened with such force it startled me.

Breaking the kiss with laughter, Hussein voiced, "Damn, it's only been a few hours an' you already hissin' and whimperin'."

Embarrassed, I replied, "Solomon, be quiet."

"Awe, the beautiful one is ashamed of the provocative noises that escaped her mouth," he joked, observing my eyes.

"Mo, be quiet!" Allie laughed, causing us to look at the pair.

"Look at yo' best friend, smilin' like a pussycat an' enjoyin' herself wit' Mo. Are you okay wit' her missin' out on an enjoyable two-day getaway because I wasn't upfront 'bout a fuck-a-ling?"

"Two days?" I asked with a raised eyebrow. "I thought it was just for today and tonight."

Picking me up, Hussein shook his head and replied, "Nawl, I added another day. It's time fo' you to live a lil' at my expense."

"At your expense, huh?" I smiled.

"Yep. If you wanna go shoppin', tell me how much you want an', you can get it. You want to do a lil' spa thing, just say it. You want to visit an expensive restaurant, shid, I'll cash out. Whatever you want to do, I'm payin' fo' it," he voiced as we arrived in front of our chatty and vibrant friends.

"What's up, Ava?" Mo pleasantly stated, softly smiling at me.

"Hi, Mo," I responded, waving.

Flashing his golden smile, Mo asked, "So, we outta here fo' two days or nah?"

"That's up to Ava. One phone call from me; my children are taken care of," Allie happily stated, eyeing me.

Hopping, Hussein asked, "What's it gonna be, Ava?"

As my titties bounced, I stared into his content eyes. They screamed for me to say yes. While observing the big kid chanting 'yes' and jumping, I thought about the pros and cons of going on a two-day getaway with Hussein, Allie, and Mo. Upon realizing it was time to step out of my comfort zone and try to live a little, I kept my eyes on Hussein as I smiled. "Allie, I think you should make that phone call."

"That's what the fuck I'm talkin' 'bout!" Mo and Hussein exclaimed as they bumped fists.

"You ridin' wit' me or Allie to yo' crib?" Hussein inquired, ogling me.

"Allie," I softly replied, searching his eyes.

"Okay," he stated, placing me on the ground.

While Allie talked to her mother, Mo pulled me aside and sincerely announced. "I don't want to put you in a bad mood, but I want to tell you this … as a man who has an' still is in yo' shoes, wit' time, it becomes easier. Yes, you'll miss yo' child, but life will become bearable."

Shocked, I said, "I'm so sorry for your loss, Mo. How long has it been for you?"

"Six years. Mo Junior was two years old. He had a bad heart. We been knew 'bout his condition before he was born. The doctors said he wouldn't make it to one. God gave us two years wit' him. His mom couldn't take being in my life after we buried him. She said seein' me was too much fo' her to bear. Lil' man looked just like me. To this day, I haven't talked to her. Take it a day at a time, Ava. If talkin' to Allie an' Hussein isn't enough, reach out to me. I know what it feels like to see yo' child's pictures, go into his room, or see other boys his age. I know the demons you are battlin', an' what go through yo' head. I'm gon' tell you like this, Ava: even though Mica's time was cut short, you were blessed to have him. To be his mother, nurture, love, an' kiss on him, but most importantly, y'all created seven years of great an' lovin' memories. Reflect on those memories, an' you'll breathe a tad bit easier."

I hadn't noticed the tears cascading down my face after searching Mo's content, light-brown eyes and taking in everything he said. After wiping them away, he hugged me, saying, "You will have the life you've dreamed of. You will be able to smile an' be happy without feelin' guilty. I can promise you that."

As we pulled away, I smiled politely, "Thank you. I needed to hear everything you said. Trust me; I will reach out to you. The road does get tight and difficult to drive on."

"On holidays an' birthdays?" he questioned more so than stated.

"Yep."

"On those days, don't shut down. Open up mo'. Buy one gift an' bring it to his grave."

Nodding, I sighed deeply and said, "I will do that."

"A'ight." He smiled. "Ready to begin this new adventure?"

"I think so."

Chuckling, Mo responded, "Shid, you better be because Hussein's all in."

Looking at the handsome man, placing his duffel bag in the trunk of his car, I smiled. "Yes, he is."

"He's dedicated to you, mo' than you'll ever know," Mo voiced.

"Oh, I know, and it scares me a little," I confessed, unable to take my eyes off Hussein.

"Why?"

"Because I don't want to be so happy that I forget my son, or I don't want to get so caught up in what I'm feeling that I miss the signs of leaving him alone." I lowly breathed, slowly planting my eyes on Mo.

"Sweet face, no matter how happy you are ... you won't forget Mica. You are his mother; you can't forget him. From what Allie told me about Mica an' Hussein's relationship, you will never forget Mica because Hussein won't allow it. Now, Ava, one thing about Hussein, he don't play 'round wit' people's hearts. If he tells you, he wants something an' that only that's what you will get. Hussein's been that way since high school. He's not yo' ordinary guy. I'm sure you've figured that out by now. So, Ava, will you do me a favor?"

"What's that?"

"You can't continue to go back an' forth wit' yo'self. That's not healthy. Cease the negative thoughts an' feelin's the moment they surface. Stop feelin' like you ain't meant to be happy or deserve good things to happen to you. Open up yo' heart an' let love back in. Be spontaneous an' enjoy life. You an' I both know how precious it is. Each day is a blessin'. Take life by the horns an' ride that motherfucka 'til you can't anymo'. It's time fo' you to step into the new life you didn't ask fo'. Make the best of it wit' those who cherish the ground you walk on. Create the life you'd always wanted. Don't be stuck in the past while grievin'. Heal, Ava."

With teary eyes, I gasped, "It's really hard to heal, Mo. Really, really hard."

"I know, but you have to be willin' to try. You have to change yo' routines to heal. If you don't, you will destroy everything being sent yo' way. I know that firsthand. I do not want you to do what I did. You will lose out on good people being in yo' life. Dwellin' on hurt will leave you one miserable an' lonely soul. I was a miserable an' lonely person fo' three years after my son passed."

"How did you overcome it?" I inquired, wiping my face.

Staring into my eyes, Mo replied, "I packed my shit an' left the house that held all the memories an' kept me stagnant. I kept my son's pictures, but everything else that belonged to him, I gave away. Then, I saw a therapist. She recommended joinin' a support group, but I didn't. She had done her job just fine. Now, look at me, on an adventure wit' a woman I have been had my eyes on fo' a lil' over six months. Start healin' now, Ava. So, yo' life can begin again."

In my little ass mind, I thought we would be staying in Alabama, not with Hussein behind the wheel of his car. Close to ten hours and well over twenty minutes, thanks to the bathroom and smoke breaks for the guys, we arrived in the community of numerous condos and a few beachfront houses in Bradenton Beach, Florida. Even though it was well into the wee hours of the dark morning, the area was far from quiet, and one could see the beauty of the place. I was in awe of the gorgeous layout of the two-building beachfront building owned by Hussein's grandparents.

"So, this is where you were trying to get me to come to after we buried Mica?" I questioned Hussein as we retrieved our luggage. At the same time, a group of people to the left of us laughed as they listened to reggae music at a nice listening decibel.

Nodding, he replied, "Yes. Do you like it?"

"Do I like it? What kind of question is that? I haven't seen all of it, and I'm already in love," I honestly replied as we stepped out of the way so Allie and Mo could receive their luggage.

"Just wait 'til you get inside," Hussein voiced, eyeing me.

"So, dude, yo' family loaded fo' real?" Mo stated as he closed the trunk.

"If you want to say that," he chuckled as a brief chirp sounded from his vehicle, indicating he had locked it.

"So, durin' the summers, this was where yo' ass was at?" Mo probed.

"Not all summers, just a few of them," Hussein replied, leading the way towards the doors.

"How many bedrooms in this place?" Allie inquired as we neared the uniquely designed glass door with one hell of a spiral art.

"Nine."

"Shit!" we exclaimed, looking at him.

Laughing, he unlocked the door and said, "Good thing, the housekeepers are due to come on Sunday. They will earn every gotdamn penny."

Upon stepping across the silver threshold, my mouth dropped as I observed the front entrance of the main building. Standing a few feet from the door made me feel at peace. The earth-tone décor gave me a serene feeling. The pictures on the walls were vibrant but homely. Everything about the place gave me a welcoming feel.

"Tour time," the beautiful being announced before kissing the back of my hand.

"Let's get on it," Allie and I announced, smiling.

There were numerous well-sized bedrooms decorated homely yet elegantly. Two large living areas were on the ground floor and one upstairs. The living area upstairs had a dining area with a spectacular gulf view; six white lounge chairs were on the balcony. I couldn't wait until the morning to view the area as the sun shone brightly. As we looked down, a volleyball net was secured in the sand. My eyes lit up like a car's headlight on a high beam as Allie lost her damn mind.

"I see we will be beatin' y'all's asses later today, huh?" Hussein joked, grabbing my hand.

"I don't think so. Allie and I are going to run circles around you and Mo." I smiled.

"Bet on it?" Hussein chuckled.

"Hold up, woe, don't bet shit," Mo chuckled. "I ain't shit when it comes to chasin' a ball in pure hellish heat."

Hussein led the way back inside the plush building as we laughed. Our next stop was the bedrooms on the second floor before we investigated the rooms on the first floor. Just like the bedrooms were laid to perfection, so were the bathrooms. I had plans of sitting my ass in the tub soaking, which I was sure I would need after Hussein was done with me.

"The finale of the tour is to look around the side of this spot. After that, we can turn up a bit or go fo' a walk on the beach an' then turn up," Hussein stated as we traveled outside.

"Jesus," Allie cooed in awe.

"Right," I replied, ogling the pool area, which gave off a tropical paradise vibe.

In front of the pool were two palm trees. On the sides of the pool were two expensive, four-chair brown wicker circular tables, and numerous lounging chairs placed in the sun's path. I knew my body would enjoy the clean, blue waters slapping against my cinnamon-brown skin.

"This is the hot tub area," Hussein voiced, pointing at a triangle-shaped area on the far-left side of the pool.

"Mann, this place is wicked as fuck. I'm diggin' the hell out of it." Mo smiled as he grabbed Allie's hand.

"I'll be sure to tell Grams an' Pop Pop that," the handsome being voiced, briefly looking at Mo.

"I can't cook, but what, um, what that kitchen lookin' like?" Allie giggled.

"You have three kids, an' you can't cook?" Mo questioned, seriously eyeing Allie.

"I can cook, but not like Ava," she giggled.

"Can you cook a holiday meal?" Mo asked as Hussein laughed while toward the door of the large place.

"Nope," Allie replied as we followed behind my handsome friend.

"So, you a chicken nugget an' French fry type of cook?" Mo probed.

"And seafood," Allie responded.

"I see now we gon' have to tighten yo' cookin' skills up. Not gon' have me starvin' lookin' like roadkill," he joked, causing Hussein and I to laugh hysterically.

Mo was in for a rude awakening, trying to teach Allie how to cook. Simply, that damn woman disliked everything about cooking. I ran out of patience trying to teach her to be patient when cooking. Allie had always been a fast-food type of person; her deceased fiancé was the cook. Allie and I often bumped heads about her dislike of cooking; that would run a man away quickly. It surely would put a dent in your pockets, especially when you have multiple mouths to feed.

"Here is the kitchen," Hussein voiced as we stepped into the polished and fully equipped cooking area.

"I would have a field day in here preparing meals!" I exclaimed as my eyes grew big.

"See those words is a man's best friend mo' than 'come get this pussy'," Mo voiced, which caused Hussein to walk off, laughing and shaking his head.

I could tell Allie was in her feelings because she sighed several times heavily before saying. "Well, this bitch here does not cook Moxley Anderson, and I don't have plans of learning or even attempting to act like I'm going to learn."

"Oh, you will. In due time, you will," he replied, eyeing an upset Allie.

"Ava!" Hussein called from God knew where.

"Yes?" I replied, eager to escape the tension in the kitchen.

"Come to me, beautiful one," he stated from upstairs.

"On the way," I responded, locating the stairs before ascending.

Halfway up the stairs, Mo asked Allie, "So, you in yo' feelin's?"

"Yep."

"You better get out of them."

"Whatever."

Oh Lord, I thought, hearing movement from one of the bedrooms down the hallway to my right.

As I ventured in that direction, Mo told Allie to come to him. That smart-mouth heifer gave him words that had my eyes bucked.

"Why are you lookin' like that?" Hussein inquired as I posted on the doorframe.

"They are having their first unpleasant conversation."

He laughed. "Why? Because she can't or don't want to cook?"

"Both."

"Well, shit," he stated, chuckling. "Are you comfortable wit' this room? This location?"

Sliding further into the room, I nodded. "Yes, and yes."

"Good."

"Thank you for bringing me here. It's much needed," I stated as he began to put up his clothes.

"Never thank me fo' doing things fo' you, Ava. I mean that."

Giggling, I said, "That doesn't mean I'm going to cease saying thank you, Hussein."

"True," he replied as I unloaded the items from my suitcase.

While I gathered my undergarments, Allie's loud voice traveled up the stairs. She was calling my name.

"Yes?" I responded, looking towards the door.

"Girl, where are you?"

"The first bedroom to your left," I said, walking to the brown dresser Hussein shoved his undergarments into.

"So, um, what exactly are we about to get into?" she questioned as we continued to unload our things.

"Whatever y'all wanna do," Hussein replied, looking between Allie and me.

"Drinking is on the top of my list. Mo has rubbed me the wrong way," she spat.

From behind her, he chuckled, "You will be all right. A lil' truth ain't never hurt no-damn-body. Dealin' wit' me, you better be ready fo' the truth at all times."

As Allie looked at Mo in a nasty way, Hussein asked, "Shit, Ava, I forgot to ask you … do you have any clients scheduled any time soon?"

"No."

"When will you have clients?" he voiced as Mo pulled Allie from our room door.

"Every day next week, and boy, am I booked," I stated, hearing laughter seeping from Mo's mouth.

As Hussein and I looked towards the door, I said, "Thank goodness she's mixing drinks. I thought shit was about to get rocky, and we would have to leave."

"Honestly, I thought so also," Hussein voiced, pulling me close.

"I'm happy you are here wit' me, Ava," he sexily breathed against my neck.

Ogling him, I truthfully responded, "So am I."

He lifted me from the ground and snaked his tongue into my mouth. Moaning, I wrapped my arms around his neck and lovingly attacked his tongue. While we were engrossed in the intense kiss, The Spiffz's "Twerk That" blasted from the TV. There was no doubt that Allie was responsible.

Completely out of character, I danced on Hussein as his tongue slid out of my mouth. Bending his knees, Hussein and I cut a rug while gazing into each other's eyes.

While thrusting his dick on my starving kitty, Hussein hollered, "Twerk that fat ass fo' a lil' piece of my change!"

Bouncing her special self into the room, my best friend grinned, "Here are your drinks. Enjoy!"

Immediately, I stopped dancing as I blushed. As I looked at the drinks in her and Mo's hands, Hussein and Allie inquired, "Why you stopped dancing?"

Shrugging, I replied, "I'm embarrassed."

"Fo' what?" Hussein laughed, still moving along to the beat but standing.

"Girl, drink this, and I bet you won't be embarrassed anymore," Allie voiced as she handed me a pink transparent plastic cup.

After the song ended, another twerking jam blasted, causing Mo, Allie, and Hussein to bob their heads and jig. Shaking my head, I placed the cup to my lips. Immediately, I smelled the liquor seeping from the colorful concoction. Like always, I slaughtered the semi-slushy goodness. Allie knew how to make a mixed drink; it was her specialty.

"Well, I'll be damn. Just drank it like it's water, then," Mo chuckled, causing us to laugh.

"I want to dance, Ava," Allie whined, looking at me.

Playfully, I rolled my eyes and said, "Well, I don't know what you are telling me for. I'm not about to dance. You know how I am when it comes dow—"

The liquor hit me halfway at the end of my speech, making me blink rapidly. A bubbly and the 'fuck it' attitude overcame me as Javon Black's "I Need (Sex)" blasted. Instantly, I went from not wanting to dance to dancing and hollering, "I'm so fucking lonely! Slide through and put it on me!"

As I jigged to the beat while slowly dropping to the ground, Allie was in front of me, moving along with the song's rhythm.

Feeling like I was high as a kite, we hollered, "I need some motherfucking sex!"

Closing my eyes, I lifted my head and rocked to the left, ensuring my romp clapped before bouncing. It wasn't long before I felt Hussein's body behind me, rocking with me.

"I need some fucking sex!" we chanted excitedly as the song ended.

D.C. Youngfly's "24 hrs" blared, resulting in me shoving Hussein onto the bed and giving him a lap dance.

"Gotdamn it. Get it, baby," he groaned, matching my dancing rhythm.

"Well shit, I guess they finna start fuckin' in this bitch, right in front of us, huh?" Mo laughed, resulting in Allie giggling while agreeing. Hussein and I were so in the zone with what we had going on to the point we didn't give a damn about them.

My pretty kitty was wet from his dick rubbing against my clit. My moving titties begged for his mouth to grace them. My wondering hands on his head itched to grip his head while he gave my pussy a facial. After staring into his eyes for too long and feeling the pressure between my legs, I struggle to breathe and fight the urge to snatch his clothes off him.

Hussein's eyes and body told a story I knew he would deliver. The longing to have my body pressed against his seeped from his eyes. The slow licking of his tongue informed me he was ready for it to wrestle with my tongue before his pink, wide, and long flesh found its way to my clit. The steady rise and fall of his chest told me he was ready for my mouth to place kisses on it while I watched his creamy-coated dick slowly enter before exiting me.

"Damn, baby, let me wipe yo' mouth." Hussein grinned, snapping me into reality as the song ended.

"Huh?" I asked with furrowed eyebrows, pussy throbbing.

"Oou, bitch, where did your mind dip off to? Wherever it went, that gotdamn mouth got too wet, and baby, you got to hunching this man on this bed, bitch!" Allie giggled inches from me as Mo laughed.

Embarrassed, I avoided answering Allie and looking into Hussein's eyes.

"Y'all don' embarrassed, my baby," Hussein chuckled as Guy's "Let's Chill" played.

"That song right on time," Mo voiced. "Let's go take a walk on the beach."

"Before we do that, how about we have another drink?" Allie announced.

"Sure," I happily chimed, looking at my best friend.

Giggling, she said, "This will be your last one, best friend. It's not only alcohol in it."

As the fellas laughed, I loudly questioned, "What the hell do you mean it's not only alcohol in it?"

"Let's just say it has a nice amount of THC in it, sis." Allie laughed, skipping out of the room.

With bucked eyes, I hollered, "Oh my God, this bitch got me high and drunk! Now, who can fuck in this kind of weather?"

"Shid, me." Hussein laughed, gripping my thighs before standing. At the same time, Mo laughed.

As we exited the room, I couldn't take my eyes off the handsome male as my mind was in a naughty land.

"What are you thinkin' 'bout, Ava?"

Before I knew it, I blurted out. "You fucking the shit out of me, causing me to wet the sheets and mattress."

Hussein's knees buckled as Mo spit out his drink, choking.

"Well, shit nih," Hussein sexily voiced as we reached the end of the staircase.

After his coughing ceased, Mo chuckled, "Well, I think I know why Allie said no mo' drinks fo' you."

Landing in the kitchen, Allie asked, "What happened?"

"She blunt than a motherfucka."

"Oh, and it will get worse. That's why she won't have another ounce of this concoction once she downs this one," Allie stated in a motherly tone as Hussein sopped my bottom lip into his mouth.

While retrieving our cups, Hussein asked, "How 'bout we take this cup to the head?"

"I'm with it!" my intoxicated behind shouted.

Once we slaughtered the beverage, I shivered. At the same time, Allie said, "Before we get to walking on the beach and spending our one-on-one time, I need to speak with Ava."

"A'ight," the fellas replied as Hussein placed me on a barstool.

Once they exited the kitchen, I slowly asked, "I know you probably want to tell me to slow my mind down, but before you do … I need to ask you something?"

"What's that?" she stated, cleaning the bar area.

"Sooo, what do you think about this getaway, and how are you feeling about Mo after y'all's little spat, shall I call it?" I responded rapidly.

"I'm feeling the trip, but he rubbed me incorrectly about not cooking or wanting to cook. Outside of that, he's easy to talk to; he listens and understands. Even though we had our little spat or whatever, it feels good to be wanted, like genuinely wanted … you know? Honestly, he makes me feel like Michael did, even down to the cooking. I guess that's why I blew up on him. A small part of me felt as if I was betraying Michael by getting to know another man," she softly voiced, eyes showing confliction.

"Did you know Mo was into you before the club scene?" I inquired as she mixed up the drinks.

"Yeah, but I never paid him any intention because he seemed like a whoremonger. Boy, was I wrong?" she softly smiled.

"Yep, you are big wrong," I giggled. "Based on our small conversation at the cemetery, he's a straight-up guy."

"If you don't mind me asking, what was said?"

While I told my girl about Mo's and my conversation, she completed her cleaning task while eyeing me every chance she could get. After I finished talking, Allie stared into my eyes and said, "He's right. It's time for you to start living. If I can jump off the porch, so can you. Speaking of jumping off the porch, tell me how you are *really* feeling about Hussein."

"Bitch, is that why you put THC in this drink? To make me tell my truths?" I giggled, running my hand through my hair.

Nodding and pointing at me, she hollered, laughing, "Bitch, you guessed it!"

Giggling and blushing, I bit my bottom lip and looked towards the back porch. Upon my eyes landing on the smiling and happy individual, I calmly replied, "It's a no-brainer; he's my male best friend who holds a special place in my heart. He became one of my best friends. He's always been there."

Slamming her hands on the countertop, startling me, Allie said, "Now, bitch, I know you can dig deeper than that. So, get to diggin' skeezer."

Giggling, I said, "Let's just say that … I'm nervous and scared but anxious to see how this will play out."

"If I tell your ass to dig deeper again, Ava Jane, I will knock your ass out. Dig now," my best friend demanded sternly.

Deeply inhaling, I faced Allie and closed my eyes. Dropping my head into my hands, I shook my head several times before confidently blurting out. "He's a fresh breath of air. His voice soothes my soul, allowing me to be calm and at peace. His entire existence excites me deep into my bones. His gentle yet stern touches have me not wanting him to cease touching me. Oh, his sex skills are amazing. I mean, make a bitch want to get down on one knee and ask him to marry me, type of amazing. Slow, passionate, dedicated, and pure bliss. He craves to satisfy, and I'm eager to be satisfied."

"Y'all fucked before?" Allie inquired, causing me to remove my hands from my face. I stared at her, smiling.

"Um, define before?"

"Like during your bereavement time or six months to a year later or before your world was turned upside down?"

"Oh, in that case, no; however, when we left the club … we did," I blushed.

Allie yelled, "Nih, bitch, when were you going to give me the details on that?"

"I was going to tell you, but you told me he had a girlfriend. Then, I became ashamed of sleeping with someone else's man. So, I kept that tidbit to myself."

"Oh," she voiced. "So, if you are here, that means he didn't have a girlfriend, and you believed him."

Rapidly nodding, I voiced, "Hussein isn't a typical man. He's always been thoughtful towards me. I often came onto Hussein, but he would never take the bait. He has no reason to lie to me, so yeah, I believe him."

Wickedly smiling, she said, "Now, back to this amazing sex thing. Was that why your slobber was trickling from your half-opened mouth while you gazed at the man as if he was a honey-baked ham while grinding on him."

Busting out laughing, I replied, "Something like that."

"So, how was it? Details, bitch."

"Mind-fucking-blowing. I squirted a lot. We had to put the blow dryer on my mattress," I voiced lowly before covering my face.

"Ooou, I'm jealous. I have never had that type of sex before. What was it really like?" she quizzed, removing my hands from my face.

As I stood from the barstool, I quickly told her about my sexual experience with Hussein. My poor friend cooed and whimpered. While I clearly described the euphoria I felt, the fellas walked in with curious facial expressions.

Blushing, I ceased talking and prayed they didn't hear anything I had said about the massive flood Hussein created while I was drunk off his sexual abilities and the liquor from The Gem.

"I don't know who's slobbin' the most, you Allie or Ava," Mo chuckled, looking at us.

Quickly, I looked away. While Hussein sauntered towards me, that damn Allie blurted, "So, Mo, have you ever made a woman squirt?"

I hysterically laughed. Hussein stopped in his tracks and looked at Mo, who stuttered. My partner had officially shut them up. After clearing his throat several times, Mo walked towards Allie and smiled. "Yeah, I've been known to do that occasionally. Why?"

"Just wondering. Was it a lot of or a small amount of fluids?" Allie continued as I still laughed.

Chuckling heartedly, Mo stepped closer to Allie, wrapped his arms around her waist, and asked, "Do you want to find out?"

"Yes, I do," she cooed.

"A'ight. You'll find out after we go fo' this walk on the beach," he handsomely voiced, gazing into her brown eyes.

"All right," she stated, standing on her tiptoes and placing her mouth to his ear.

After she whispered and reclined on the counter with a raised eyebrow, Mo dropped his head and laughed.

Lord, what did my friend say to him? I thought as Mo sincerely said, "I'll eat you 'til you fall asleep an' wake you up doing the same shit I did to put you to sleep. Allie, I'm the type of nigga that'll have you convertin' yo' religion. Shid, fo' you, I'll eat that ass an' suck yo' toes off the bone. A nigga been wantin' you, so everything you think I ain't gon' do to you ... you wrong."

"Sweet Jesus," Allie and I whimpered.

At the same time, Hussein hollered, "Nigga, I felt that shit in my soul! All it takes is the right female to bring that shit out of you!"

Looking at Hussein, Mo replied, "An' Allie is that right one fo' me."

"Aww," I replied lovingly, feeling warm and bubbly inside for my best friend.

While I smiled at the cute couple, I admired the way Mo gracefully interlocked their hands before placing a kiss on the back of Allie's hand. It was gentle yet loving. As I studied the pair, I couldn't help but support what they were trying to accomplish. Mo stepped in within hours and returned the sparkle to my best friend's eyes. Out of the sneaky links she's had, she'd never found the one to make her eyes twinkle like Mo.

Slipping into my presence, Hussein grabbed my hand and whispered, "Let's go fo' a walk, beautiful one."

"Okay," I responded, nodding.

As we maneuvered out of the kitchen, our vibe was different. Allie had placed everyone in a sexual mood. While we strolled along the beach, Hussein was extremely touchy with me, just as Mo was with Allie.

Delicate kisses graced my neck, lips, and the back of my hands. Gentle touches soothed my skin before our tongues clashed gloriously. Outside of the sensual, respectful rubs Hussein blessed upon my body, the serene walk was right on time. I was at peace with myself; I didn't feel guilt or resentment towards myself or hatred for my ex-husband. All was well, just as it should've been. However, I couldn't help but wonder for how long.

We ambled inside the large estate an hour later, drunk, high, and hungry. The fellas demanded we shower while they cooked breakfast. I was thankful; I wasn't in the mood to be around a lit stove.

Once I cleaned my body, I daydreamed about the lovely early morning loving I would have with Hussein. Every naughty thought that came to mind caused me to blush a time or ten. Upon exiting the tub, I walked towards the large mirror. Observing the object, I wiped off the condensation.

Finally able to see my eyes, I sighed heavily. After closing my eyes and counting to ten, I opened them and confidently said, "You have come a long way, Ava. Nothing is the same anymore, and it never will be. You will be fine. Know that you will be fine. You have Hussein."

Stepping from the mirror, I grabbed my nightwear and put it on. Three knocks sounded at the door, making me say, "Come in."

"Please tell me you have a spare razor or something?" a fully dressed Allie questioned lowly as she closed the bathroom door.

Laughing, I said, "It's a good thing I know you, huh? I didn't bring a razor, but I did bring Nair. It's in the black bag by the toilet."

"That's why we are besties. You know I be lacking in some departments. Thanks, boo."

"You are welcome," I stated before she fled from the bathroom.

Oh, Allie Jockson, some things will never change about us, huh? I guess that's why we've been best friends since the seventh grade. We complement each other like peanut butter and jelly, I thought, preparing my toothbrush.

Shortly afterward, I moisturized and sprayed my favorite sweet-smelling perfume onto the hotspots of my body. With my comfortable yet slightly provocative nightwear clinging to my body, I pranced out of the bathroom with my personal items. Once I discarded them into the proper bag, I exited the bedroom. Before I arrived at the kitchen table, Allie hollered painfully.

Running towards the bathroom with a racing heart, I yelled her name. The fellas were on my heels, asking her what was wrong. Upon entering the bathroom, a sight no one should've seen caused me to laugh. My poor friend was fanning her coochie as she cried out in pain. Quickly, I closed the door.

"Oh my God! This motherfuckin' shit don' took the hair and skin off me! What the hell? I wanted a bald pussy, not a skinned-up one!" she screeched.

"Mann." The fellas laughed, not far from the door.

The more Allie fussed, the more we howled in laughter. Eventually, I found the will to say, "Lather soap and rub it down there."

"I'm ready to go home," Allie fussed, causing us to laugh more.

"Yo' ass ain't finna go home. Bring that skinned-up pussy on. I'll doctor on it." Mo laughed, resulting in me sliding down the door, extremely amused.

Looking at me with evil eyes, Allie said, "I'm too gotdamn embarrassed. You know I hate being embarrassed, Ava."

With blurry vision and trying not to giggle, I blurted, "I'm sorry."

Standing, I cleared my throat and said, "Call me if you need me."

"Okay."

The goofy-looking, foolish men stared at me as I opened the door. Before I knew it, we busted out laughing. Closing the door, Mo chuckled, "How bad is it?"

Shrugging, I replied, "I don't know. I was too busy laughing. I think we are in the doghouse."

"Shittin' me. I'm finna go rectify this shit right nih," Mo voiced, stepping towards the bathroom door.

As he opened the rectangular object and stepped inside, Hussein picked me up and said, "He gon' take care of her. I'mma take care of you. So, Ava, you need to eat. You gon' need everything food has to offer you. I have som' things I need to discuss wit' yo' body. That's if you don't mind."

Legs trembling, I cooed, "No, I don't mind at all."

"Are there any restrictions?" he questioned, walking into the kitchen.

"What do you mean?"

"Do I have to use a rubber? Are there any positions you don't want to be in?" he probed, pulling out a chair before placing me in it.

"Yes, you have to use a condom, and any position is fine with me."

The look in his eyes told me he didn't want to use protection, and I was not about to open a can of worms when neither of us was ready for the adventure of not pulling out. Simply, I wasn't prepared for unprotected sex. An eerie silence overcame us as I began to eat. I felt uncomfortable, yet it only took Hussein to take that feeling away by the simple movements of his tongue as he whispered in my ear.

"I ain't gon' keep buyin' rubbers, Ava. I've been wearin' them damn things since I been havin' sex. Before this month out, I will be slidin' off in you without a piece of rubber on my dick. I sure as hell ain't gon' pull out either. Now that I've spoken on that matter, eat up an' enjoy yo' meal, baby, because I'm finna work yo' ass out 'til I pass out, which ain't gon' happen anytime soon."

With an open mouth and bulging eyes, I stared at him. As my heart rapidly beat, my pretty pussy was eager to be fed disrespectfully but oh-so-passionately. Biting his bottom lip and ogling me, Hussein took off his shirt before walking away, whistling. Slowly closing my mouth, I thought, *oh, Jesus. It's going to really go down tonight, and I am here for it all!*

Chapter VII

Hussein

"True love is rare, and it's the only thing that gives life real meaning."-Nicholas Sparks, Message in a Bottle

A Week Later

Upon our return home, bullshit from Lakin landed in my lap; the bitch was on a hateful tip. Any little thing she could make up to cease me from copping products from her mother, the spoiled runt tried. Her actions became so severe Nanette demanded I show my face at her well-decorated home. For two hours, I had to listen to Lakin's lies. Not a single time did I defend anything; there was no need to argue with a broad who was never relevant to me.

At the end of the useless chit-chat, Nanette made it clear to her daughter that she would always be in business with me as long as I wanted us to be. I left Nanette's home with three duffel bags filled with weed and cocaine. I hadn't heard nor seen Lakin since. Word around town, she moved back to her hometown in Pennsylvania. I didn't give a damn where she went as long as she left me alone. I was where and with whom I needed to be with—Ms. Ava Jane Langston.

Since last Wednesday, everything I ever wanted was at my fingertips. My life had tremendously done a complete three-sixty. Before Ava and I became intimate, I existed with many things on my mind. Now, with a clear purpose and my best friend returning whole again, my thoughts no longer lingered in my brain. I opened up to Ava about wanting to own a business.

The once human resource manager turned nail technician made the road much more straightforward for me, and she believed in what I needed to accomplish for our future and myself. Ava told me to write down three

78

things I loved to do the most. After I wrote them down and we observed them, we laughed while pointing at smoking weed.

It was Ava's idea for me to investigate owning a weed dispensary. Honestly, it wasn't a bad investment. However, the dilemma arose when I didn't know where to start my business since Alabama hadn't legalized weed. Therefore, we started looking into successful recreational dispensaries throughout the U.S. I hope Ava and I would find the perfect state to kick off my future as a boss within a few months.

"Damn, my guy, you all right?" my supervisor, Rico, asked as he strolled beside my forklift.

Looking at the stout, receding hairline fellow, I replied, "Yeah, just slipped off mentally fo' a minute."

"How was your vacation?" he probed as his phone dinged.

Smiling, I announced, "That motherfucka was lit. I locked down on the girl I've always wanted."

"You talking about little shorty that brought you something to eat on your lunch break last night?" he asked, texting.

"Yep," I answered as Rico looked at me.

"Bro, no disrespect or anything, but that one there is a keeper. She's good-looking."

"Yeah, she is that, but it's more than the looks fo' me. Ava's a real one. I'll be a fool to let her go."

"What happened to Lakin?"

"We were just fuckin' 'round. No strings attached. Simply put, her time was up," I confessed as my phone vibrated.

"Between you and me, I'm going through a divorce. I tried to make it work, but no matter what I did, nothing was enough. It was always something. I had to break free," he confided lowly.

Like usual, we chatted about our personal lives as our fingers glided across our phones' keyboards. While Rico talked about his depressing life, Ava had my full attention as I stared at a shiny thigh picture she had sent.

"Finally, break time," Rico voiced.

"Yes, it is." I smiled before zooming away, eager to call Ava.

Usually, I would converse with a few guys I communicated with; however, things were different since Ava accepted our newfound intimate friendship. She had my attention on all my breaks; it was the best feeling in the world. I anticipated smiling while hearing her voice. I was elated to give her a tour of the place that had a facelift since she last visited.

Stepping out of the building, a few associates called my name while I dialed Ava's number.

"I'm on an important call. Holla at me when I get back up here," I told them as Ava answered.

"I love that picture you sent me. Where the rest of it at?" I jokingly asked, walking into the parking lot.

"Waiting on you to take it," she sexily voiced.

"Fo' real?" I asked, intrigued.

"Yep."

"Hm, I might have to make a trip over when I get off," I teased ten cars from my vehicle.

"That you might have to do, sir," she giggled.

"Ava, all you gotta say is that you want me to get off early, an' I'll go 'head an' start coughin' 'round this bitch. They'll think I got that damn 'Rona. That's two weeks off guaranteed," I seriously voiced, seeing her step out of her vehicle, laughing and looking edible.

"Oh, so, you pulled down on a nigga, huh? You must tryin' to get that pussy tickled or som'?" I questioned, jogging to her four-door whip.

"I did, and maybe so," she purred before ending the call.

Damn, my baby lookin' sexy ass fuck in that short, casual brown dress, I thought as my eyes drunk in the sight of her.

Sashaying in a pair of gold sparkly two-strap sandals, Ava walked towards the passenger door of my car. While I unlocked my whip, I grabbed her waist while planting several kisses on her neck. Pulling her from the passenger door, I whispered, "I want you to drive while I tickle that pretty pussy."

"Oh my," she stated as I led her towards the driver's door, handing her the keys.

After she hopped in and started the engine, I closed the door and skipped towards the passenger side. As I was about to hop in, I heard Rico yell, "Gotdamn it, Hussein, I see ya'!"

Laughing, I chunked the deuces and hopped in the passenger seat. As soon as I closed the door, Ava said, "You have put the wrong person in the driver's seat."

"No, I put the perfect person in the driver's seat," I stated as Jeezy featuring Plies' "Sexé" played.

Immediately, Ava looked at me and asked, "Why isn't the trunk bumping?"

"I shut off the amp. Do you want it on?"

"Yes," she happily answered, rapidly nodding.

Laughing, I showed her the knob to turn on the speaker amplifier. Upon doing so, my lady started the song over, turned up the radio, and dropped the gearshift into the drive position. The sexy being skirted off, rocking her head while grooving. Like many times before, I admired the beauty while she drove my whip as if she were the owner. The gorgeous, heavy foot driver opened the motor on my shit and zipped past a few of my co-workers driving the speed limit.

"You know you sexy wit' yo' sexy ass," I whispered into her ear as I slipped my hand underneath her dress. My dick bricked at the realization her hairless, smooth pussy didn't have an ounce of cloth covering it.

As she kicked off her left sandal and placed her left foot on the seat, Ava briefly and sneakily looked at me before blowing me a kiss.

"What you want from me, Ava? I'll give it all to you. Just tell me what you want," I whispered as I inserted two fingers into her wet fortress.

While Ava rolled her body along with the beat, my fingers matched her rhythm. In seconds, she was shaking and making the beautiful sex faces I loved. Reaching the sharp curve in the road, Ava leaned to the left, granting my fingers full access to the right corner of her pretty and delicious treasure trove.

"Ooou, Hussein," Ava cooed, biting her bottom lip.

Working her middle perfectly, I licked her ear before saying, "I swear you make me hate a rubber. A nigga wanna feel this wetness on his dick. My man jealous that my face and fingers get all of the goodness."

Upon her mouth forming an O, I knew what time it was. Thus, I turned down the radio and thuggishly growled, "Give it to me now, Ava."

"Not yet," she moaned, fighting the nut.

"I said, give it to me now, Ava," I hissed.

"Not yet, Hussein," she whined, body shaking violently.

When it came down to pleasing her, I didn't like to be told no. Therefore, I leaned closer to her and said, "You better focus on the road, Ava, an' give me what I demanded."

"Why would you sa—"

While fingering her, my mouth clamped onto her clit. As I sucked on it like the pink bud was a pacifier, Ava touched my head and squealed, "Husseinnn."

"You," I voiced in between sucking on her clit.

"Ah," she breathed.

"Gon'," I stated, fingers tapping on her G-Spot.

"Oou, Hussein, please," Ava hissed, damn near sitting upright in the seat.

"Learn."

"Hussein, I can't take this while driving," she whined, body shaking as I felt the car slowing before she hopped into the slow lane.

"To."

"Please stop. Too many big trucks around and behind us," she whined, gripping my neck.

Removing my mouth off her delicious pussy, I looked around, turned on the hazard lights, and said, "Pull into the emergency lane."

"What?" she stammered.

"You heard me," I replied, laughing.

"Hussein?"

"Huh?"

"Are you serious right now?" she asked, shocked.

I didn't respond. I slid the passenger seat backward.

"Oh shit, you are."

After Ava pulled into the emergency lane, I unbuckled her seatbelt and commanded, "Sit on my face."

"Wait? What?"

"You heard me," I sternly implored, raising an eyebrow.

"Hussein, really?" she asked worriedly, looking around the interstate.

"Yep. Come on an' let me get that tension off you."

After six minutes of going back and forth with Ava, I snatched her ass from the driver's seat and placed her on my face. She tried her best to resist, but my mouth game got her ass right. With two palms filled with ass cheeks, I ate her moaning-and-shaking behind up like I'd been doing for the past week.

"Good, Jesus," she whined, riding my face.

Lifting her higher, I slid my tongue from her clit to her asshole.

"Oh, my God!" she loudly voiced, shaking more.

While repeating that action several times, I unbuckled my belt before unzipping my denim shorts. As Ava moaned, she couldn't move. Pulling out my dick, I worked my mouth to get what I wanted from her.

"Husseinnn!" she provocatively hollered, giving me what I sought—her sweet rainfall.

"Mhm," I groaned, swallowing the sweetness her body provided.

Upon being satisfied with an incredibly saturated face, I placed her pretty kitty close to my dick. Knowing she wouldn't let me go in raw, I gripped her hair and sucked her tongue into my mouth. While driving her crazy with my tongue dancing around her mouth, Ava slid her pussy up and down my naked guy.

Try. Now, I thought, slowly lifting her and gently rubbing the head of my dick against her wet treasure trove.

Shaking her head, she broke the kiss. Quickly, I sucked her bottom lip into my mouth and continued with my mission. Her repetitive cooing in my mouth was why I slipped my guy into Ava's oven. Breathlessly and with bucked eyes, she looked at me and said, "No, take him out. You don't have on a condom."

"Nope an' so," I groaned, slowly moving in and out of her.

"Solomonnn," she moaned, matching my thrusts.

Smiling, I asked, "You still want me to take him out?"

"Nooo," she whimpered, dropping that pretty kitty on my thirsty guy.

The slow pumps were all good until Ava leaned onto the dashboard, spread her legs, and provocatively uttered, "Get it, Hussein."

"An' I'm finna fuckin' get it," I growled, snatching her towards me before putting her on the passenger seat.

In the emergency lane, I bobbed and weaved inside Ava's sweet place as if we were in a bed. I didn't give a damn about my car rocking. All I cared about was giving her everything she lacked in her marriage. I needed Ava to know I wasn't in between her legs for me but for her and her only.

"Hussein, we rockin' the shit out of this car on a highly traveled interstate," she breathlessly spoke, body convulsing.

Gripping her hair and deep stroking her coochie, I clenched my teeth and said, "Ask me do I give a fuck. Caterin' to yo' needs is all I care 'bout. Do you understand?"

"Yess," she howled, arching her back.

I was in that thang good when Ava's body locked to the point her eyes bucked, and she struggled to speak.

Mischievously smiling, I said, "You scared to let that motherfucka come out, huh?"

"Yes," she struggled to say.

"Oh well. Guess what I'm finna do? I'mma snatch that motherfucka up outta you," I replied as I placed her legs on my shoulders and wore that pussy out.

More aggressive than I should've been, I gripped her neck and loudly growled, "Gimme that wet ass pussy, Ava! All of it! Now!"

With the tsunami escaping her pink tunnel, splashing onto my body, Ava's sex noises bounced through my car. Feeling myself, I danced in the pussy, all the while telling Ava a few things.

"From now on, when you see me, you better get ready to wet som' shit up because that's what the fuck you gonna do. I don't like to repeat myself, Ava. I make myself be heard loud an' clear the first time. Ain't no mo' fuckin' rubbers slidin' off in you. I'm done wearin' them bitches. Understood?"

Tears streaming down her face and pussy throwing up beautifully, she nodded.

"Good." I smiled, slowing my pace and kissing her forehead.

A few more slow strokes later, I looked at the clock. I had twenty-five minutes to get back to work. We had been on the side emergency lane for ten minutes, and I wasn't close to nutting. My stamina game was a motherfucker unless I beat my dick head against her G-Spot!

Clearing my throat, I gazed into the ditzy-eyed woman and said, "I hate to do this, but I'm going to give you one mo' nut before I get back to the job. Cool?"

"No. I want you to nut too," she sweetly voiced, holding tightly to the back of my neck.

"I don't do that rushin' shit wit' you fo' a reason. I can really hurt you, Ava. You know this."

"I do, but I said what the fuck I said," she softly voiced, eyeing me.

My girl, I thought as I placed my hands in the crook of her knees and pushed her legs back. After positioning her body just right so that the head of my tool slammed into the desired spot, I gave her the business. Thus, her body gave my seat all of its wetness.

"Good gotdamn," she moaned loudly and repeatedly as her body shook before locking.

Feeling my soldiers rising, I placed my lips on hers and asked, "I'm 'bout to nut. Can I nut in you, Ava?"

Immediately, the whimpering woman wrapped an arm around my neck and breathlessly said, "Yes."

Stunned at her answer, I probed, "Are you sure?"

"Yes," she moaned, nodding.

Deeply and sensually, I hungrily French-kissed the woman of my dreams as I slingshot my protein shake off in her. Upon breaking the steamy kiss, I placed a delicate smooch on her forehead and slowly pulled my guy out of her. While I climbed into the driver's seat, Ava set the passenger seat upright and rolled her neck from side to side.

"You good, baby?" I asked, fixing my clothes.

"Yes," she yawned, opening the glove compartment box and pulling out a feminine wipe.

Chuckling, I voiced, "No wonder you didn't bring yo' purse. You stashed the pussy wipes in the glove compartment."

"You want me to remove them?" she asked gently.

"Nope."

"Okay," she stated, cleaning that bomb good good in between her legs.

Once she placed the used wipe into the package, Ava sat it in the cupholder. Biting her lip, she looked out of the window.

"Come here," I demanded, patting my lap.

While she crawled into my lap, I patted her soft bottom. Secured where I needed her, I dropped the gearshift into the drive position and turned off the hazard lights. As TK Soul's "I Wanna Hold My Baby" played, Ava kissed my neck and dropped her head onto my right shoulder. Turning up the speaker knockers, I looked at the rearview mirrors before zooming away from the emergency lane.

Flying like a bat out of hell, my mind was on the heavily breathing woman sitting on me. As I rubbed her back, I focused on where I wanted us to be within a year. I saw a baby, an engagement ring, and a house that didn't have horrible memories attached to it. I saw a whole new life for Solomon Hussein Hampton and Ava Jane Langston. A life that didn't require me trapping weed or working for a fucking millionaire because Ava and I would be the millionaires.

As I entered my job's parking lot, I decreased the radio volume and softly called Ava's name.

"Yes?" she sleepily voiced.

"You good enough to drive home, or do you want me to clock out an' take you home?" I questioned as I slowly drove towards her car.

"I think I'm good enough. I'm going to sit in the car for a while to wake up," she yawned.

"Nawl, that ain't an option," I stated, turning into the row where her car was.

"I'll be good. I promise. I'll text you the second I pull into the driveway," she breathed.

"That's not good enough fo' me. If something happens to you because of what I just did ... I'mma be fuckin' sick. So, I'mma go clock out," I replied, looking down at her.

"Nope, you have been off for a week. Time to get back to the money. If you are that pressed about me making it home safely, you can sit in the car with me."

Seeing we would go back and forth, I said, "Drive my car home. Turn the speaker knockers up. Keep the window halfway down. Don't turn on the air conditioner."

"Hussein, you are overreacting," she giggled lightly.

"When it concerns you, I'll always overreact. So, take your house keys off your key ring and put them on mine. I'll call you when I pull up in your driveway. Non-negotiable," I stated as I placed the gearshift into the park position."

Ava opened the door and said, "No need to do that. I can use the code to get in the house."

"You sure?" I inquired as I stepped out of my whip.

"Yes," she announced, gazing into my eyes.

Pulling her close, I kissed her deeply and squeezed her butt. Breaking the kiss, Ava said, "Go ahead before you are late. You have ten minutes to make it inside, sir."

Nodding, I asked, "Do you need to get anything out of your car?"

"No, my purse at home. My ID and bank card tucked safely into my bra."

"A'ight. I'll see you when I get off."

"Okay. Before you come over, go to your place and grab clothes. It's been three days since I laid next to you overnight. Sooo, um...."

Smiling, I asked, "Is that why you sent me a thigh picture, came out here with no panties on ... knowin' damn well I can't keep my hands off you?"

"Something like that," she giggled, sliding into the driver's seat.

"Yes or no."

"I said something like that."

"You know what, woman, I'mma let you have that one. Let me get in here and knock out these next few hours. Drive safe. Text me the second you pull into the driveway," I responded before bending into the car and kissing her again.

"Okay," she voiced before saying. "You know I can drop you off at the front of the building, right?"

"Yeah, but I'll walk. I'm finna smoke a cigarette an' admire you drivin' my car without me being in it."

"All right. See you later," she stated, which sounded more like a question,

Instead of treating it as such, I smiled. "See you later, baby."

As she pulled off, my woofers breathed as the tweets announced the song. Firing up a cigarette, I smiled and shook my head. As I inhaled the nicotine, the volume on my radio increased. Walking towards the front of the building, I jigged along to the beat as I looked at the semi-busy highway. Due to the many cars having the right away, Ava patiently waited to make a right turn.

Arriving before a group of niggas, still watching the road, they said, "Nigga, you don' started som' shit. You ain't gon' never drive yo' whip."

"Gotdamn it, that woman found the rim light switch. Oh, she finna stunt in yo' shit." Rico laughed as I choked on the cigarette smoke. At the same time, Ava sped off, hopping in the fast lane. Once again, her heavy foot ass opened the motor up in my shit, resulting in me shaking my head.

"Shid, that's bae right there. She can do that," I happily implored, walking off and flicking the cigarette into the garbage can.

"Mane, what the fuck you got in that trunk?" Rico asked as we walked towards the entrance door.

"Som' shit that has already given me eight noise ordinance tickets in one damn day," I chuckled.

"Eight? Shid, finna be nine on that tag before the night ends," Rico chuckled.

"An' I'mma pay that motherfucka." I laughed, sliding through the metal detectors, eager to get off so I could lay under the one that had my nose wide open.

Chapter VIII

Ava

"All happiness depends on courage and work."-Honoré de Balzac

I intended to go to Hussein's job for a hug and kiss. However, when I parked beside his car, I knew that wasn't the real reason I had shown face at his job and sent him a picture of my thigh. Surely, I didn't expect him to take me on a 'eat and fuck the shit out of me in the emergency lane' trip. However, I wasn't mad or disappointed. Yet, my poor body and mind were gone; if Hussein wanted my nose wide open, the motherfucker was.

As I blasted his speakers and drove like usual, I was fully awake and mind doing numbers. Looking at the clock on the radio, I sighed heavily as a surge of emotions overcame me. In need of my female best friend, I bypassed the exit to go home. I had to make sense of what was really happening to me. I needed someone to tell me to slow things down between Hussein and me.

I'm not an irrational or careless person. I am not, I thought, as Basic Black's "Special Kind of Fool" sounded.

Gunning towards Allie's job, my eyes were focused on the road, but my mind was elsewhere. As I rehashed every moment of Hussein being in my life, a part of me knew we weren't rushing. The other part was eager for me to begin a life with him. Yet, I needed confirmation that it was okay how we moved.

Hussein isn't someone new in my life. He's been here since October 26, 2013. He became my best friend in 2014. You started feeling... I thought, exhaling sharply.

The less I thought, the better. I didn't want to overthink anything between Hussein and me, especially how we became so close. Needing to have a clear mind, I changed the song. Upon Ronnie Bell's "Cotton Candy" blasting, my thoughts ceased. In tune with the jam, I sang.

When I arrived at the four-star, two-floored hotel parking area, I decreased the radio's volume. Shutting off the engine, my cell phone vibrated and rang. Looking at my device, resting in the cupholder, I saw Hussein's name boldly displayed. As I opened the door and answered Hussein's call, a smiling Mo walked from inside the hotel.

"You made it home yet?" Hussein inquired as I walked towards the hotel's entrance door.

At the same time, Mo chuckled, "Well, I'll be damn. You got this nigga whip. Oou, you doing big things, Ava. I see you glowin', my friend."

I nodded at Mo, but responded to Hussein. "No. I came to Allie's job for a brief moment."

"Boy, she beatin' the damn block down." Mo laughed, holding the door open for me.

Hussein laughed. "Oh, so you doing it like that?"

Blushing, I said, "Yes."

"Wait, did you say you are at Allie's job?" Hussein questioned.

"Yes."

Chuckling, he replied, "Well, shit nih. Text me when you make it home."

"I will," I sweetly replied as Allie stared at me with a massive smile.

"So, we are doing shit like this now, Allie?" I giggled as Mo's phone rang.

"Girl, what are you talking about?" She grinned. My best friend glowed, and it looked good on her.

At the same time, Mo said, "Nigga, don't you supposed to be workin'?"

"We know who is on his line. So, tell me how you ended up with Hussein's car?" she asked, stepping from behind the desk.

Wiping my forehead, I tee-heed. "Whew, honey. Now, that's an interesting story, which I will get into later. I came here for advice. So, listen carefully because I will have to stop talking once Mo comes in."

"Go."

Within two minutes, I told Allie everything I'd
experienced with Hussein before and since we slept
together. I ended with the truth of me allowing him to nut
in me. The expression on her face was priceless as Mo
sauntered into the hotel, informing Allie he would be back
as soon as he could with her food.

"Okay, be careful," she genuinely replied as he strolled
towards her.

After they kissed, he told me to be safe on the way
home—if I was to leave before he returned. Upon
responding that I would be careful, Allie and I didn't talk
until Mo started his engine.

"From my understanding, we out here just risking it all,
huh? Doing the damn most. Whew, I don't feel like a fool
anymore."

Thrown off, I said, "Elaborate."

"Well, in Florida, I didn't get asked, can I nut in you. I
simply got it with the promise of not going anywhere and
caring for the three kids I already have."

"Oh, so we were careless with the pussies, huh?" I
giggled, fumbling with my hands.

"Basically."

"I came here for advice, but unfortunately, it seems you
can't give me anything because you are in the same boat
I'm in."

"Truthfully, I'm taking things slow with Mo, but the
way he makes me feel has me like a puppy, eager to be
trained and rubbed on. I'm done overthinking everything
in life. I make sure my children are well cared for and
loved. I please everybody, all the while not being happy.
It's time for me to put myself first. If things go sour
between Mo and me, I can honestly say I enjoyed his
company. I enjoyed having his arms around me. I will
cherish the pillow talks and the few times I shed tears
from the passionate and wholeheartedly sincere
statements he made. I said all that to say this: Ava stepped
out on a whim with Hussein. From what it seems
like *and* what I've semi-witnessed with my own eyes,

you've already taken a liking to him before everything turned horrible. You are a single woman. Why continue to fight what you feel for him?" she kindly spoke, rubbing the back of my hand.

"True," I deeply inhaled, lost as to what we should discuss.

"You are scared of how Hussein makes you feel, aren't you?"

"A little."

"You think it's only a matter of time before he shows you something different?"

Shaking my head, I responded, "Not really. I'm scared of us rushing and shit falling apart. You know?"

"I do. Once again, we are in the same boat. Based on past relationship experience, I won't focus on the 'what ifs'. I'm simply going to enjoy it. You should do the same. Ava, I've been around you since the seventh grade. I've experienced every heartache that came your way. Also, I experienced joyous times. Since you moved to Grove Land, there had always been one person who would put that twinkle in your eyes. The twinkle Jak could never place in your beautiful peepers. So, riddle me this ... why be scared of the way Hussein makes you feel? From where I'm standing, it looks mighty damn delicious and bitch; I'm eager for Mo to give me my sixteen servings of that!"

Smiling, I replied, "Well, I heard that."

My best friend and I chatted until Mo arrived with her food. After we issued hugs and goodbyes, I exited the hotel's lobby with Mo on my heels, asking about my mental health. Unlocking Hussein's car, I faced Mo and responded, "I'm a little conflicted, but overall I'm okay."

"Conflicted 'bout startin' a life without Mica being here, correct?" he inquired, searching my eyes.

"I haven't gotten that far into my thoughts."

Nodding, he voiced, "Trust it will come, an' that's when you need to call me. You will shut down, an' that's not a good thing."

"Okay," I sighed, removing my hair from my face.

"Ava, talk to me. I can tell something else is wrong, an' you are tryin' not to show it."

"I'm fine, really. The aftermath of a situation is more complex than I thought it would be. I really thought I would be okay with it."

"Talk to me. I have time. Allie's stuffin' her face," he announced, propping up on the side of Hussein's car.

My mouth opened and closed many times. I couldn't find the right words to say, or it could've been that I didn't want the most intimate thing between Hussein and me placed in the air just yet, even though I had already told Allie.

Clearing my throat, I placed my hands on my head and said, "In the heat of the moment, I think I did the most stupid shit ever. I … I … shit, Mo, I don't know what I just did before coming here. All I know is that I'm conflicted about my choice based on being so lonely, Hussein's sexual abilities, and I really care about him. Possibly love him."

"From what I was told, you an' Hussein have history, so I'm not surprised that you may 'possibly love him' as you put it. Ava, it's okay to love him because y'all were friends before anything; he's giving you every reason to love him. I can honestly tell you this, that nigga worships the ground you walk on. I'm not a new nigga in Hussein's life. I've been knowing that fool since our school days. The way he is wit' you; I've never seen him like that wit' no females. Ever. It's like I'm starin' at a whole new guy. While we were in Florida, he finally let me into a small part of his personal life that involved you. One thing I can tell you, you were never lonely. You didn't pursue the one person who always told you to call him whenever you needed anything. You never reached out to him; he had to contact you. Ava, Hussein has always had yo' back an' always will. Why do you think he was pullin' up at his grandparents' house at odd times of the night? Why do you think he ensured he was over his grandparents' house every weekend, bright an' early? Yeah, he loves his grandparents, but he loved you an' Mica mo'. Those were the words out of his mouth. I don't know what happened in yo' past relationship, an' I don't want to know. What I do know, my boy got it bad fo' you, an' you are fightin' what you have fo' him because you are scared that yo' past relationship will come into a new one. You want him, but you are afraid of him. The whole point of livin' is to let go of the past hurts. If you don't let go, you won't find happiness. You'll be stuck in misery with an unstable ass mind."

After Mo read me like a book, my emotions got the best of me. Tears slipped down my face as I sighed sharply.

"Clear yo' head, look at the sky, an' count to twenty. When you are done, hop in yo' nigga's car an' go home. Text Allie when you make it."

After doing what Mo commanded, I said, "Thank you."

"No problem. Now, go home," he demanded politely.

"Headed that way, boss number three," I joked, smiling.

Upon patting the car's hood, Mo stepped away and lit a cigarette. As I slid into the front seat, I started the engine and welcomed Keith Sweat's voice on "I'll Give All My Love to You". Slightly rolling down the window, I placed the gearshift in reverse and released my foot off the brakes. As I sang the song, my hand was itching to increase the volume. Dropping the gearshift into the drive position, I honked the horn twice while driving off. Not far from the hotel's entryway, I turned up the volume and sped off in the non-existent traffic.

While the song played, my eyes were fixated on the road, but my mind was on Hussein. Zoned out, I sat upright and drove his car as if on an emergency ride to the best hospital in Birmingham, Alabama. Within fifteen minutes, I was turning onto my street. Slightly turning down the radio, I dreaded going into my house. The three-bedroom, two-bath family home was quiet, clean, and fucking lonely.

"I do not want to go in here," I stated aloud before I saw my car parked in front of the garage. Instantly and drastically, my attitude changed.

He's home, I thought, smiling before I happily announced, "God, you were on time with this one."

Rushing to exit the car, I sped into my driveway. As I parked behind my car, Hussein walked out of my house, smiling and holding two glasses. Quickly, I hopped out, closed the door, and skipped towards the man walking towards me. At the same time, I ensured his vehicle was locked.

Look at this here, I thought as my heart raced as I asked, "What are you doing off?"

"I felt like you needed me here."

"You felt?" I probed as he extended a wineglass to me. Upon taking the glass and swirling it around, the wonderful smell of the dry, fruity wine enticed my taste buds.

"Ava, I know you better than you think. I don't pop up just because. I peep things an' then I pop up or slide on over here," he stated, searching my eyes.

An eerie silence overcame us as Hussein drank from the wineglass and gazed into my face. Shortly after swallowing the liquid, he made an ugly facial expression before asking, "What the fuck kinda shit did I purchase an' consume?"

Laughing, I said, "A dry wine."

"How can you tolerate this mess?" he asked, grabbing my wineglass before pouring the contents out of his glass into mine.

"I have a peculiar set of taste buds, I guess," I softly replied, admiring how his fingers felt touching mine. The tension between us was extremely thick. It was apparent there were some things on his mind.

"You can have this nasty mess," he stated, interlocking our fingers and pulling me towards him.

"Okay," I breathed against his chest.

Looking down at me, Hussein joked, "Did you get a noise ordinance or speedin' ticket?"

Giggling, I shook my head and replied, "Not a cop in sight."

As we strolled to the porch, he stated, "That's the first. Seems like every time I hop in that motherfuckin' car an' be itchin' to beat the block down, they are everywhere."

"I think they love getting your money," I voiced before sipping from the wineglass.

"Sounds 'bout right," he sighed deeply before sitting in my favorite lounge chair.

Pulling me onto his lap, Hussein gently asked, "You know you can talk to me 'bout anything, right?"

"Yes," I responded, turning to face him.

"Then, tell me what's on yo' mind."

"Well, um, after I left your job, my mind started to race and rehash. Not in a bad way. I was thinking of all the times you've been present to alleviate a lot of shit I was feeling. Also, I realized that you meant more to me than I have led on. Solomon, I used to feel ashamed for the feelings I housed for you, being a married woman. Sometimes, I purposely didn't come to the front of the yard when my husband was home. Although we were respectful, I didn't want to act differently towards you. Um, shit, I don't know where I'm going with this, but deep down, there's a huge something there, and I'm a tad bit afraid of it."

"Why?"

Shrugging, I replied, "Because I feel things are going too fast."

"Ava, you an' I are not strangers. When y'all first moved to this neighborhood, we were. We became acquainted through civil talks the first week of y'all livin' here. It increased drastically when I started realizin' certain things."

"Certain things like what?" I inquired before gulping the entire contents of the wineglass.

As I placed the glass on the ground, I could tell Hussein was uncomfortable with the conversation we were about to have. Soothingly, I rubbed his face and said, "Certain things like what?"

After profoundly exhaling, Hussein replied, "I could tell things were off in yo' marriage, not at yo' expense. I could tell you were lonely, an' I didn't like that. I noticed when a man isn't interested in his wife. The numerous times he wasn't here or the times he came home were key indications. I saw you an' Mica mo' than I saw you, Mica, an' yo' ex-husband or yo' ex-husband an' Mica. Thus, I made it my business to keep you company, in a friendly way, an' interact wit' Mica on a big brother type of thing so you could have som' time to yo'self. Granted, I always found you attractive, intelligent, an' funny. God knew I wanted you an' Mica all to myself. I did, Ava; I ain't gon' lie. I motherfuckin' did. I knew you wanted me to bed you, but I couldn't because you were spoken fo'. However, that didn't stop me from being yo' rock an' Mica's 'big brother'. There's a lot of things I did that you don't know 'bout. Who do you think put the trash can on the curb every Thursday? Who do you think had a hand in the grass being cut every Wednesday? When you used to work at Bigco Distribution Center, who do you think paid a human resource employee to ensure no one said a word 'bout who placed items on yo' desk? When I realized that nigga Jak was slippin' big time, I silently stepped in an' handled his job. I did his fuckin' job proudly wit' no regrets."

With teary eyes and a smile, I shoved my lips upon his as he wrapped his arms around my waist. While we engaged in a fiery kiss, everything Hussein spoke about slammed into my head ten-fold. Plenty of times, the grass had grown higher than my ex-husband would've liked. The next day, the grass was cut by an unknown man. Naturally, I assumed the man of the house had a hand in it; how wrong was I. In reality, which didn't come out until two days after Mica died, the man of the house didn't have a hand in anything other than privately humiliating me behind my back.

"I want a family wit' you, Ava, an' I'm willin' to wait 'til you are ready fo' that. If that means I have to pull out, I will, but I'm not puttin' on a condom," Hussein whispered against my lips as he stood, holding me tightly.

"Okay," I voiced as he walked towards the front door.

"Do you want me to put our cars in the garage?" he asked, ogling me.

"Nope," I announced, shaking my head.

"So, it's like that now?" He smiled.

"Hussein, get in this house so I can relearn how to gargle dick," I seriously voiced.

His knees buckled as he grabbed the screen door's handle. Laughing, I said, "Yeah, it's going to be one of those nights. Me pleasing you as you've pleased me all these years by talking, being there, and recently with your sexual prowess."

After slipping into the house and locking the door, Hussein sexily looked at me and groaned, "Shid, have yo' way wit' meee."

"And I'm going to do just that, sir," I provocatively stated as I climbed out of his arms, eyeing him. "But before I do, I need you to complete these tasks in the order I give them. First, take a shower. Then, fix a drink, step outside, and smoke a blunt. When you are done, come back inside, sit on the sofa, and watch a little TV until you receive further notice."

Saluting me with a pleasing facial expression, Hussein slowly licked his full lips before responding, "Say no mo'."

I twirled my hair as I turned on my heels while sashaying away.

"Keep on wit' that sexy ass attitude. A nigga ain't gon' make it to the bathroom, much less to the kitchen to fix a drink, Ava," he thuggishly spoke.

Cheesing, I didn't acknowledge him. I continued sauntering towards my room with sweaty palms and a hopeful plan of truly satisfying Hussein as I proclaimed I would. My sex skills were beyond rusty.

Shit, I need to call Allie's freaky ass for some sex advice, I thought, entering my room.

Upon closing and locking the door, I quickly dialed Allie's number, all the while feeling giddy. On the fifth ring, my breathless friend answered.

I giggled, "I just know damn well you are not doing anything you don't have any business doing while you are supposed to be working."

"You made it home safely?" she asked breathlessly.

"Bitch, are you fucking ... like right now?"

"Did you make it home?" she questioned louder, which sounded more like a moan.

As I laughed, I replied, "Yep. Now, I need a huge favor."

"What's the favor, Ava?" she cooed.

"Oh Jesus, Allie. Why in the hell did you answer the phone? You know what? Don't answer that," I quickly stated as I shook my head and continued. "Um, what did you do with all that freaky shit I told you to take out of my closet?"

"I left that shit in your closet but put it in a shoebox. It's in the far back, right side of the closet. Ava, I hate to end this call, but I really gotta go. Love you. Talk to you later," she rapidly spoke in a shaky tone before ending the call.

Deeply inhaling with a slight smile, I placed my phone on the dresser before stepping into my closet. Nervously, I followed Allie's directions to retrieve the box that held the freaky items. I had only used a few of those items, maybe four times with Jak, plenty of times while he was absent, and zero after Mica died. Jak never received the ultimate freaky side of me; he had always shooed me off. He wasn't interested in spicing up our marriage if I wasn't on my back or his dick down my throat. It was always about Jak Morris and never me.

In a flash, my fingertips graced the sized eight stiletto heels silver box. With glee soaring through me, I rapidly snatched the box from the far end of the closet. As I removed the lid, I retrieved three needed items before tossing the box back into its rightful place. After placing the items on the bed, I walked to the tall, six-drawer dresser, fearing that I wouldn't do a great job pleasing Hussein.

Grabbing a lingerie outfit I had never worn, I looked into the clean mirror and skittishly spoke, "Well, it's been five years since I purchased this. Now, it's time to be seen in it. I hope Hussein likes it and everything else that comes with this outfit."

Chapter IX

Hussein

"Is sex dirty? Only when it's being done right." -Woody Allen

With a clean body, I had drunk half of the bourbon whiskey from Ava's kitchen cabinet. After smoking a blunt and thumbing through several channels on the TV, I became impatient. I was eager to see my lovely lady and snake my tongue through her mouth before sliding it inside every hole in her body. Upon patiently sitting in the dimly lit front room, a brother was curious about what Ava had planned for us. Whatever her plan of action was, it had to be damn good because she had been in her room a little over an hour, rearranging shit and laughing. A few times, I was sure she was on the phone with Allie, getting advice.

This woman finna drive me fuckin' insane tonight, I thought as my phone rang.

Grabbing my device off the arm of the sofa, I saw my brother's name. On the third ring, I answered Gideon's call.

"Well, shit, nigga, about time you answer the phone. Damn, you can't return phone calls or pop up being annoying like you usually do. What's good with you?" he asked, laughing.

Chuckling, I replied, "I'm sorry. Baby brother has been ducked off an' livin' life to the fullest."

"Wit' Ava?"

"Indeed."

"So, y'all in a relationship?"

"Not yet. As bad as I want to rush things, I'm not going to. She needs to be mo' secure 'bout us."

"Cool. Make sure things stay good between y'all."

Smiling, I looked down the hallway and responded, "No doubt."

"Um, have you talked to Mom and Dad?" he chuckled.

"Ma an' I texted earlier, and I chatted briefly wit' Dad this mornin'. Why?"

"She's ready to lose her religion over Sister Catamine. Momma cursed for the first time tonight."

Laughing, I replied, "I know you fuckin' lyin'."

"No, I ain't."

"What has Sister Catamine did now?"

"Still after Dad. He had to pull Mom away from the old bat today. Mom gave the broad a nice set of Satan's words. Dad said Mom left the grocery store praying and didn't stop until a little before she cooked dinner."

Knowing that my mother was a tender and loving woman, I would've paid a thousand dollars to see her act out of character. It was rare Momma lost her temper. She was very composed, always had been.

"Man, I wished I was there to witness that. I would've been eggin' her on before she slapped the shit out of me." I chortled.

As my brother talked, Ava sexily yelled, "Solomon Hussein Hampton!"

"Uh, bruh, I'mma talk to you later," I rapidly spoke before ending the call.

If he knew me, he knew what would go down and why I didn't wait for his response.

"Yes, Ava Jane Langston?" I voiced, dropping my cell phone on the sofa.

"I think it's time you see me and feel what I have planned for us," she provocatively announced.

"I'm wit' it," I groaned, dick rising like cornbread in a 450-degree heated oven.

"Good. You stay put. I'm coming to you," she sassily replied.

"A'ight," I responded, smiling and looking towards the hallway entrance.

Shortly afterward, "Impatient" by Jeremih and Ty Dolla $ign played at a nice listening decibel from her room. Immediately, I bobbed my head. With the remote control in my hand, I tapped the controller against my thigh.

When she sang the hook, I saw multi-colored lights illuminating the hallway. Focused on that direction, I anticipated seeing the most gorgeous woman I had the pleasure of being around strut to me wearing a provocative outfit. I longed to see her out of her comfort zone, or it could've been I longed to see the real Ava. Upon Ty Dolla $ign's voice gracing the speakers, Ava sexily pranced into my vision. Immediately, I stood, mouth open, as I gawked at the skimpily dressed woman.

My good *gotdamn.*

From head to toe, Ava was the shit. Her recently blonde hair was slightly curled. Never been the type of woman to wear makeup, Ava's lips were glossed to perfection. Silver, large hoop earrings dangled from her ears, and a beautiful choker secured around her narrow hickey-filled neck. The silk, black robe perfectly clung to her curvaceous body, making me eager to untie it. Ava's slender, long legs were oiled very well. Her toes and natural fingernails were polished with a glossy coat on top of the midnight polish. Her average-sized feet were black stiletto heels with a thick, silver jewel-studded strap across the toe area. Her right ankle held the same unique design ankle bracelet as the choker around her neck.

She modeled her outfit slowly while walking towards me—erotically looking at me and dangling a black satin blindfold.

"My, my, my," I groaned, walking towards her.

Creeping towards me, Ava dangled the blindfold and provocatively purred, "Solomon Hussein Hampton, may I blindfold you?"

Through clenched teeth, I groaned, "Fuck yes."

"Solomon Hussein Hampton, may I take you to another world?" she asked, stopping a few inches from me.

"Hell yes, you can," I responded.

"Solomon Hussein Hampton, kneel, please," she authoritatively hissed.

"Yes, ma'am." I grinned, dropping to my knees.

"Oou, I love a man who obeys," she cooed, ogling me while walking beside me.

When Ava arrived behind me, Avant's "Don't Say No, Just Say Yes" sounded, and the lovely woman securing the blindfold over my eyes sweetly sang. Sexily, she purred the hook into my ear while dragging two fingers across my neck.

"Is that so?" I probed before licking my lips and gripping my guy.

"Mm-hm." She held out as I felt her hands crawling towards the top of my head. Immediately, chills crept through my body. I had never encountered a sexual act as enticing as the one Ava blessed upon me.

Slowly skating her fingers down my face, she calmly articulated, "Solomon Hussein Hampton, please stand. When I grab your hands, I need you to trust me to lead you from here until we reach the bedroom. Will you have a problem with that?"

"Not a single problem," I replied, standing.

"Damn, I love a man who isn't afraid to let a woman lead." She seductively moaned, resulting in my dick becoming harder than it has ever been before.

Ava's soft and loving touch caused me to groan her name as she interlocked our fingers. Ava asked, "Solomon Hussein Hampton, are you in love with me?"

Nodding, I honestly replied, "I am."

Pulling my hands, she asked, "When did it happen?"

Following her blindly, I voiced, "About a year and a half after y'all moved in."

"Could it be an infatuation?"

"Fuck no," I voiced as she slightly turned my hands to the right. "Ava, I have been fuckin' since I was fourteen. I have never been in a relationship. When I saw you, I was like, 'shit, that's the type of woman I would have on my arms'. Then, I got to know you; that turned into likin' you. Then, it turned into a crush followed by me lovin' you, which landed me to be in love wit' you. By that time, I really wasn't hearin' a relationship wit' anybody if it wasn't wit' you. So, I became the nigga who never had a girlfriend but had quite a few females ridin' his stick. All because I needed you to be my one an' only girlfriend before I upped that relationship status—like to marriage."

As Chris Brown's "Wishing" played, Ava whispered, "Oh my, Solomon Hussein Hampton."

"What that, baby?"

Dropping my hands, Ava softly said, "I'm speechless right now."

"Why?"

"The things you've said, I don't know how to verbally respond to them. So, I guess that's a good thing since actions are the best way to show a person how you really feel about them. Right?"

"Right," I replied as she grabbed the waistline of my gym shorts and boxers.

While she passionately licked me from my chest, Ava slowly pulled down my garments. When she arrived at my pussy clogger, the sweet-smelling woman pulled my garments towards my ankles. Then, she licked before kissing my overly happy guy before questioning, "Oh, Solomon Hussein Hampton, what do we have here?"

"Some grade-A dick," I cockily replied as Bobby Valentine's "Beep" played.

"Yes, it is," she hissed before directing me to lift my left leg. Shortly afterward, Ava instructed me to raise my right leg.

Free from my clothing, the sexy woman politely voiced, "Solomon Hussein Hampton, take four steps backward."

Upon doing so, Ava commanded, "Hold out your arms."

Oh, shit like that, nih? I thought as I grinned.

After the handcuffs were slapped onto my wrists, I laughed. "Oh, we playin' that gam—"

"Good, gotdamn," I groaned as Ava's wet, minty, and warm mouth graced the mushroom-shaped head attached to the lovely tool my parents made.

"Mmm," she moaned, lifting my bound arms and sliding her head between them.

By her doing that simple action, more of my dick slid into her mouth, resulting in me throwing my head back and softly moaning, "Ava."

The sexy, innocent-looking broad took me for a ride I wasn't ready for. At first, she took her time with sucking and licking my tool, all the while massaging my balls and rubbing the upper portion of my legs. A nigga was beyond weak by the sixteenth time she made love to my man with her mouth. Then, she amped her dick-sucking skills and drove me wild. She spat on my shit and sucked it off, moaning and whimpering.

The repetitive, slow, head-twisting antics of deep-throating, dirt biking, and delicately sliding her teeth down the shaft of my tool had my knees buckling multiple times. While I balled my fists, my toes curled. My mouth was drier than a bitch's pussy during menopause. My mouth hadn't closed since she had sucked on the head like an infant starving during her nightly feeding. Under the black blindfold, my crazy behind opened my eyes as if I could see. My medium-beaded peepers were crossed while I shook my head from side to side, wishing I could see Ava's facial expression while she ate my dick up.

"Avaaa," I groaned as she sucked my tool and made a popping noise.

"Hm?" she announced, still sucking nastily while her fingers glided towards my ass.

"Ah, Ava, what you got going on?" I inquired, not feeling whatever mood she was trying to set.

Still jacking my dick, Ava removed her mouth from him and replied, "Just relaxing you. That's all."

"A'ight," I replied before clearing my throat.

The dick-sucking goblin continued her business while massaging my lower back. A brother was relaxed like a mug, to the point I wanted to lie down. There was only one thing on my mind throughout the ordeal—loving the woman who had a rough marriage and a horrible loss. While I was in my thoughts and enjoying what she was doing to me, I hadn't realized that damn woman had

spread my ass cheeks until I felt severe pain in all five of
my damn right toes.

Man, I'm propped up like a hoe. Oh hell nawl, I
thought as I tried sternly to say, "Ava, get the fuck from
back there."

Instead, I moaned that shit. I was beyond embarrassed
and uncomfortable. I couldn't lie; the shit she did felt good
than a motherfucker. Still massaging the area between my
balls and asshole, the whimpering, sexy fucker had my
dick knocking a hole in her throat. The more pressure she
put on the 'no go zone', the more I found myself bending,
reaching fo' my ankles, and whining her name. I felt like a
skeezer in her room; she had me begging and pleading for
her to stop. The more I was close to nutting, the more her
fingers slid towards my asshole.

"Ava! Don't you dare touch that motherfuckin' asshole
of mine, an' I mea—"

"Ooou, shit. Ooou, shiiii. Our Father, who art in
heaven, hallowed be thy name; thy kingdom come; thy
will be done on earth as it is in heaven. Give us this day
our daily bread, an' forgive my bootyhole's trespasser as I
try to forgive her who trespass against it." I moaned, head
dropping, knees shaking like a leaf on a windy day, and a
dick ready to vomit in Ava's mouth.

Ava placed her forefinger over my asshole and rapidly
moved it from left to right, saying, "My dick."

The tables had turned, and I'll be damned if I hadn't
become the weak bitch. Everything I ever made a female
say flew out of my mouth faster than a skillful driver
whipping a Lamborghini.

"Ava, baby, please don't cease us. I'm beggin' don't," I
whined as my knees buckled too hard as I felt my boneless
friends rise to the occasion.

No longer sucking my dick, Ava slid underneath my
bound wrists and demanded, "Solomon Hussein Hampton,
touch your toes. I want to suck that monster of yours from
the back."

Oh my damn, I thought, doing as my lady requested.

Gracefully gripping my dick and pushing it between my slightly ajar legs, Ava blew on the head before she attacked him.

"Good God," I groaned, bending closer to the ground, allowing Ava to put more of my dick into her mouth.

"Mhm," she voiced, sloppily sucking while jacking my dick and tugging my balls with the other hand.

"Avaaa," I moaned weakly.

In a smooth move, Ava spread my ass cheeks, slapped her tongue across the 'no-go zone', and ate a nigga's ass extremely beautifully but disrespectfully. The sexy woman had her way with me, and there wasn't anything I could say or do. My hands had never gripped my ankles in my entire life, but I'll be damned if I wasn't holding onto those fuckers as tears cascaded down my face.

"Ava, baby, please," I moaned weakly as she alternated between eating my ass, sucking on my dick, and inhaling my balls.

The moment Ava slowly inserted a finger into my ass, I shot up like a rocket with much to say. However, as quickly as I stood, I gripped my ankles back. That woman found a spot in my asshole that had me hollering, moaning, and whining like a bitch. With my dick deep down her skillful mouth and middle finger aggressively tapping on my P-spot, my knees buckled as I howled her name. At the same time, my protein shake filed into her awaiting warm mouth.

"Mhm, mhm, mhm," Ava sensually announced, still fingering my asshole.

"Ava, baby, unhand me. Just ... motherfuckin' unhand me," I weakly voiced, body trembling.

The sexy broad took her time releasing my dick and asshole. When she did, Ava softly demanded, "Solomon Hussein Hampton, slowly stand up."

As I did so, I felt like a shameful whore; I was sure my face was red. I had never busted that hard; moreover, I never had a female play around my 'no-go zone'. Badly, I wanted to bury my face into a pillow.

"Are you okay?" she softly inquired.

I felt some way, but I couldn't process what I felt. Thus, I calmly spoke, "I have no idea. That shit is new to me, so I don't know how to interpret it or my feelings now."

"Understandable. Do you feel I violated you?" she probed, removing the blindfold.

With the ability to see, I didn't look at Ava. Clearing my throat, I replied, "I really don't know."

"Hussein, look at me," Ava softly stated.

"I can't," I stated as she removed the handcuffs.

Laughing, she asked, "Why?"

"I can't look at myself, much less look at you, Ava. Look at it from my angle; you had me bent the fuck over, eatin' my ass an' suckin' on a nigga dick. Oh, let's not forget you played hopscotch wit' my prostate. You had me in this bitch hollerin', whinin', moanin', an' all that girly shit. I guess I'm in my feelin's behind that shit." I huffed, glaring at the wall.

Ava placed her hands on my wrists, and I damned near lost it. "Ava Jane Langston, "Go wash yo' hands. I don't want my ass secretions on my wrists."

As she skipped towards the master bathroom, fake coughing, concealing her laughter, I shook my head and snatched my clothes off the floor. Exiting the master bedroom, I questioned my masculinity; I didn't like that one bit. Once in the guest bathroom, I tried to think with a level head but couldn't. The more I thought about Ava's actions and my body's response, the more confused I became.

"Hussein?" Ava softly voiced, knocking on the bathroom door three times.

"Yeah?" I answered, turning on the water knobs.

"Would you like me to come in, or do you need time to yourself?"

"I need time to myself, Ava."

"Okay. For what it's worth, I didn't try to make you feel uncomfortable. I know I did, and for that, I'm sorry. Will you forgive me for making you feel uncomfortable?"

"Yes," I replied, stepping into the shower.

"Thank you. Are you hungry or thirsty? I can whip up something for us … if you like," she softly announced.

"Nawl, I'm good. Thanks, though."

"You are welcome. Well, um, whenever you want to talk to me, I'll be ready to listen. Cool?" she nervously stated.

"A'ight."

What the fuck? I thought as I cleaned my body.

"Hussein?" Ava called lowly.

"Yes, Ava?" I replied in an agitated tone.

"Just because you enjoyed what I did doesn't make you gay. Don't be confused or embarrassed by what I did. I don't view you as a weak man. You will always be dominant when it comes down to us. I … I just wanted to please you. That's all," she tenderly implored.

Man, I thought as I replied, "Okay."

Thirty minutes later, I stepped out of the shower with one thing on my mind—going home. Rapidly, I put on my clothes before leaving Ava's bathroom the same way I did before I entered—free of water and a clean tub. Sauntering into the living room, I saw Ava sitting on the sofa, twiddling her thumbs as she nibbled on the right corner of her mouth. Her peepers planted on me; they begged me to look into them. Feeling like a kid in trouble, I refused to look at Ava. I was too ashamed to place my eyes on her.

My cell phone rang as I scurried to my shoes beside the sofa. Ignoring the device, I slipped my feet into my shoes while snatching my shirt off the arm of the couch.

In the process of throwing my shirt over my head, Ava bleakly asked, "Are you leaving?"

"Yes," I nodded.

"Because of what I did?" she calmly probed, still eyeing me.

"Yep," I replied as my cell phone ceased ringing.

"Can we at least talk about it before you go?"

"There's nothin' to talk 'bout. I'll call you when I make it home," I told her, snatching my gun from underneath the sofa.

She touched my back and replied, "There's much to discuss. I made you uncomfortable. It was wrong of me to do that to you without asking your thoughts."

Without looking at her, I kissed her forehead and said, "I'm finna go."

"Hussein, don't go. Let's talk. Please," she begged as I walked away from her.

"I told you, Ava, there's nothing to talk about. I'm good. We are good. Okay?"

"Not okay, Hussein. If we don't talk about how you feel, you will always be closed off about it. You will always be on edge, and I don't want you to be that way while we are intimate. So, please communicate with me. Tell me how you are feeling."

Ring. Ring. Ring.

Between my annoying ass device and Ava not letting me leave, I lost it. Turning to face her, I sternly and slowly said, "Don't you ever fuckin' do that shit to me again, or I swear this shit will be over. Fo' good. Do I make myself clear, Ava?"

"But I thought it felt good to you. You were moa—"

"I don't give a fuck how my body reacted to that shit! Don't do that to me again, Ava! My asshole is meant fo' shit to come out of it, not to have a broad's tongue cruisin' through it before she finger fucks it! You had a fuckin' field day eatin' my ass, an' my wimpy ass was just bent over like a three-dollar whore, takin' that shit an' moanin'! That shit was so not cool in my eyes, Ava," I spat, observing her facial expression.

She tried her best to stifle the laughter, yet it didn't work. That fine, freaky motherfucker busted out laughing while cupping her mouth. I didn't see shit funny. She played with my manhood. Even though the shit felt damn good, I was uncomfortable with her thinking she would slip her finger into my asshole anytime she wanted. I didn't want her to think she would have me in the buck or bent over again. Those would be her positions for life!

Shaking my head, I dryly announced, "I'm glad you see this shit funny. I'mma holla at 'cha, Ava. I'll text you when I make it home."

While strolling to the door, my cell phone rang. Ava no longer laughed as she spoke apologetically, "Hussein, I'm sorry. I really am. You should choose different words to use when you are serious. I can't take you seriously when you say funny stuff."

Ignoring Ava's comment, I looked at my phone and saw Mo calling. I answered the call to cease hearing Ava's voice as I left her house.

"Mo, you blowin' me up. What's wrong?" I inquired, unlocking the doors on my whip.

"Hussein, let me make it up to you. Come back in. I don't want to be alone tonight," Ava said, standing on the porch.

At the same time, Mo said, "Shid, that's my question to you. What's wrong?"

Ignoring Ava's comment, I squinted my eyelids as I turned to look at her. Slowly, I asked, "Did Allie receive a phone call or was on the phone textin' between thirty to forty minutes ago?"

"Yeah, a phone call."

"After that phone call ended, did Allie tell you to call me?"

"Yeah."

"Did she tell you why?"

"Nawl. Just that you needed someone to talk to before you lost yo' shits."

Clearing my throat, I turned and walked towards the porch. My eyes landed on a worried Ava.

While Mo called my name, I shook my head and said, "I'm here."

"What's wrong, bruh? Why are you 'bout to lose yo' shits?"

"Hold on fo' one minute, bruh," I rapidly told him before placing the phone on mute.

Observing Ava's peepers, I asked, "Did you tell Allie what happened between you an' me?"

Nodding, she slowly said, "Yes."

Fuming, I inquired, "All of it?"

Ava nodded.

"What the fuck, Ava? It wasn't any of her fuckin' business. Why would you tell her? You wouldn't like it if I told my partnas how you are in the bedroom, would you?" I inquired, feeling more embarrassed.

"No, I wouldn't. I only told her because I needed advice on making you comfortable with what I did."

"Man." I held out, unmuting the call and walking from the porch. "Bruh, where you at?"

"Shid, at Allie's job in a room. You need me to come out fo' a bit," he yawned. At the same time, Ava called my name.

Ignoring her, I spoke into the phone, "I did, but since you yawned, that means yo' ass is tired. On som' real nigga shit, I'm gucci. I'll chop it up wit' you later."

Chuckling, he said, "Nawl nigga, yo' ass ain't gucci. Som' shit don' popped off an' you don't know how to handle that shit."

Ceasing my strides, I spoke through clenched teeth. "What did Allie tell you, Mo, an' don't lie to me."

"That Ava Mortal Kombat yo' ass while you was touchin' them ankles." The black bastard laughed.

I had never ended a call so fast as I strolled towards my car, feeling like a fucking punk. There was no way I would lie underneath Ava for the next couple of days. She would feel the pressure of not having me at her disposal for the stupid shit she pulled tonight.

"Solomon, I don't want to be alone tonight. Please, don't leave me here by myself. I'm begging you don't leave me … here … by myself," she whined hopelessly.

Fuck. She hit me wit' that Solomon shit, I thought, sighing heavily and ceasing my strides.

As I sat on the hood of my car, Mo's ass called back. Stuck between feeling like a punk ass nigga and hearing Ava call my first name in a damsel in distress tone, I was at a crossroads.

Shaking my head, I answered Mo's call.

"Yeah?"

In a serious tone, Mo said, "Bruh, I ain't call to joke. Honestly, I have no room to do so. You wasn't the only one grippin' ankles tonight, nigga. Well, I wasn't grippin' my ankles, lil' motherfucka had me holdin' up my own damn legs. My Jesus, I was in this gotdamn room justa moanin' an' hollerin'. My boy, my hard-up ass got slutted out tonight. I mean slut-the-fuck-out, woe!"

Before I knew it, I powered off my phone, laughing. Locking my car doors, I sauntered towards the porch, eyeing Ava. In the proximity of her, I cleared my throat, cupped her face, and announced, "Yeah, I liked that nasty ass shit, but I don't like the aftermath of knowing that I liked it. That was new to me, Ava. You can't just drop som' shit like that in my lap an' not discuss it wit' me first. The next time som' off the wall shit appears in' yo' head, talk to me 'bout it first. Understood?"

Gazing into my eyes, she nodded, "Understood."

"Get yo' nasty ass in the house, Ava Langston," I voiced, shaking my head.

As we stepped inside, I thought, *man, I don' let this guh slut me the fuck out. Jesus!*

Chapter IX
Ava

"Sometimes the questions are complicated and the answers are simple." — *Dr. Seuss*

As the water trickled down my back, sliding between my ass cheeks, my breaths became unsteady while my mouth hung open. With each water droplet slipping into my mouth, my head became heavier. The tighter my right hand gripped my ankle while my left hand gripped the side of the tub, the deeper Hussein's dick traveled inside my exhausted yet still starving pink walls.

Planting kisses in the center of my back and gripping my waist, Hussein etched his name into my pussy and asked, "My, oh my, Ava. You good down there?"

With a trembling body and a pretty kitty eager to cum, I struggled to speak like the many hours before; thus, I nodded.

"You can't talk, baby?" he chuckled, increasing his thrusts.

Rapidly, I shook my head as my knees gave out. Holding onto my waist, Hussein aided me on all fours while rapidly fucking me.

"Ah, Ava, baby, you ain't gon' give up like that, is it?" Hussein chuckled, slipping a finger in my asshole and placing his leg on the side of the tub.

I tried to drop my bobbing head onto my hands. However, Hussein ceased that by digging deeper into my pussy and gripping a fistful of my hair. He sexily growled, "Oh, fuck no, Ava, baby, I want yo' ass just like this. I love seein' the water slam onto yo' back before going into every direction on yo' body, especially that ass. I want you in this position, so every time I hit this pussy, I see them waves."

"Oh Jesus," I cooed, eyes crossing.

Popping my behind, Hussein spoke through clenched teeth. "What the fuck I told you 'bout callin' Him. He ain't got nothin' to do wit' this."

Seventeen more pumps and nasty kisses later, I had to tap the walls.

"Oh no, you ain't tappin' out. I didn't tap out when you was eatin' a nigga ass up like you were at a fuckin' buffet. Nawl, baby, you gon' take this dick. You gon' take all of it!" he savagely spoke, beating up my pretty kitty until I breathlessly squealed that I couldn't take any more.

"Oh, Ava, baby, be a big girl an' take this dick. I know you can," he sang, removing his pussy clogger.

Oou Lord, I know You see me in this tub helpless. Help me out. Let him catch a cramp or something. He'll stop then, I thought as Hussein slung the shower curtain back, bent, and wickedly smiled.

Oh Lord, why he ain't cramped up yet? I thought as Hussein said, "It's time to come out of this tub. By the way, Ava baby, I ain't don' wit' you yet."

Tears welling, I whined, "But Hussein, you have been in me for hours. We've nutted so many times. Shit, the fucking sun is up, and we still haven't been to sleep. I'm so gotdamn hungry and thirsty. My legs and arms feel like Jell-O. I believe I've pulled out a patch of hair. My throat muscles are tired; I've been in this damn house for hours upon hours upon hours upon fucking hours, moaning, screaming, and yelling. Baby, you have worn me out. Please let me get some sleep. I have clients coming today, starting at ten. I need to sleep, Hussein."

Standing, Hussein calmly said, "Okay. Let me help you out the tub so you can go get some sleep."

After helping me out of the tub, I poorly stood on a dry towel. My legs weren't worth a fuck, and I surely wouldn't flee from the bathroom without having a secure balance. Therefore, I didn't move.

"You want me to carry you to the bed?" he sweetly asked, standing beside me.

"Shit, the bed is wet up. I can't lay in that mess," I huffed, realizing I would have to lie in the guest bedroom.

Hussein stepped forward and asked, "Well, do you want me to carry you into the guest bedroom?"

"No, I can manage. I need to use these fuckers anyways. You had them in every direction," I answered, running my shaky hand through my wet hair.

"Ava?" Hussein softly called from behind me.

"Yes?" I voiced, turning to face him.

Sneakily grinning, that fine bastard shoved me against the sink, spread my legs, and dropped to his knees.

With fluttering eyelids, loudly and erratically, I cooed, "Gotdamn it, Huss—"

In a flash, I was back in the position that caused me to be worn out. Hussein's mouth had my back arched on the sink as my toes twitched and my hands pushed his head further into my pretty pussy.

"I thought this would get that mind of yours right," he chuckled, slipping fingers into my asshole and pussy.

"Good God," I stated, spit flying out of my mouth as I involuntarily sat upright, eyeing the demon between my legs.

Intensely working my middle and rear end, Hussein increased his finger movements. While narrowing his eyes, Hussein asked, "Now, Ava, why you keep callin' that Man in our fornication sessions, guh?"

"I don't know," I voiced poorly.

"Okay," he said before he attacked my body beautifully.

My toes and fingers balled, and my body felt as if it was sizzling. In seconds, my body went limp. By the look in Hussein's charming eyes, he knew one hell of an orgasm was on the verge of showing itself. Quickly, there were no fingers stuffed into my pussy or ass. Yet, his clogger was slowly entering my treasure trove.

"After this one, I won't have any choice but to let you sleep," he chuckled, placing my left foot on the wall and my right foot on his chest.

Planting his nose on top of mine, Hussein eyed me while sliding my body towards the edge of the sink. Slipping his hand towards the back of my neck, he lifted my head and sexily growled, "You will be sleep before I get all of my nut out my sacs an' into you, which I will successfully do. Now, I need to say this to you while yo' eyes are open. Ava Jane Langston, you are fuckin' mine. You belong to me; I belong to you. I've always belonged to you; you've always belonged to me. So, baby, I don't give a fuck what go on … you better never shut me out because I'll never shut you out. Understand?"

"Yes," I whimpered, breathing erratically.

With his dick head hitting my G-Spot, Hussein sexed me faster and genuinely voiced, "Good. Now, one mo' thing, I've been dyin' to say this fo' so gotdamn long that I can't hold it in anymo', an' I won't say it to yo' sleepin' body. Ava, I love you. I've always loved you"

He finally said it, I thought before moaning, "I love yo—"

Oh my God. Oou, my Jesus. Oooh, I thought, staring poorly into his loving peepers while he diminished the little energy I had left.

Orgasm after orgasm spilled out of me before I found the will to holler his name as tears streamed down my face. Ensuring to keep my peepers open to see him cum inside me, I focused on his facial expression as he passionately talked. I drank everything he said as I felt his dick pulsating while his hand gripped my waist.

Wiping my tears, Hussein kissed my lips before moaning, "You are mine, Ava. You are mine."

"I'm yours, Solomon," I erratically breathed as my pretty kitty doused Hussein's athletic physique. At the same time, my eyelids grew heavy.

Placing his mouth to my ear, Hussein moaned, "I'm finna cum in you, Ava."

Weakly, I mouthed, "Okay."

"Sleep well, beautiful one," was the last thing I remembered.

When I awakened with slobber crust in the corners of my mouth, it was because of the pounding on the front door and the doorbell buzzing repeatedly.

"I hope I hadn't overslept," I groaned, running my hand through my messy hair.

Thank goodness. It's only 7:30, I thought, looking at the clock on the black, three-drawer nightstand.

As I yawned and flopped back onto the bed, I wasn't worried about whoever was at the door. Curling underneath Hussein, he kissed my forehead and groggily asked, "You do hear that, right?"

"Yes, and I don't care who it is. This is not the time to talk to anyone. Just ignore it," I yawned as the knocks and banging ceased.

"Lift up. I'll look out the blinds to see who it is. Those knocks sounded very personal," he wearily spoke.

"Solomon Hussein Hampton, I don't care who is at the door. Lay down," I replied, planting my hand on his chest and tapping it twice.

Upon doing what I said, Hussein wrapped his arms around me. At the same time, we heard knocks from my bedroom window and my mother's screechy voice calling my name.

Shit, Hussein's here. She's going to show her ass. Fuck, his car is in my driveway. Damn it, I thought, slapping my hands over my face, and said, "Fuck."

Chuckling, Hussein replied, "Go get the door."

"The hell you say. She'll get the hint and go on. Later, I'll feed her some lie about why I didn't come to the door," I whispered as Hussein's cell phone vibrated. As he rolled over to grab his device, my mother pressed the doorbell, allowing it to chime continuously.

"Oh my God, Momma, please go home," I begged as Hussein answered his phone.

The doorbell ceased as Hussein replied, "Yes, ma'am."

His grandmother or mother, I thought, closing my eyes.

Busting out laughing, Hussein stated, "Go 'head on nih, Grams. You play all day."

A few seconds later, Hussein sat upright and said, "What? Man, Grams, I know you lyin'."

Looking at me, Hussein laughed. "Baby, yo' Momma on the phone wit' the police. Talkin' 'bout, she think you missin'. Man, please go to the door before them folks kick the door in."

"Are you serious?" I shockingly inquired, throwing the covers off me.

As I scrambled out of bed, he replied, "Yep."

Shit, I can't deal with my mother while Hussein is here. She's liable to fuck up my entire day. I can't afford for her to put me in an unpleasant mood, I thought as Hussein told his grandmother that he would come over before he left the neighborhood.

"Stay in this room, Hussein; do not come out," I quickly spoke before rushing out of the room.

Halfway down the hallway, it dawned on me I was naked. Shaking my head and sighing heavily, I didn't have time to turn around to put on clothes. The last thing I needed was for the police to come over because of a false call. Arriving at the door, I overheard my mother on the phone, using her Caucasian voice.

"Ma, get off the phone with the police. For the love of God, I'm home," I spoke, unlocking the door.

As she informed the dispatcher that I was home, I fled to my room, searching for something to put on. Genia Langston nosily inquired loudly, "Care to tell me why my preacher son's car is in your yard, Ava?"

No, the fuck, I don't care to tell you, Ma, I thought, nearing my room.

While my eyes landed on a naked Hussein standing at the doorframe with a curious expression plastered on his handsome face, I asked, "Momma, what is the nature of this early morning visit?"

"I came by because your brothers and I hadn't heard from you in a few weeks. Now, answer my question … why is my preacher son's car in your yard, Ava?" she probed, raising her voice. At the same time, I skipped by Hussein without looking at him. I was eager to get rid of her.

"Momma, I don't know why Hussein parked his car in my yard. Honestly, I don't care. His vehicle isn't bothering a soul. As far as my brothers calling me, they haven't dialed my number. You know they only call me when they want money or try to finesse me into watching their kids," I inhaled, skipping toward the tall raven dresser.

"You are their sister; hell, you should be offering to spend time with your niece and nephew. Anyways, so you don't know why his car is in your yard, and you don't care, huh? Well, you should. That boy runs with the wrong crowd, honey. Before you married that bastard, Jak, you used to not take shit from anybody. Since Jak skipped out on you, you've let yourself go and let folks do what they want, huh?" she nastily spoke as I hurried to dress.

Shut up, please, I thought, throwing an oversized shirt over my head.

The more my mother talked her noise, the more I wanted to shout for her to leave my house. Running out of the room, I wondered what I could say to get her gone without being rude. When I arrived in the living room, eyeing the woman who had given birth to me, she shook her head and huffed, "You just woke up all right. You've never gone to bed without wrapping your hair."

"Momma, you see me. I'm fine. Please stop speculating. I'm not up for a social visit at this hour. Can you please belittle me after one o'clock? Thanks," I voiced while walking towards the door.

As I stepped closer to her, Momma stopped me from walking. While she suspiciously eyed me as if I lived underneath her roof, her eyes landed on my neck. Lord knew I was grown, but Genia Langston had a way with her mouth that I had to respect because she was my mother.

"For someone to have been sleeping, you surely have a lot of hickeys on your neck, Ava," Momma hissed with an ugly expression. "I'm no fool, Ava. Hussein's car is in your driveway because he's in your house. Heard what I said *your house.* You were a fool once; don't be a fool twice."

"Wow. You've seen me. I'm breathing. It's time for you to leave. You are barking up a tree you don't want to climb this morning, Momma," I spoke through clenched teeth.

"I'll leave when I get good and darn ready, Ava Jane Langston. Now, you better listen up well. I don't know what you have cooking up with Hussein, but I know one thing: you better cease that before he do you like Jak did you." She scolded as a gym-short and socks-wearing Hussein stepped into my line of vision, causing my heart to race.

I told his ass to stay in the room and not to come out. Now, she really won't fucking leave, and God knows what's going to escape her mouth, I thought as Hussein greeted my mother, showing his beautiful teeth.

"Ah," Momma gasped, eyes bucked. The hard-up woman didn't speak, which resulted in Hussein chuckling before placing a kiss on my cheek.

Oh my God, Momma is going to blow a gasket, I thought as Hussein rubbed my back and said, "Baby, what would you like to eat?"

"*Baby?*" Momma sarcastically spoke. "It's a must I don't leave until I tell you a thing or two about yourself, Ava."

I removed his arm and replied, "I'm not hungry. Text me when you make it home, please."

Taken aback, Hussein stared at me for a while before nodding and walking towards the sofa. Aggressively, Hussein shoved his feet into his shoes and retrieved his gun from underneath the cushion sofa, followed by snatching his keys off the table. While he did those things, I couldn't take my eyes off him, and Momma didn't take her eyes off me.

Hussein, I'm so so sorry, I thought, watching him walk out of my house. It hurt me when he didn't look my way or say goodbye.

My miserably bitter mother said, "Ava Jane, you should be ashamed of yourself. He's way younger than you. What could you two possibly accomplish together? You have surely lost it. You are that desperate for a man, honey?"

"I won't do this today or any other day with you. You have come into my safe haven and disrespected *my* company. This is my house! The driveway those two cars are parked in that's mine, also. I got this property through the divorce settlement, along with a hefty amount of alimony. So, take your judgmental attitude elsewhere because it's not welcomed here. Furthermore, my son is dead! I don't have to watch nobody's gotdamn kids! I'm far from desperate, and I have *not* let myself go. You, dear mother, have let yourself go. I didn't lose my mind and threw myself into a church because my husband was secretly sleeping with his best friend, who is a man. That was you, Mother. I didn't swear off men and a happily ever after. That was you, Mother. My failed marriage didn't change me drastically; it hurt me. I pay attention to the males *I* choose to have in my life. Your failed marriage destroyed you! You will not bring misery to my doorstep because you are unhappy. Don't you dare talk down on me. Ever! You have officially worn out your welcome. Don't you bring your ass to my house again if you can't act like the guest that you are! It's time for you to go, and I mean right now!" I angrily spoke as Hussein's car roared to life before reversing out of the driveway.

Shocked at my tone and the truths I spat, Momma left my house without saying a word. Upon locking and closing the door, I searched my room for my cell phone. As I tore up my room, I badly needed to talk to Hussein. While I retrieved my device from the head of the bed, blasting speakers bumped down the road. Without a doubt, I knew it was Hussein. Peeking out of the blind, I saw his car pulling into the driveway.

Exiting my room, I sighed deeply and prepared myself for whatever he had to say. After all, he heard the bullshit that escaped my bitter mother's mouth, and I didn't defend him. Before he could knock or ring the doorbell, I had unlocked and opened it.

Staring into his eyes, I said, "I'm sorry you had to witness that."

"It's all good," he quickly stated before pulling me close, sucking my bottom lip into his mouth.

Breaking the kiss, Hussein nonchalantly said, "I'll talk to you later."

"Hussein, stay."

Shaking his head, he replied, "Nawl. No tellin' who else gon' pop up an' you gon' try to hide me or not defend me. I just came back fo' a kiss an' to tell you … don't let yo' mother's words get to you. You know where I stand wit' you. Have a good day, Ava."

"Hussein," I called as he walked away.

"Hussein!"

"I'll talk to you later, Ava," he voiced, not looking at me.

Hopping into his idling car, Hussein turned up the radio and rapidly reversed out of my yard. While I watched him zoom down the road, I pounded my fist on the doorframe and yelled, "Fuck!"

My mother had shown her ass so severely that I didn't want to conduct any business today. For most of my working hours, I wasn't in the mood to talk; however, I did. Throughout my chatting time with my clients, my mind was on Hussein. In between clients, I texted the disappointed man. He viewed the bulk of my texts and responded to only a few.

Usually, when he arrived at work, he would let me know. Today, he didn't; thus, I knew I was in the hot seat with him. To ease the damage I allowed my mother to create, I texted Hussein the code to get into my house when he clocked out for the night. Like the other texts, he viewed it but didn't reply.

After my last client left, I entered my home drained and frustrated. I wanted to call my mother and give her another set of choice words, but I let her ass be. She was dead wrong for coming at me the way she did. Ever since I could remember, my mother would be down my throat about tedious shit. My father always came to my rescue, telling her to stop being so hard on me. It was safe to say that my mother showed favoritism when it came down to Kyle and Jordan.

Unlike me, my older brothers never received a hard time from Momma. She let them get away with murder as she calmly and respectfully talked to them. In the beginning, I never understood why she treated me harsher than she did them. I was more independent, smart, and well-mannered. My brothers did or said things I would never do; I had more respect for people and myself.

However, the day came when I learned why my mother treated me like she did. By me being the last child and a girl, Momma felt my father should've married her instead of continuing to date her. When he never proposed, all the hurt and blame were thrown at me. It was a stupid reason for her to treat me like she did. Yet, Genia Langston did what she wanted—left her misery at my feet.

My brothers had our father's last name, and I had our mother's last name. Rumors spread around the city that my father wasn't my dad since I didn't have his last name. The stories didn't bother me because I knew the truth. I resembled my father more than my brothers.

Upon turning ten, I received an earful of unpleasant information one day after school as I strolled into the house. Momma was hysterical, throwing everything towards my father and Jacob, his male best friend. The hurt woman hollered about my father having sexual relations with Jacob while still having unprotected sex with her.

According to my mother's loud rants, which could be heard from the sidewalk, my father had been sleeping with Jacob the entire time he dealt with her. That day was the last time my mother spoke to my father or any man. That was the day Momma swore she would never date or have sex again, and she didn't. That was twenty-two years ago. In addition, it was the last time I heard my father's voice and saw him. He made it his business not to communicate with my brothers and me. I didn't know if Momma had a hand in him not being in our lives, but we caught hell trying to find him. Over the years, I gave up looking for him. There was no need to run behind a man who didn't want to be loved by his daughter.

Ring. Ring. Ring.

Shoving my hair from my face, I skipped towards the kitchen while removing my cell phone from my back pocket. Staring at Allie's name, I answered.

"What's up, boo?" she excitedly asked as I opened the chrome refrigerator.

"Girl, about to lose my damn mind in this house," I sighed, snatching a bottle of water from the door shelf.

"Why?" she inquired as her seven-year-old daughter, Noni, called her name repeatedly.

After sternly telling Noni not to interrupt her while she was on the phone, Allie spoke agitatedly, "I'm about to beat her ass. I haven't been on the phone all day, and here her ass comes with that mess. Now, why are you about to lose your mind, Ava?"

"First off, Genia showed her ass earlier this morning, which prompted me to shut down in front of Hussein. He isn't really communicating with me, and Allie, I don't like that," I confessed, opening the bottled water.

Allie quizzed, "Now, I need to know blow-by-blow details."

As I walked out of my kitchen, I briefly closed my eyes and spilled the terrible events from this morning. While I did so, I received a text from Hussein. Feeling giddy, I read his message. Just as quickly as I felt pumped, it went away. The three words he sent me caused me to frown and shake my head.

"I know damn well she didn't say all that shit, Ava!" Allie loudly voiced, shocked.

Maybe another time.

I glared at the text message Hussein sent me as I replied to Allie, "Oh yes, she did. I had to lay her ass out, and truthfully, I'm still itching to tell her some more things she needs to hear."

After blowing raspberries, Allie said, "No, ma'am. Let her miserable ass be. If you feed into her shit, all hell will break loose. Your mother's mouth is too much for me. Once you lay her ass out, you will crumble. So, don't pay that bitter hag any attention. Do you hear me?"

Nodding, I said, "Yes."

"Now, finish telling me the rest of the story," she demanded.

As I did so, I relaxed on the sofa and stared at the ceiling. When I finished, Allie hollered, "Oouu, baby, that nigga has placed you in the doghouse. Shit, Ava, how will you wiggle yourself out of the mess you in?"

Shaking my head, I replied, "I have no idea, but I'm going to come out of it."

"Well," she sang before continuing. "How about we figure out how to get you out of this jam at Auran's Bar and Grill tonight?"

"Sure. It's not like I have any plans since Hussein isn't coming over," I pouted.

"Okay, well, it is close to six o'clock. Are we leaving at the usual time?"

"Yep."

"Well, you know I change into fifty 'lem outfits before I settle on the final one," she giggled.

To save my best friend the hassle of swapping clothes every five minutes, I sat upright, voicing. "I'm wearing a white crop top shirt and cut-up, whitewash denim shorts, and white open-toe heels."

"Oh, so, bitch, we finna show out tonight, huh?" She laughed.

Smiling, I responded, "If that's what you wanna do, then you know ya girl is all for it."

"Nih, bitch you know I am all for the fuck shit. I'm with it. Let me get off this phone so I can put this outfit together real quick and secure this newly purchased wig."

"All right. You know what? Get ready earlier than normal. I want to go out to eat first."

"Now, bitch, you know you are speaking my language. What time do you want to step out?" she hollered before laughing.

"Seven-thirty, okay?" I questioned, walking towards my room.

"Sure is. I'll see you then."

"Allie?"

"Yessss," she hissed in a funny tone.

Giggling, I announced, "Will you stay the night with me?"

"Bitch, I'm not finna get on you," she lowly spoke in a raspy voice, resulting in me busting out laughing as I posted up on the hallway's wall.

"I hate you right now! I swear I do. Please, please, don't say that shit tonight. Do not embarrass me, Allie! Folks swear we are fucking around as it is."

"Girl, fuck them folks. Yes, I'll stay the night. With that being said, watch me act a fool tonight! Now, bye!" the heifer laughed before ending the call.

Slapping my forehead, I sauntered towards my room, asking myself, "What have I gotten myself into for the night? This best friend of mine is going to have my face blue-black."

At nine-thirty, a tipsy Allie and I slid into the crowded, diverse atmosphere of Auran's Bar and Grill, looking great and smelling fantastic. Bodies of all shapes and hues swayed from side to side as the DJ played urban music. Plenty of partygoers were drunk while a few held tightly to cigarettes or Black-N-Mild's while bobbing their heads. While walking towards one of the bars, I scanned the nice-sized establishment. As usual, I didn't see anyone I knew and was beyond thankful.

After Allie and I received two drinks apiece before strutting towards the sitting area, we saw our usual table and the surrounding tables closest to the dance floor occupied. Deciding to sit higher within the seating area, we climbed the eight steps. Upon landing on the last one, DJ Unk's "Don't Hide That Pussy" blasted.

Immediately, I classily swayed my body to the beat and gulped a nice amount of my drink. Meanwhile, a grooving

Allie drew attention to us. I didn't like all eyes on me, whereas Allie lived for that shit. Therefore, I let her do her thing while I stood beside her and ensured no one violated her.

Three songs later, my best friend and I visited the bartenders. For the life of me, I had zero idea why I allowed Allie to talk me into taking four shots of Crown Apple. After we took the shots, she ordered four more drinks of Crown Apple with Sprite. Before leaving the bar, she demanded we slaughter one of the cups before returning to our sitting area. Like a damn fool, I did what she commanded.

"Good gotdamn it, Allie!" I hollered, giggling, as I felt the effects of rapidly gulping liquor.

Oh my goodness, I can't do that shit again. If we are to make it home safely, I can't let Allie sucker me into taking shots and downing an entire cup of Crown Apple and Sprite, I thought as she bounced her rounded bottom towards our seating place.

Bobbing my head to an unknown song, I scanned the club. My breath was taken away as I saw Hussein standing beside Mo at the pool table. With numerous females in their presence, I felt some type of way. Quickly, those feelings went away as I remembered his words about who belonged to him and who I belonged to. There was no need for me to act a fool or negatively towards a man who had clearly told me on many occasions where his heart lay.

As we climbed the steps, I sipped from the little red straw and vibed harder with the song's beat. While I sat at the table, Allie stood still, zoned ahead, and mouthed something. I was sure she saw Mo and Hussein. She placed her mouth to my ear and said, "Mo and Hussein in the joint."

"I know."

"Oh my. Chile, I'm gonna sit back and pay attention to some shit for a minute," she stated, sitting in the chair— for the first time since we arrived.

Song after song, my best friend didn't say anything as she watched the pool area. I couldn't lie as if I didn't have my eyes placed that way. My handsome guy had my full drunk-ass attention as he held other females' attention. While Hussein laughed and chatted with the pretty-looking females, a few tried touching him. Quickly, he moved their hands while shaking his head. Immediately, a smile crept upon my face. Wanting to know his facial expression, I decided to pull some slick shit. Retrieving my phone, I texted the attractive being.

Me: How's work going?

While I put my phone on the table, I stared at him.

Leaning over, Allie laughed into my ear. "Bitch, you just texted him?"

Not taking my eyes off Hussein, I nodded. Ten minutes later, he texted: *It's all right.*

Stunned, I shook my head and felt like a fucking fool for sleeping with a gotdamn liar. That simple lie made me ponder everything else that slipped from his mouth. Furious, I flung my phone into my small handbag before downing my beverage. I was officially pissed off with myself. I had made an absolute mess with things between Hussein and me. Now, it would be hard for us to return to being friends!

I should've never opened my gotdamn legs to him, I thought as Allie asked, "What's wrong?"

Angrily, I placed my mouth to her ear and said, "I texted him how was work, and he replied, it's all right."

"Are you fucking serious?" she loudly asked, shocked.

Nodding, I replied, "Yep. Next round on me. Four shots of Crown Apple and four cups of Crown Apple and Sprite, right?"

"We don't need anything else to drink, Ava," she spoke, shaking her head.

"I do. So, are you drinking or not?" I inquired, trying to hold in tears.

"I see you need it, so yeah, we are drinking. Come on," she voiced, standing.

I sexily yet carefully sauntered down the steps with my head held high, moving along with the rhythm of an unknown jam. Not a single time did I look towards the pool table; I kept my eyes on what was in front of me. Upon arriving in the long line at the bar, I tried to keep my mind from racing. Most importantly, I did my best to keep my mother's words from today and the past out of my head.

"Whatever you are thinking about, please let it go," Allie whispered as she grabbed my hand.

"The sooner we get our drinks, the better," I told her, glancing into her pretty face.

"Okay," she mouthed before turning around.

My best friend didn't turn her head for some time. I was sure she was looking in the direction of the pool tables. While I faced the bar, out of my peripheral vision, I saw Allie shaking her head as she mouthed, "Wow."

"What's wrong?" I probed, placing my eyes on her.

Allie didn't respond as she gently tapped a few White guys on their shoulders. Once she had their attention, she said something to them. After they smiled and nodded, that damn heifer flashed them her titties. Spit flew out of my mouth as snot shot out of my nose. As I held onto my nose, Allie grabbed my wrists and led me in front of the men. Shocked at my best friend, I grabbed napkins from a holder before wiping my nose. While she placed the orders, I stared at her. I had to know what she saw and why she flashed those White men.

Whispering into her ear, I said, "Really, Allie? So, we are back to showing titties to skip the line? I saw your facial expression; thus, spill now."

As the bartenders placed our drinks in front of us, I retrieved my banking card before putting it into the dry palm of the stocky bartender. While Allie hadn't responded to me, I watched her down the four shots before gulping the entire contents within the first cup.

As I patiently stared into her face, the bartender handed me the card and a receipt to sign. At the same time, Allie calmly spoke, "I saw Mo groping some chick's pussy before whispering in her ear."

Beyond stunned, I looked at her while I poorly signed the receipt. We had officially landed ourselves into some shit neither of us was prepared for. After downing the four shots and the first mixed drink, we skipped away from the bar dancing; I led the way. Instead of walking towards our seating area, I strolled in the other direction—where Hussein and Mo were.

Absolutely outside of myself, I let the alcohol talk to me, and I'll be damned if it took everything in me not to listen. Allie slid before me as Tweeday & Hollyhood Bay Bay's "Roll" sounded. While she pranced toward the guys who had us looking like fools for them, Allie sneakily looked back at me while we swayed to the beat of the jam. In the proximity of the males eyeing us, I winked at my best friend before blowing her a kiss. Being cordial and smiling, we waved at them before sliding to the dance floor. I didn't dance in front of people; however, with the liquor cruising through my body and eyes on me, I showed my ass. I felt as if I was a teenager—carefree and ready to enjoy the night without a single fucking worry.

Shit, we should get drunk more often, I thought as Hussein rolled behind me and Mo strolled behind Allie.

Looking at my friend, I laughed, chunked the deuces, and walked off, dancing. Allie wasn't far behind me. The goofy-ass characters were in tow while we climbed the stairs to our sitting area. As Allie stood beside me, minding her business, Mo was in her ear. At the same time, Hussein stood behind me, talking some shit I didn't want to hear.

Sucking down the rest of my drink, I faced the handsome young guy. After draping my arm around his neck, I placed my mouth to his ear and slowly said, "I don't deal with liars. I let that shit go when I signed those divorce papers. I was sitting right here when I texted you. You gave me a strong face lie. So, I will tell you a strong face ass action; then, I'll tell you a strong face truth. Get the fuck from around me and stay the fuck away from me.

You'll never slide off in me again. You most definitely don't have to worry about touching your toes again. Now, bye."

Aggressively, Allie grabbed my wrist. Stepping back, I looked at my angry friend. She mouthed, "Let's go before I turn this bitch out."

Nodding, I planted the cup on the table and began the journey of leaving the packed seating section. As we strutted between a pile of handsome men, I started to have a double vision.

Ah fuck, I thought, sighing deeply.

After I issued out many 'excuse me's', Allie and I was outside as it seemed the dry heat suffocated my drunken body.

"Man, y'all are too drunk to drive. Who whipped up here?" Mo inquired from behind us.

Neither of us said a word as we continued walking towards my car.

"Bitch, waittt! Whew, girl, those drinks got me!" Allie drunkenly voiced from behind me.

Laughing, I slowed as I saw my friend holding on to the back of a nice-looking Ford truck. At the same time, Mo slid behind Allie to aid her in standing.

"Don't put your motherfucking hands on me, Mo. Why in the fuck are you in my presence anyways? Go back inside and continue groping the chick's pussy you were up on. No malice this way, my guy. We gucci. Thanks for the good time, though," she spat as she took a step backward and fell.

Lord, how in the hell are we going to make it to my house like this? I thought as Hussein and Mo were at Allie's alcohol-infested body.

"I got it. I got it. Thanks for the help. I'm good now," she voiced, staggering.

"Man, Ava, please tell me you are driving?" Mo asked calmly.

"I am," I replied, lifting my head and closing my eyes.

"She can't drive. She's drunk too," Hussein softly said, inches away from me.

"Ava, be honest wit' me. Can you drive?" Mo inquired. Shaking my head as I felt like laughing for no damn reason, I replied, "Nope, but trust me, I will. I've done this quite a few times. Isn't that right, Allie?"

"Sure the fuck has!" she sang.

"Hussein, gon' drive yo' car, Ava," Mo ordered.

"I'm driving my own gotdamn car. Don't need a daddy; gay motherfucker never wanted to be a daddy, to begin with. He wanted to shove dick in his best friend's asshole. Don't need a man; I had one, but he fucked half of the stewardess before calling it quits after I killed my son ... so he likes to say. Plus, having a man is fucking overrated. All y'all do is lie, cheat, and make promises you worthless piece of shits can't keep. Oh, shit, I forgot y'all good for dick and mouth if it's giving out. Don't need a brother; those fuckers are a waste of a human body. So, y'all can politely fuck off!" I spoke slurred, eyeing Mo and Hussein as Allie finally made it before me.

"Ava, you are not fit to drive. Hussein, gon' drive yo' car," Mo stated sternly.

"Sir, go fuck yourself." I laughed, turning on my heels while I grabbed Allie's hand.

On our heels, those assholes wouldn't let us slide inside my car. Mo, Hussein, and I went back and forth for quite some time. Meanwhile, Allie's ass sprawled on the hood. All it took was for Allie to start vomiting for me to loosen the grip on my keys. As I moved to assist Allie, Mo snatched my keys. Anger consumed me, but I couldn't act out because my best friend sounded like she was vomiting up a lung.

Once Allie ceased throwing up, I drunkenly said, "Mo, your job is simple. Drive my car home. Don't talk to me about shit. I mean absolutely shit because I don't give a fuck about nothing, and when I say nothing. I mean, not a gotdamn thing. Since Allie doesn't want to be around you, which I don't blame her, she will ride with Hussein. Once we are safely inside *my* house, y'all *will* motherfucking leave and continue to have a great night. Won't be no lingering around my motherfucking place."

As Mo handed Hussein his car keys, Hussein looked at me and said, "We need to talk, Ava."

"Oh no, boo. One thing about my crazy-ass mother, she knows bullshit when she sees it. I should've listened to her when she had all that shit to say about Jak. Maybe I wouldn't be so fucked up mentally. Anyways, thanks for the banging ass sex this cobwebby pussy hadn't seen in so many moons," I announced before walking away, feeling sullener than the day I received those divorce papers from Jak two days after we buried Mica.

I will never ever be this gotdamn dumb again! I knew I should've kept my distance, but oh no, I had to experience everything I had fantasized about. Now, look at my stupid behind, already getting lied to after suddenly opening my fucking legs and mouth. What in the absolute hell, Ava Jane Langston? Just plain damn dumb, once again.

Chapter XXI
Hussein

"There is hope, even when your brain tells you there isn't."-
John Green, Turtles all the Way Down.

Sunday, July 26th

It had been a challenging nine days without talking to or seeing Ava. She didn't respond to any of my calls or texts, which she viewed. She wouldn't answer the door. I tried using the code she had sent me a week ago, but it didn't work. Late nights, she wasn't on the porch, drinking that nasty-ass wine while looking at the sky, thinking. She wasn't at any of the clubbing joints she'd frequented.

Every day at noon, I slid through Mica's grave to see if she was there; she wasn't. I chopped it up with my little buddy for an hour before I planted a toy truck on his final resting place. Every day, several times a day, I asked my grandparents if they had seen Ava, and their response was always the same—no. Literally, Ava was off the grid, and that worried me.

Today was no different; after I visited Mica's grave, I posted up at my grandparents' house. An hour after being at their home, Mo, moping ass, pulled up. We faced a few blunts while discussing Allie and Ava before rolling Grams two joints. My partner's stupid ass was in his feelings since Allie ceased communicating and stopped him from showing up at her job. I lied about being at work, whereas his stupid ass dared to touch on another bitch's pussy. Like I told him, I didn't blame Allie for throwing his ass in the trash. He did some foul shit for a nigga who proclaimed he really liked her. True enough, I shouldn't have lied to Ava about being at work; I couldn't give her a legitimate reason as to why I lied. I was a man; I admitted I was dead wrong for that. For that, my chances of being back in her good graces were slim; however, I still had to try to get her back into my hands.

"Grandson, I know why you are here. I've also noticed your car ain't been parked over there. So, tell me, what happened?" Grams inquired, flicking the lighter.

Deeply inhaling, I looked down the street and said, "I lied about being at work when I was inside a bar."

"How did Ava know you lied, Solomon?"

"She was in the joint," I confessed, seeing Ava's and Allie's cars bypass my grandparents' house.

"Boy, why did you lie? You must've been in there with another female or had one coming up in there?" Grams curiously inquired as Mo hopped to his feet.

"There, they go," he said.

She won't talk to you if she gets that car in that garage. Get your stupid ass in the garage, nigga, I thought, eyeing Ava's garage door.

As it opened, I spoke to my grandmother. "No females. I have no idea why I lied, Grams."

"Just plain damn dumb, boy," she voiced as I took off running.

Ava blasted her horn as her front fender almost caught my right leg. Losing my footing, I tripped. Thanks to my reflexes, I caught myself before I fell.

My grandmother disappointedly spoke, "Dumb ass boy, you are close to being D.O.A."

As Ava angrily pointed toward my grandmother's house, I shook my head. While we played the staring game, Allie parked her vehicle in the driveway. Shortly afterward, Allie and her children exited the four-door sedan vehicle. The kids greeted me with a smile while waving enthusiastically; smiling, I greeted the always happy children.

Throughout the entire time, my grandmother fussed about my stupid ways. It seemed the second Allie's children were out of sight, Grams said, "Mo, I don't know why you are still in my damn yard. You shouldn't be hounding nobody to talk to your dumb ass. Touching on a pissy-tail girl's pussy while dealing with someone else. Allie shouldn't have one nice thing to say to your stupid Black ass. You can't tell a woman you want her and only her and go touching another bitch's coochie. You just don't do shit like that, Mo. Whew, y'all young boys make me sick. Don't know the first thing about loyalty and patience. Just pull your dick out and wonder why it's itching and burning. Mo, get off my property; I'm beyond pissed at you. I thought you would have some sense after that girl left your ass for all that unnecessary cheating you was doing while y'all's son was barely clinging to life."

By the time Grams was five sentences into her speech, Ava was out of her car, eyes glued to a stunned and trembling Allie staring into Mo's shamed face. I was thankful Allie's kids weren't outside because they would've learned some things I was sure their mother wanted to keep hidden. Just as the ladies learned something about Mo, so did I. I was astonished; thus, I couldn't imagine what Allie felt.

"Aye, woe, I'mma holla at cha," Mo voiced as he shook his head, chunking the deuces.

"Yeah," I voiced, shaking my head. "Allie, before you ask me, I didn't know anything my grandmother spoke about. I promise you I didn't. If I did, I would've never put you in the line of fire."

As she tried to put on her game face, Allie skipped past us without looking into our eyes or saying anything to my comment. The expression on her face hurt me. I knew they had done some very explicit relationship-type sexing and held deep conversations. Without a doubt, I was sure Allie's mind was not settled. I knew she felt every horrible emotion that had consumed her.

"Allie," Ava softly voiced, leaving her car as it idled, walking towards the garage doors.

"Not now, Ava, not now. Hussein lied to you about being at work. You can easily forgive him for that and continue to see him. I dealt with someone who lied on a different level and touched another female even though he didn't know I was in his presence. Those things are forgivable, but I shall never talk to him again. You do not know how I really feel. You have no idea the lies that were said to me. You won't ever know what's swirling around my mind. Once you finish talking to Hussein, I will not discuss what we heard or how I feel. I was a complete fucking fool. There shouldn't be a reason I did half of the things I did so fucking quickly. I am angry, Ava. I am motherfucking confused. I feel the way I feel because *I* was so gotdamn desperate for something else, only to land back in dog shit. On top of all that, my womb was and still is unprotected! I didn't have common sense to use a damn condom. So, no, Ava, we shall never talk about what the fuck we heard nor the things I've done and allowed him to do!" she softly sobbed before walking towards the door.

"I'm sorry, Ava, for how Allie's feelin' an' lyin' to y—"

"Did you really not know ... what your grandmother said?" Ava asked, looking inside her garage while fondling her hands.

While walking closer to her, I shook my head and honestly replied, "I had no idea."

"Jesus, Hussein. She was really into him. I mean, really, really into him. It took a lot for her to date a guy. Sex is one thing, but to try to start over again is something else." Ava's lips quivered as I wrapped my arms around her before pulling her close.

"I know," I voiced, rubbing my chin on her head and snaking my hand across her belly.

Ava eyed me and sincerely said, "Hussein, I forgive you for lying. As Allie said, that's forgivable. I've believed so many lies in my life until it's unbelievable. The first time Jak lied to me, I still remember what it was. It sticks with me. All it took was for me to believe that one small lie, and I believed the bigger lies. I said that to say this; you didn't have to lie. You could've been truthful, Hussein. What could I do about you being out and not responding to me? I wasn't in a relationship with you; there was no need for me to go off like you were my man. We were sleeping together; that's it. I knew what type of day you had with me. I respected being in the doghouse until you would talk to me. All you had to do was tell me the truth. I wouldn't have shoved you out of my life. Now, we have spoken. Now, you can leave."

"Ava, I don't want to be out of your life. You know this," I announced, searching her sad eyes. Eyes, I swore I would never make sad.

Ava blurted out while aggressively clapping her hands. "I have trust issues, Hussein. You should know this by now. You are not a new person in my life. You have witnessed my ex-husband take me to Hell and back. You have witnessed him collect all of his shit while his new bitch was in the driveway we used to call our driveway. You had seen me at my absolute worst before Mica died and surely after. So, you know I have to let you go because Allie's situation, Mo's antics, my past, and the little white lie you told have placed me in a mindset I never thought I would be in. I don't trust myself, and I'll never be able to trust you—all because of a little white lie you told. We can no longer be the way that we were trying to be. Within six months, I can be the friend I was before we incorporated sex into our lives, but I can't be your woman. I just can't."

Pushing from me, she continued, "One should never bring their past hurts into a new relationship, situationship, or whatever. You've caused me to bring my hurt into whatever we were trying to create, Hussein. I'm not mentally fit to be in a relationship with anyone because my hurts from my first everything runs so deep that it leaks out of my pores. Side note: Jak told the same little lie you told. Yet, he was out on an outing with the very bitch he's married to now. How I know? He took pleasure in airing out his dirty laundry when I took too long to sign the divorce papers. The fucked up part about all of this, Hussein, I really tried to move past the hurt. I did. I gave us a chance because I like you and don't want to be my mother. Now, I'm starting to think the old bitch has a point. The less I deal with men, the less I will hurt. I hurt for no gotdamn reason! I shouldn't have to hurt the way I do, Hussein! For the record, the past few weeks I've spent with you, I didn't hurt! Before we started having sex and were just friends, I didn't hurt when you were near. Now, all that pain and horrible thoughts are back tenfold, and it fucking sucks! I have spoken all I can say without going into a dark hole. I have someone inside my home that needs her best friend. You have a good one, Hussein."

I slid my hand across her waist as she tried to step away from me. I soothingly said, "Ava, I completely understand that I rubbed yo' entire mind the wrong way. However, I can't do six months of not being able to please you while I put a smile on yo' face. I ain't okay wit' not being at yo' beck an' call. So, fo' the moment being, I'm going to let you be, but know this … I ain't gon' give up on creatin' the perfect life fo' *us*. I'm not going to sit back an' let you be without me. Nawl, baby, there is no Hussein without Ava. If you, Allie, or the kids need anything, text me, an' I'll bring it."

"Hussein, you are making things harder than it has to be," Ava replied, removing my hand from her waist.

As she stepped away, I responded, "Nawl, I ain't, baby. I'm just tellin' you what I'm going to do an' what I need from us. You are worth fightin' fo' Ava. *We* are worth fightin' fo'. So, like I said, if you, Allie, or the kids need anything, let me know, an' I'll bring it. Have a great day so Allie's kids can enjoy y'all."

Walking away, I wanted to place a kiss on her lips. I wanted to go inside her house and keep the kids company while she consoled her best friend. Importantly, I needed to make my girl whole again. To do that, I knew I had to step back and let Ava breathe while allowing her to realize I was the man for her.

I didn't step inside my grandparents' house until I saw Ava pull her car into the garage. With Ava still running wildly in my head, I plopped on the sofa beside my grandfather and sighed heavily. The old man chuckled several times before pulling his glasses off his face to stare at me.

"I thought I would never see the day Solomon Hampton was in love. What can Pop Pop do to see that you get the girl you've lusted after since you were seventeen?"

Rubbing the back of my head, I steadily spoke, "Help me get her back without me drivin' her away."

"Oh, Grandson, that's easy. You make her see what she's missing by not being with you. Continue doing what you did before you started parking your car in her driveway," he voiced as my grandmother yelled his full name provocatively.

As he answered her, I whipped my head towards the direction she called him from and said, "Man, what she got going on?"

At the same time, Grams tried to sound erotic as she yelled. "Honey!"

With bulging eyes, I hopped from the sofa as if I had been shot several times in the chest. The images that appeared in my head of my grandparents getting it on didn't sit well with my stomach. As I traveled towards the front door, gagging and disgusted, Pop Pop chuckled, "Boy, if your grandmother and I didn't get it on ... your ass wouldn't be here. Now, we'll pick this chat back up later. I'm sure you will be back for dinner."

Shaking my head repeatedly and vigorously, I said, "Null, I ain't comin' back tonight. My mind an' stomach won't be right to sit underneath y'all. I'mma holla at cha another time. Y'all go 'head on. I'mma lock the door."

Laughing, he sent me off with good wishes and a solid promise that I would have Ava back in my life as needed. After fleeing my grandparents' home, I rushed towards my whip. Upon taking a seat in my car and starting the engine, I sent Ava a text. Upon seeing she had viewed it, I shook my head while cranking my speaker knockers. While sending her a message through Usher featuring Plies' "Hey Daddy (Daddy's Home)", I rolled down the window and reversed out of the yard.

Strolling down the road, doing the speed limit, I had a hopeful mindset and a somewhat content heart while observing the street's environment on a sunny and humid day. Many people outside enjoyed the beautiful day as kids rode bikes, skateboards, played in kiddy pools, or ran through a sprinkler. The adults were either on the porch or underneath tents, enjoying their company. All was well in the suburban area, making me eager to feel half as good as them.

Upon reaching the stop sign, I turned down my radio and retrieved my phone. Dialing Jerrard's number, I pulled off. On the fourth ring, he answered. His background was noisy, which meant I had to head his way. My partner knew how to have a good time, and I was in need.

"Where you at, foolie?" he hollered drunkenly.

Smiling, I replied, "Shid, hearin' yo' tone an' the noise in the background, I'm headed yo' way. What I need to bring?"

"Yourself. Your brothers, their wives, Mo, an' a heap of my family an' their friends are here."

"A'ight, I'm on the way." I responded, turning from my grandparents' street.

"Okay. See you when you get here."

"A'ight," I voiced before we ended the call.

Dropping my phone into my lap, I zoomed towards the west side of town. My phone didn't rest in my lap long before it vibrated long and hard. Briefly looking at my screen, I rushed to answer the call from Ava.

Turning down the radio, I breathed, "Hello."

"Solomon," she lowly announced.

She needs me, I thought, quickly making an illegal U-Turn in the middle of a busy street. "Yes?"

"Can you come assist me, please?" she voiced as I overheard Allie sobbing.

"Yes. Ask Allie is it okay if I take the kids out fo' a bit."

"I'm very sure she won't mind. They don't need to see her like this. I'll make sure they are ready when you pull up."

"Okay."

"Solomon?"

"Yes, baby."

"Thank you," she genuinely stated.

"No problem. I'll see you in a bit."

"Okay."

Planting my phone into my lap, I rapidly thought of several things I could do with Allie's kids while Ava tried to help her best friend get her mind right. While I pondered on kid-friendly activities, I went over the speed limit. Once I re-entered the neighborhood, I had zero clues about where to take the kids; thus, I decided it was best to let them tell me what they wanted to do. It wasn't like I was a stranger to Allie's kids. I often took Mica and them to the park or other entertainment places so their mothers could have a few hours to themselves.

As I pulled into Ava's yard, her front door opened, and the eager children and a stressed Ava stepped onto the porch. While the kids ran to my car, I stepped out, anxious to start joking and being goofy. After they were settled in the car, I strolled towards the porch. In arms reach of the most exquisite woman I had ever known, I ogled her tired eyes.

"When do you want them to come back?"

"Can you handle two hours with them?" she inquired, searching my eyes.

Smiling, I responded, "Shid, the question is … can they handle me fo' two hours?"

She grinned, "Yeah, that is a good question. Lord, have mercy on those kids. They have no idea just how childish you can be."

Shaking my head, I replied, "Nope, but they are going to find out. I'll have them back in one piece within two hours."

Biting her bottom lip, Ava's body language informed me she wanted to say something. As I waited to see if she would say what was on her mind, she shook her head and sighed heavily. "Y'all be careful, Solomon."

Damn it, she's fightin' that mind of hers, I thought as I winked and said, "Always."

Turning away from her, I strolled towards my car. As I arrived in front of the hood, Ava loudly said, "Solomon."

"Yes," I replied, looking at the conflicted woman.

Seeing her tightly balling her lips and fumbling with her hands, I said, "Ava, I'm not going anywhere. You'll see. Go be a best friend. I got the kids covered. I'll have them back in two hours."

Nodding, she replied, "Okay."

Tapping on the hood of my car three times, I continued on my journey of being a big kid. Once inside my chilled car, I unhooked my phone from the Bluetooth device before placing the radio on a kid-friendly radio station. Before I pulled out of Ava's yard, I looked at the curious children.

"So, tell me what y'all in the mood to do?"

At the same time, they hollered, "Go get something to eat."

Dropping the gearshift into the reverse position, I asked, "Okay, so we finna grub. What's after that?"

"Laser tag, go-karting, and possibly paintball," ten-year-old Jonah voiced.

"I want to go to the mall," fifteen-year-old Mariah stated as she held her phone inches away from her face.

"The pet store!" Noni's badass squealed.

Driving down the road, I announced, "Well, it looks like we have a full schedule. So, where are we going to eat at?"

"Zaxby's!" they chanted, causing me to laugh.

"Zaxby's it is," I voiced as the edited version of "CoCo" by O.T. Genesis played.

"Oou, Hussein, turn it up, please!" Jonah and Mariah excitedly hollered, bouncing their shoulders.

"You ain't got to tell me twice." I laughed, doing as they requested.

One day, I'm going to be an amazin' dad, I thought, dipping out of the neighborhood, feeling whole and vibrant.

Chapter XII

Ava

"May your choices reflect your hopes, not your fears."-Nelson Mandela

While my best friend outstretched across my bed, I rubbed her back and softly said, "Allie, I'm so sorry you are feeling the way you are. I honestly don't know what to say. I don't, and for that, I'm sorry."

"There's nothing to say, Ava. Absolutely nothing. I feel like such a fool. I've never been the type of woman to do the things I did so quickly with Mo. That's what got me so mentally fucked up. Like how in the hell was I so trusting of him. How did I let him come into my world so easily without proving himself first? Am I really that damn desperate for a man and an amazing life? I can't figure out why I didn't see any flaws in him. I'm good at scoping that shit out," she sniffled.

Shaking my head, I said, "Mo hid his shit well. Even Hussein didn't know the true Mo. By the way, the kids are with Hussein. They'll be with him for two hours."

"Okay. Tell him I said thank you, and I'll pay him back for whatever they suckered him into doing," she replied, sitting upright and wiping her eyes.

"Now, you know, just like I know, he isn't going to take your money."

"True, but I'm still going to try my best to put the money back into his pockets," she sighed, looking into the mirror.

As she studied her appearance, I observed my distraught best friend. I was thankful that I trusted and believed Hussein when he said to call him if we needed anything. There was no way I could allow my godchildren to see their mother in her condition, especially Noni's bad and curious behind. I didn't have to worry about Jonah and Mariah because their cell phones occupied them.

Placing her hand on mine, Allie stared into my face and lovingly said, "I know I'm the last person who should be given relationship advice. But bitch, I have to say what is needed. I heard everything you told Hussein. You should recant the bulk of your speech. You don't need him out of your life for six months. Hell, you don't need him out of your life at all. Yeah, I understand you are afraid of having your heart broken again. Yeah, I know Hussein triggered horrible past events, but one damn thing I can say … Hussein isn't Jak or a Mo. He would never be a Jak or a Mo. That man loves your dirty draws, girl. He's beyond genuine when he talks to you, holds you, and stares into your eyes. He's always been the man for you. Let him back into your world because God knows you don't want to be like your mother. Cease letting your fears overtake a beautiful union between y'all, Ava. From day one, seven years ago, I saw the hunger in his eyes for you. The day we lost Mica, I saw the hurt in his eyes as he held you all night. The man stayed out of work for two weeks to be at your beck and call. Let that damn man back in, best friend. Let Solomon Hussein Hampton be your everything because bitch you are surely his everything. That nigga took three kids off our hands because *you* needed him to. *You,* bitch, *you.* That man has been at you like crazy since he told a small white lie. Deep down, your ass knows Hussein isn't anything like your ex-husband or Mo. He was raised better than that."

Putting my eyes on the immaculate large-sized mirror, I rubbed my forehead and nodded. 'I know, Allie, I know. Also, stop being so hard on yourself. Mo pulled one over all of our eyes. The only thing you can do is protect your peace and hold your head high."

Putting her head in my lap, Allie sighed deeply and sadly asked, "What if my period doesn't come on? What in the hell am I going to do with a fourth child?"

"Your best friend going to be right there to help you raise him or her," I truthfully said, rubbing her back soothingly.

As she nodded, silence overcame us. Apparently, the quietness rubbed Allie the wrong way because she sounded like Bane from *The Dark Knight Arises* as she voiced, "Bitch, you ain't finna get on me."

Tickled, I hollered, "Oh, bitch, you feeling a little better! Get your crazy ass off me!"

Engrossed in laughter, we hopped off my bed and ran out of my room. The silliness between my friend and I didn't cease until we heard Hussein's speakers bumping. When he shut off his car, we strolled towards the door. Immediately, we heard the excited children chatting loudly. She was eager to see her kids; I was anxious to see Hussein. Upon opening the door, our eyes landed on the four beings that didn't leave the same way they had returned. Everyone wore different clothes and shoes as they clung to different shopping bags.

"What in the hell did y'all get into?" we quizzed, stepping aside to let them in.

"We had so much fun, Mommy!" Noni happily stated while jumping.

As the children told their mother about their day, Hussein calmly asked, "Can you step outside? I won't take up too much of yo' time. I promise."

"Sure. Solomon, you could never take up too much of my time," I blurted, eyeing him.

While displaying his beautiful smile, Hussein extended his hand. Leisurely, I placed my hand into his. As we walked towards his car, he quizzed, "Is she feelin' better?"

"For the moment, she is."

"Good. I got something fo' y'all."

Stunned at the man standing beside me, I ceased walking and said, "You didn't have to get us anything. You taking the kids off our hands was enough, Hussein."

"I know I didn't have to, but I needed to. I'm not like most men, Ava. You should know that by now. I come from a two-parent household. I know how the matters of the heart are supposed to go. I know the do's an' don'ts of dealin' wit' someone. Hence, I don't play wit' females feelin's. I've known Allie just as long as I've known you. Just like you, she's a hard workin', good woman. Just like you, she didn't deserve to be stomped on by the actions of a man. So, I need y'all to genuinely smile fo' me before I dip," he said, opening the back passenger door.

The most beautiful flowers I'd ever seen grace his floorboard. As he retrieved the two bouquets of flowers, which had several balloons attached to the clear vase, he lovingly said, "The kids helped me pick out everything."

This man here. Always, always thoughtful, I thought, blushing and eyeing the gorgeous plants.

Lovingly, I responded, "These are beautiful, Hussein. Thank you."

Sternly looking at me, he questioned, "What I told you 'bout that thank you shit?"

"And what did I tell you about thinking I'm going to stop thanking you?" I replied, biting my bottom lip and ogling him.

As we stared into each other's eyes, Hussein sighed deeply while handing me the flower vases and balloon sets. Ensuring my hand lingered on his for a moment, I needed to tell him some things, mostly about how I felt and to recant pushing him out of my life. Yet, my courage got the best of me, resulting in me not opening my mouth.

Clearing his throat, Hussein quizzed, "Please, tell me why Noni so damn nosey?"

Shaking my head, I giggled, "Hell, when you finally find out, please let me know. I've been wondering that ever since she started talking."

"He bought a what? Y'all asses better be lying!" Allie hysterically stated from the living room.

"Oh shit, I think I'm in trouble." Hussein laughed as his trunk opened.

"What did you buy?" I giggled as I walked towards the back of his car.

At the same time, Allie ran out of the door, calling Hussein's name.

"Huh?" he loudly stated, looking at Allie.

"I just know them kids are lying," Allie voiced.

"Oh, my God!" I squealed as I stared at a large tank with a gerbil in the corner.

With her hands on her hips, Allie stood beside me and goofily hollered, "Who in the hell finna take care of this damn rodent? I ain't dealin' with that fat fucker, Hussein! No, sir, you have to take this thang back! See, you play all damn day! You know I can't stand shit with more legs than me!"

As Hussein and I laughed, Allie fussed, "Lord, whatever those kids ask for … there your ass go buying it. Six months ago, it was a gotdamn bird. A year ago, it was a fish tank and all the trimmings. Don't make any sense. They just have their fucking way when they are with you. Now, I'm the gotdamn animal keeper because their ugly asses will forget about it after a week. Lord, have mercy."

"Mommy, you like it, Nemo Nemo?" Noni yelled as she ran out of the house.

"You have already named the ugly creature?"

"Yes, ma'am. Ooou, yeah, Mommy, we picked out some pretty flowers and cool balloons for you and Auntie Ava," Noni excitedly spoke as she played with multi-colored slime.

"Oh, really," Allie softly grinned, looking at Noni before placing her eyes on Hussein.

Hussein's handsome self pointed at me and replied, "I hope you like the flowers and balloons."

Gawking at the different colored flowers, Allie softly said, "Everything is perfect. The assorted roses are such a sight to see. I absolutely love them. Thanks, Hussein."

"You are welcome," he genuinely voiced as Allie looked at me with a wicked smile.

Shortly afterward, she said, "Noni, go in the house."

"But Momm—"

"I said, get yo' ass in the damn house, Noni," Allie sternly voiced, glaring at her daughter.

"Okay," the spoiled seven-year-old responded, head dropping as she slowly walked away.

Out of earshot, Allie stepped back and looked between Hussein and me. I knew she was on the verge of saying something stupid. Thus, I patiently waited as Hussein started laughing. After all, he knew Allie enough to know when she was up to no good.

"Ava finna get on you," Allie spoke, impersonating Bane's voice.

"Man!" Hussein hollered, laughing.

I shook my head and giggled as spit flew out of my mouth.

Hopping on Allie's level, Hussein spoke in a Bane tone. "And I'mma let her!"

Walking away with teary eyes, I loudly laughed. "I'm not about to play with y'all today. I'm not!"

As I arrived on the porch, Allie said, "Tell my rugrats to come on; I'm sure you want some one-on-one time with your honey. Since y'all have a lot of things y'all must talk about."

While I relayed the message to my godchildren, Allie fussed about getting the tank and the rodent into her car and home. Quickly, Hussein offered to unload and load the rodent into Allie's living quarters. Upon her thanking the handsome being, we prepared to leave my house.

"Ava, will you drive, please?" Hussein sexily asked as I arrived at the opened passenger door of his car.

Eyeing him, I nodded and said, "Okay."

While I scurried away, I felt Hussein's eyes on me. Slowly looking back, my eyes met his. The fine being provocatively licked his lips and nodded.

"What's the nod for?"

"Fo' me to know an' you to find out," he chuckled, sliding into the passenger seat.

Oh, Jesus, I thought, hopping into the driver's seat.

While I started the engine and dropped the gearshift in the reverse position, Allie pulled from my yard. As I followed her, Hussein grabbed my hand and kissed the back of it before interlocking our fingers. Immediately, butterflies floated in my stomach, and my pretty kitty was anxious for him to touch her. However, we had to talk severely before I spread my legs.

"Why are you fidgetin'?" he sexily asked as I halted at the stop sign.

Shrugging, I nervously voiced, "I don't know."

"I think you do," he voiced, eyeing me.

"Hussein," I softly stated, turning off my street.

"Yes?"

"Um, I…"

"Whatever you think you want or need to say, don't speak. I won't pressure you to do anything you don't want. I'm simply here as yo' friend, helpin' out yo' best friend. When we unload the rodent, I will take you back home, an' I'll leave," he announced, still looking at me.

That's not what I want, sir, I thought, feeling the need to change the subject to something less tense.

"Have you talked to Mo since he left?" I inquired, briefly looking at him.

"No."

"Oh."

"Have he reached out to Allie?"

"I'm not sure," I responded, exiting my neighborhood.

"Ava, you listenin' to me?" Hussein voiced, placing our hands on his leg.

"Yes."

"You will never have to worry 'bout me doing anything to hurt you or make you cry. Hold up, I recant that crying part. Oh, you gon' cry, but it won't be a sad type of cry. When those orgasms start hittin' you back to back, like they been doing, you gon' cry. When I up an' surprise you out the middle of nowhere, there's a possibility you gon' cry. To be very clear, the only time tears gon' run down yo' face because I'm pleasin', entertainin', an' makin' you happy. I'm not an asshole. I wasn't raised to be one. When I'm dealin' wit' one female, it's just her an' no one else. One thing I won't do is cause you intentional pain an' a mind that makes you think 'bout the past. Yo' history is over because yo' future is right here. *I'm* right here, an' I'll never hurt you. If you need six months away from me, I'll have no choice but to take it like a man. I'll be waitin' whenever you are ready to pick up where we left off," he sincerely breathed, ogling me.

I'm not going anywhere, I thought, nodding and squeezing his hand.

Right then, in that calm moment, was the time to express to him that I forgave him for the little white lie, and I wanted to resume what we had. On the other hand, I wasn't sure if I was ready to count my eggs before they hatched. Therefore, I thought about everything Hussein had said to me from the first time I met him until now. I reflected on his actions. I analyzed everything about the person he was.

In my soul, I knew Hussein was perfect for me; however, I wasn't sure if I was ready to take on everything that went along with a relationship. The possible hurt that came with being in a committed relationship I wasn't up for. Yet, Hussein made me want to take all those risks because he completed me. Solomon Hussein Hampton brought back the old Ava Jane Langston; I loved her.

I remained quiet until we arrived at Allie's three-bedroom, two-bath trailer home. After thirty minutes of Hussein and the kids getting the rodent situated in Allie's front room, Allie stepped onto the porch. Looking at us, she asked, "So, my parents are having a little get-together. Would y'all like to attend?"

While standing, looking at the fine being sitting in a folding chair, I nodded and said, "If Hussein's cool with it, so am I."

Smiling, he nodded. "I'm cool wit' it."

"Good, because I need my drinking buddy. Today has been one hell of a day," Allie voiced, running her hands through her jet-black, long wig.

"Yes, it has," I replied, eyeing Hussein.

As Allie called her children's names while walking inside her home, Hussein strolled towards me, eyes saying a million things. The closer the handsome being ambled towards me, the more my heart raced.

Nearby, Hussein said, "What's on yo' mind? Do you really want me to go to this lil' gatherin' wit' you? Or would you prefer to go by yo'self? Whichever you choose is fine wit' me."

Playfully rolling my eyes, I announced, "Hussein, shut up. If I didn't want you to attend, I would've said so."

As he dropped a hard dick onto my stomach, I gasped; he chuckled, "What's wrong wit' you?"

"Now, you know damn well what's wrong," I breathed erratically.

"She hungry, huh?" he inquired as the kids stepped out the front door, resulting in him stepping back.

See, this is the type of shit that is turning me on. He knows when to tone down his antics. My God, I thought as he chuckled and walked off the porch.

Exhaling heavily, I slowly descended the few steps. Upon reaching the dirt, I sauntered towards Hussein's driver's door while running my hand through my hair. With much to say to him, my mind raced with the best opening sentence. I didn't want to come off as an unstable creature. So, I needed the perfect words to roll out of my mouth correctly.

You got this. Just be open with him like you've always been, I thought, opening the door.

Taking a seat, I started the engine and stared into the smiling man's face.

With his eyes locked on me, I opened my mouth to speak, but Hussein stopped me from talking. "You are tongue-tied. The best thing you can do is not say anything. Let's just attend the lil' gatherin', Ava."

Shaking my head, I genuinely replied, "That's not good enough for me. You see, Hussein, I shouldn't have brought my past relationship into our world. Yeah, I was hurt by your little white lie, but I shouldn't have tried to put us in the deep end. I'm not sure if I should apologize for trying to alienate you. What I am sure of ... is that I don't want you out of my life as my friend or anything else. I told you once I value what we have, and I don't want to lose that. I don't want to lose my male best friend. I can talk to you about anything. You don't judge me. You don't push me to do anything I don't want to do. I'm comfortable around you, so the right thing to do is to forgive you for that little ass lie and allow us to continue to create something beautiful."

"Are you sure that's what you want to do right now?"

"Absolutely," I voiced, searching his eyes. "Hussein, I'm sorry how I made you feel when my mother came over. I'm sorry I didn't defend you sooner than I did. I hope you don't think I was ashamed of you because I wasn't. I just didn't want to deal with the bullshit that still came from her mouth. My mother makes me feel as if everything that happened was my fault. I don't like her playing those cards, and most importantly, I didn't want you to witness me being the weak little girl her mother birthed."

Reaching across the seat, Hussein's gentle hand graced my face. "I forgive you. Fo' the record, I could never think you are weak. You are far from that. You've shown me just how strong you really are, Ava."

"Can we start off slow? Like, no more nutting in me? Just us exclusively dating one another without starting a family, just yet," I inquired softly.

"I agreed to not nut in you all the other times, but it was you who told me to do so. So, Ava, when I'm in the process of pullin' out, don't get to hollerin' 'nut in meee, Hussein' because I'mma fill yo' ass up," he seriously stated. "I hope you ain't finna take the 'no condom' thing away because I can't handle that."

As Allie reversed from the yard, I laughed. "As long as you pull out, I'm fine with you not wearing a condom."

"Okay." He smiled as I reversed.

While we traveled the short distance to Allie's parents' home, I tried to hide the smile on my face by biting my bottom lip. Knowing that I was on the path to overcoming my fears brought much joy to my spirit. This time, Hussein didn't save the day; Allie did, and for that, I must thank her a million times over. She was why I stepped out on faith and got my knight in shining armor back after nine long motherfucking days.

Chapter XLII

Hussein

"What's a fuck when I want love?"-Henry Miller

To be near the one you really love was the best feeling in the world. No matter how many females I fucked, none made me feel what cruised through my body from what Ava rendered. I was sure Allie had a heartfelt conversation concerning me. Deep down, I know the distraught woman needed to see her best friend and me together, and I would give her just that.

"I thought Allie said this was a lil' gatherin'," I voiced, noticing the numerous people and cars parked in a vast green grassland.

Giggling, Ava said, "Shit, I forgot to tell you, a little gathering with Allie's parents really meant a party. There will be food and drinks for days."

While she parked my vehicle close to the road, Allie crept towards the front door of her parents' yard. Briefly, I pondered why Ava didn't follow behind her friend. As I did so, I scanned the faces of those in my sight. Immediately, I caught a glimpse of four females I had knocked down. To this day, those broads were spiteful towards me.

As Ava shut off the engine and opened the door, I cleared my throat and said, "Ava, I see at least fo' females I slept wit'. Those hoes hate me with everything in them because we didn't get into a relationship. I'm very sure they will be on som' spiteful shit."

"Okay," she calmly replied, eyeing me.

To clear any unwanted thoughts, I honestly voiced, "No, I don't want to leave unless you are ready. I'm just givin' you the heads up."

Smiling, she responded, "Hussein, you come with a past just like everybody else. Whom you slept with doesn't affect me because I'm getting the dick now. I'm getting that once-virgin mouth. I'm getting it all. So, I'm not pressed. You know what will press me, and it surely isn't spiteful females."

"A'ight," I replied, smiling as I opened the door.

"By the way, we won't be down here long. I came to show my face briefly," she casually stated before stepping out of the car.

When one of the bitches I used to fuck with saw me stepping out of my whip, her eyes roamed towards the driver. The bullshit began, but I was prepared for it.

"Y'all look at this shit here! I know damn well a female ain't drivin' Hussein Hampton's car! Not the nigga who don't want to be in a relationship wit' nobody!" the shapely, short, and disgruntled bitch, Nia, sarcastically yelled while clapping her hands.

As Ava walked towards the front of my whip, I shook my head, looked at the useless broad, and replied, "I've never dated anyone because what I saw was a bunch of nothings. Now, the female drivin' my car is everything. Thus, she gets this bitch whenever she wants it. So, Nia, take that petty ass shit elsewhere. Enjoy the party; you might find yo'self a lick out here."

"Boy, whatever," she smacked, rolling her light-brown, medium-beaded eyes.

Scurrying towards the front end of my whip, I extended my hand towards Ava; I wanted to know if she would place her hand in mine. Upon her doing so, I smiled. "My girl."

"Where are the rest of the females you slept with?" Ava lowly asked as we walked further into the yard.

"One comin' down the steps an' the other two, we finna bypass. They are sitting on the hood of that black Nissan Versa."

"Oh my God, Hussein. The one comin' down the steps is Allie's sister. The one closer to the windshield is Allie's

158

niece, Tawatha's hot ass. Jori, her cousin," she shockingly voiced, ceasing her strides.

So, I don' fucked Allie's sister, niece, an' cousin. Man, I'm wild as fuck, I thought, feeling as if I possibly made a bed I couldn't get out of.

To ensure I heard Ava correctly, I said, "Come again?"

Before she could repeat herself, Allie's sister, Jamecia, hollered while walking towards us. "Oh no, Ava! No ma'am! That nigga don't wanna do nothin' but fuck! Trust, I know all about Hussein Hampton! You've been through enough; that nigga is not the one to start over wit'! Go 'head an' send him back to the streets!"

Hopping off the cars, Jori and Tawatha hollered, "Jamecia, hold up! Wait! You fucked who?"

"Y'all heard me," she voiced.

"I'll be damn," I voiced, shaking my head as I looked at a calm Ava.

At the same time, Jori and Tawatha replied, "I slept with him too."

Realizing what had come out of their mouths, Jori and Tawatha stared at each other before placing their eyes on me.

Standing before us, Jamecia hugged Ava and said, "This nigga ain't no good, Ava. You don—"

Holding two fingers and repeatedly shaking them, Ava shook her head and said, "Listen, this is what we are not going to do. You are going to respect your parents' home. I completely understand if you do not wish for Hussein to be present. We will leave. Everyone has a past. It may not be pretty, but everyone comes with one. Now, I will tell you something you would never know because I don't like people in my business. I didn't and haven't received what you and many other females received. Before I arrived at the lowest point in my life, it was Hussein who was present. During the hardest point in my life, Hussein was there every step of the way. He's not a new person to me. I've known him since I moved next door to his grandparents. What y'all witnessed is completely different from what I've seen and still see. Now, Jamecia, Jori, and

Tawatha, are y'all uncomfortable with Hussein being here?"

"Sure, the fuck is." They smirked.

Nodding, Ava said, "Okay, but before I leave, I must say this openly as I've always talked to y'all. Stop opening your legs if a man presents you with rules and regulations. He's telling you upfront that's all he sees in you. Know your worth, and you won't be bitter. There's no amount of pussy, ass, and head in the world that'll make a man want to be with you. He has to need you. On that note, love y'all, and enjoy the party for me."

Oou, that baby classily stepped. She finna get nutted in.

While the females looked dumbfounded, Ava squeezed my hand, looked at me, and said, "You still want me to drive?"

Licking my lips, I smiled. "Shid, that's yo' car. I told you that one time before."

"Okay," she nodded as we turned around.

Halfway towards my whip, Allie was why we turned around and faced her.

"Um, so y'all wasn't going to tell me the juicy ass tea before y'all left?" she spoke with her hands on her hips.

"Mann," I chuckled, shaking my head.

"Girl, I'll call you later," Ava giggled.

"No, bitch, I want the information now because I'm really feeling some type of way. Those skeezers don't want him here because he told them what he wanted and didn't back down. Like, there are other niggas out here that smashed and passed their asses. So, why try to stunt on Hussein?" Allie casually inquired, looking between Ava and me.

Ava smugly looked at her nails before holding them before her face. "Whew, best friend. I know why they stunt on him. I know exactly why they are upset. Trust me, my recently used coochie knows why your sister, niece, and cousin are highly pissed. However, they surely didn't get the full-throttle Hussein. That's for damn sure."

Chuckling, I said, "Y'all wild."

At the same time, Allie hollered while laughing. "Nih, Bitch!"

"I'll call you later, Allie," Ava giggled, blowing her friend a kiss.

"Oh no, bitch, you finna explain some things to me."

"Allie, we are getting ready to leave. My stomach is touching my spine right now," Ava continued, giggling as we arrived at the doors of my vehicle.

Plopping her hands on the car's hood, Allie said, "Now, Ava, is it th—"

"It's the type that'll make you say 'I Love You', and y'all aren't even in a relationship. The type that'll make you stalk him, knowing damn well y'all aren't even together like that. That's that ... 'oh my god, yeah, you can nut in me' dick. So, yeah, they are pissed pissed," Ava quickly stated, resulting in me howling in laughter.

"Best friend, good-damn-bye. Now, the next time I invite y'all's asses to one of my parents' parties ... I don't give a damn who doesn't like it ... y'all asses gon' fall through an' stay put. Understood?" Allie commanded, observing us sternly.

"Understood," Ava and I replied in unison.

"Good because this little gathering will pick back up next Saturday around three o'clock. Seafood upon seafood," Allie stated as she backed away from the car.

Looking at Ava, I watched her sensually lick her lips before she asked, "What do you need us to bring?"

"Seafood, any kind."

"Um, how about I give you the money now? I'm sure you can do your friend a solid and pick up the items for me," Ava voiced, rapidly blinking.

"Guh, this damn seafood boil is next Saturday."

"I know. I might be tied up or something," Ava mischievously voiced.

Dropping her head, Allie zoned into Ava's face with a wicked smile, causing me to laugh at the silly chick. While I observed the two non-verbally communicating women, I adored their friendship. Truthfully, they were more like sisters than friends. They did everything together; I could only imagine their text message thread.

"It's Sunday, and you are already planning to be fucked out before Saturday gets here! Well, baby, I ain't mad at all." Allie laughed as Ava reached into her purse.

"I know damn well you ain't givin' her yo' money, an' I'm right here, Ava," I sternly voiced, pulling a wad of cash out of my pocket.

Oddly looking at me, Ava seemed as if she was stuck. Why? I had no idea. Strutting over to the ladies, I asked Ava, "How much were you going to give her?"

"Two hundred should cover a nice amount of seafood on top of what they already will have. Hussein, you know how I am about seafood."

"I do," I replied, peeling off two crisp one-hundred-dollar bills. "Allie, seafood is expensive. Will two hundred suffice?"

"For your greedy ass girlfriend, yes, it will because she wants all the damn trimmings," Allie voiced as I extended the bills to her.

"I'm going to assume you will prepare mine just how I like, right?" Ava smiled.

"And I am," she quickly responded to Ava before addressing me. "Any special way you like your seafood boil?"

In unison, Ava and I replied, "I'm allergic."

"Well, shit. That must suck."

"Not really. The shit stank anyway," I replied, chuckling.

"Sir," they replied, eyeing me.

"Hell, it does," I chuckled before telling Allie bye and walking away.

"Okay. Well, if you get a breather, call me Ava," Allie stated as I was close to my vehicle.

"Okay. Love you, chick," my future wife voiced, pressing the unlock button on the key fob.

"I love you the most," Allie sang beautifully.

True friendship, I thought as Ava and I slid our bodies into the warm vehicle.

"Next time, don't you dare go in yo' purse fo' no money. You come to me fo' that. Understood?"

As she turned over the engine, Ava nodded.

"Understood. Now, I'm starving. Where shall we eat?"

"You pick the place. I'm buyin'," I responded as she pulled away from the road.

"I'm in the mood for dick … shit, I mean steak. I'm in the mood for *steak*, a baked potato, and a salad. So, is one of those steakhouses good?" she inquired as I laughed at her supposedly fuck up.

Ava's facial expression informed me she was embarrassed. I didn't see a reason for her to be. It wasn't like she wasn't with a man who wouldn't give her what she wanted whenever she wanted.

Still chuckling, I said, "You said it right. Yo' ass in the mood fo' dick. Don't think I ain't been catchin' the way you've been eyein' me. So, do you want dick fo' an afternoon, evening, or late-night snack?"

"Truthfully, I want the dick now, but I'll wait until after we eat," she voiced, exiting the small community Allie's parents' lived in.

"Are you sure?" I quizzed, ogling her.

"Yes, Hussein. I'm sure," she announced, briefly looking at me.

"Okay. Before I let you get on me … I need you to show me what you 'bout at that bowlin' alley. From day one, you always talked a good game but never joined me when I told you to come show me what yo' strike game like," I voiced, interlocking our hands.

"Hussein, you might need a little more practice before coming at me like that," she giggled.

Placing my mouth to her ear, I whispered, "Bet som'."

"Bet," she responded.

"Kick off the bet then, dear," I breathed in her ear before sucking on her earlobe.

"If I win, you will sponsor a spa day for me. If you win, I'll sponsor whatever you want to do," she responded.

"Nope, you can get that without a bowling bet. Dig a little deeper, Ava," I provocatively voiced before sucking on her neck.

Stuttering, she said, "If I win, you can stay a week at my house."

"Not good enough for me, Ava. So, I'm going to dig fo' you."

"Jesus," she whimpered as she accidentally mashed on the gas pedal.

Chuckling while sliding my hand between her legs, I replied, "How 'bout if you win, you stay a week at my apartment. If I win, you still stay at my apartment fo' two weeks."

Without hesitation, Ava relaxed further in the seat and moaned, "Okay."

"Can I play wit' her fo' a minute?" I inquired, massaging her thigh.

"Yess," she whimpered.

"You think I can kiss on her fo' a minute too?" I softly voiced as I unbuttoned her shorts.

"Yess."

Sliding my hand into her panties, I asked, "Ava, you gon' put yo' dirty clothes into my dirty hamper?"

"Yess."

Slipping two fingers into the most delightful cookie jar I'd ever encountered, I quizzed. "You gon' walk 'round my apartment naked as if yo' name on the lease?"

"If you want me to."

"That ain't what I asked you. So, I'mma ask yo' ass again. You gon' walk 'round my apartment naked as if yo' name on the lease?" I questioned, tapping on her G-Spot.

"Yess, Husseinnn," she moaned, body shaking.

"When you get into my apartment, promise me you won't freeze up on me," I slowly spoke as I beautifully stabbed the one spot I knew had never been touched by anyone other than me.

"I ... I promise," she stuttered, foot coming off the gas pedal; she was beyond relaxed, which wasn't good.

"You are too relaxed to be behind the wheel. You can't handle this pressure, so I will pull my wet ass fingers out of you. We are going out to eat, bowl, an' then we are going to yo' second crib. Understood?"

Vigorously shaking her head, Ava voiced, "I can handle the pressure."

As I tried to remove my fingers from her treasure trove, Ava pushed them back in and started to fuck them.

"Jesusss," I hissed, dick growing. "Ava."

"Husseinnn," she loudly moaned as she neared an intersection.

Seeing what she needed, I was one eager nigga to give it to her. "Hop out of this lane and turn right by this gas station. I'm finna give you exactly what you want. Ava, to be clear, we ain't going out to eat or bowlin'. You will be exhausted. However, we can order the food from any steakhouse of yo' choice an' eat in. We can tackle bowlin' another day."

Going in the direction I told her, the sexy woman's eyelids fluttered as she cooed, "Hussein, I'm cummin'."

"You better keep yo' eyes focused on the road, Ava Langston," I growled, making her cum.

"You see that dirt road to the left, up ahead?" I questioned, finger fucking her intensely.

Biting her bottom lip, she nodded.

"Turn on that dirt road. It's private property; my mother and her siblings own it. It was passed down from their parents. Only a few of us have keys to this place, the responsible ones, as my mother likes to say. My brothers, three of our much older cousins, and I are those people besides the siblings. When I unlock this gate, there's a big house, 'bout a mile an' a half, sittin' to the right. You will turn into that yard."

"Okay," she voiced as she neared our destination.

Once I removed my saturated fingers from her pussy, I stared into Ava's face and sucked the sweet liquid off my fingers. The sexy woman moaned, which resulted in me smiling. Afterward, I retrieved the master keys to the deadbolts on the black iron wrought gate. Upon Ava pulling into the dirt road close to the gate, I hopped out, running with a hard dick.

After rapidly unlocking the locks, I pushed one side of the gate back and motioned for Ava to slide through. When she did, she stopped a short distance ahead while I secured the locks on the gate. As I jogged to the car, I hoped Ava would like what she saw. Once we made things official, I would ask my mother for permission to build Ava a house on our land before I stepped to my three aunts and two uncles.

"Oh wow, it's so much land out here. Why haven't they done anything with it?" Ava stated, astonished, slowly driving down the dirt road.

"They want to keep it as is; we use it for family reunions, which is coming up soon," I told her as she pulled into the only concrete surface on the many acres of land.

"Am I invited?" she jokingly asked, placing the gearshift into the park position.

"Why is that even a question, Ms. Langston?" I provocatively voiced as I opened the door.

"It was a joke, Hussein," she breathed, stepping out of the car.

Chuckling, I replied, "If you say so."

As we closed the doors on my vehicle, I gazed at the beauty whose shorts were unbuttoned and hair slightly tossed everywhere. Upon her arrival in arms reach of me, I analyzed her face. "Do you want yo' lovin' inside of the house on any piece of furniture, outside on the porch, or on the hammock beside the apple tree?"

"What are the odds any other keyholders will come by?" she inquired, looking towards the wooded area.

"Um," I stated, retrieving my phone.

After opening a text thread between my brothers, cousins, and self, Ava questioned, "Um, what, Hussein?"

While my fingers swiftly glided across my keyboard, I said, "Give me a second."

"Okay," she responded as I sent an important message, eager for their reply.

Once I received it, all smiley faces and thumbs up, I announced, "Not a soul will pull up."

"How sure of that are you?" she questioned, eyeing me.

"I just sent them a text tellin' them who I was wit' an' where I'm at an' not to show face. Thus, you don't have to worry 'bout anyone poppin' up," I voiced as an eighteen-wheeler's horn sounded.

"Oh, well, in that case, on the hammock beside the apple tree is absolutely fine with me." She smiled, kicking off her shoes before removing her shirt and dropping it on the ground.

Following my lady's lead, I kicked off my shoes and climbed out of my shirt, dropping it on the ground. The further along we were to the hammock, the more pieces of clothing we shed. Strolling past the apple tree, I stripped out of my boxers and ogled Ava as she wore laced white panties. The woman could've been a model. Her body was exquisitely fit and well-proportioned. Her smooth, cinnamon-brown skin was meant to be shown to millions worldwide; she didn't have to be naked for them to see her natural beauty.

"Solomonnn," she purred, sitting on the hammock with her ankles crossed.

"Yes, beautiful one."

"Are you going to stare at me or come to me?"

"Boffum," I chuckled, moving towards her.

Inches away from her, I demanded. "Open yo' legs fo' me, Ava."

Those slender limbs spread like melted butter on bread. Kneeling, I eyed her before kissing her pussy through her panties.

"Solomon," she cooed, gripping the back of my head.

"Yes?" I voiced, placing my hands underneath her butt.

"Annihilate me."

"Then, take yo' sexy panties off fo' me, Ava," I groaned, dick begging to be inside her.

After she did so, Ava didn't have time to throw her panties onto the hammock before I slid between her open legs. Slowly and sweetly, I delivered kisses to her forehead before planting a trail of smooches to the center of her neck. I ensured to suck on it while my hands caressed the round jiggly, soft ass. After having enough of her succulent neck, I gave her twins a great show, thanks to my hands and mouth.

"Husseinnn," Ava squealed, legs trembling.

Dropping her head back, Ava moaned, "Jesus."

As I ran my tongue down the center of her body, I popped Ava's thigh and asked, "What does He have to do wit' this?"

Arriving at my destination, I eyed the glistening pussy and announced, "Look at me taste you."

With an open mouth, Ava slowly dropped her head. Her peepers were locked onto me. I took my time spreading her fat pussy lips before I slid my tongue as far as it could go inside of her.

"My God," she whined, legs trembling violently.

With my mouth latched onto her pussy, I gazed into her face as the tip of my tongue had a party inside her sweet land. While I sucked on her goodies, I slowly slid her back onto the hammock. As she wrapped her shaky legs around my neck, I took pleasure in taking Ava to the places only I had been taking her on. I enjoyed taking my time tasting the one woman I would taste for the rest of my life.

"Solomonnn," she loudly and sexily announced, slowly rocking on my adventurous tongue.

"What, baby?" I asked while lifting her legs, allowing my tongue to travel further south.

Landing at her back door, Ava gripped her hair and cooed, "My God."

As I French kissed her asshole, two fingers found their way inside her as my free hand traveled toward her twins. While I ate Ava up, my name was the only thing coming out of her mouth. I had lived to hear her moan my name the way she was doing. I had lived to please her until I couldn't anymore. I strived to give Ava Langston nothing but the best, sex included. Today, she would get all of me because she fucking deserved to have every ounce of Solomon Hussein Hampton.

I didn't cease feasting on her body until I felt in my soul she was ready for the finale of the first round. When that time arrived, Ava's back was up against the apple tree with her legs firmly pressed beside her head. Slowly, I rolled my mid-section while digging in her guts, nice and slow.

"Hussein, please," she begged, hands tugging on her hair as she moved her head from left to right.

"Please, what, baby?" I voiced, surfing through her ocean.

"What you want from me?" she cried, eyes searching mine.

"You. Me. Forever."

Those three words caused the floodgates from her face and her pretty, pink walls to flood me. I didn't stop; I kept going. She wasn't weak enough. I needed Ava unable to breathe. I needed her throat raw from screaming, hollering, and moaning my name. I needed her limbs to be as if they were cooked noodles. I wanted her eyes puffy because she had reached a point in our lovemaking that all she'd done was cry because she was beyond pleased. I need her beautiful eyes teary because of the glorious things I had blessed upon her body and the promises I made her. She knew that I would never break a promise to her. That glorious moment came after round three, which she begged me to nut in her. I did that shit while massively grinning!

With my mission and so much more accomplished, I carried the exhausted woman into the house and bathed her. Once I dressed and placed the sleepy woman onto the sofa, I cleaned my body while rehearsing my speech to ask her to marry me.

Many minutes bypassed before I carried a lightly snoring Ava from the single-family home. While leaving my family's land with the woman cradled in my lap, I was more at peace than ever. Thus, I flipped on my speakers.

The sounds of Tank's "Fuckin Wit Me" blasted, resulting in me smiling harder.

Life is good! Real motherfucking good! I'll be a married man before I know it, and she will be in her final marriage! With a man who has eyes for her and her only!

Chapter XIV

Ava

"If I know love, it is because of you."-Herman Husse

A Week Later

Living with Hussein was a blast, and there was no doubt that we had to continue living together. Nothing changed about us; we were simply Ava and Hussein. There was never a dull moment. I freely and comfortably blew up his bathroom while he showered. If he farted, I would giggle. If I passed gas, I would tell him to catch it before running off. There was nothing we didn't do together.

Our play wrestling always turned into a steamy lovemaking session, no matter where we were. Thanks to those lovely sexual sessions, quite a few of his wall paintings were knocked down before meeting their fate on the floor. We rocked two of his table legs loose, resulting in him catching me in mid-stroke. Due to him banging my back loose while I was on the edge of the sofa's arm, we damned near put a hole in the front room's wall.

Outside of our goofy and lovemaking antics, I loved every aspect of being in his one-bedroom yet spacious apartment. The living room was mainly our hangout spot; it was cozy. He had the most amazingly comfortable dark gray sofa. Whenever I outstretched or sat on it, I grabbed the Auburn War Eagles blanket from the back. Once I curled underneath the thick blanket, it wouldn't be long before sleep found me.

His room was my favorite. It was homely, well-cleaned, and organized. In addition, he had two gorgeous gold-framed pictures of Mica and him on the edges of his dresser. Each morning and night, I would kiss my son's photos and tell him how much I loved him. Not a single time did I shed a tear by seeing my boy's picture or even cry about him not being alive. I would sit on Hussein's extremely comfortable, king-size bed and smile at Mica's photographs.

When I had to leave to attend to my independent hustle, I would miss Hussein the moment I stepped outside of his apartment. The same happened when I was left alone in his apartment when he had to work. Yet, I found solace knowing he would return to me after his shift.

He didn't know I dreaded going to the old house filled with horrible memories and no life. He didn't know a dark cloud would overcome me when I entered the driveway. He didn't know that I no longer wanted to live in that house and that Grove Lang was no longer a place I needed my name attached to. Once my workday ended, I would flee the house, heading back to my second crib, as Hussein liked to say.

Being everything he needed started the moment I walked through the door. I set my alarm clock to blast thirty minutes before he was due to walk through the door. His blunts were rolled and waiting for him when he strolled into the bathroom. After bathing him, I would prepare dinner for the next day since I would conduct my independent duties. Life was becoming bearable, and I appreciated every moment of it.

"Gotdamn it, Husseinnn!" I passionately screamed with my hands firmly planted on his chiseled, tattooed chest. I was running from the dick he beautifully yet savagely delivered me.

"Stop all that motherfuckin' runnin', Ava," Hussein growled. Aggressively, he grabbed my arms and wrapped them between my spread legs while dropping his dick off in me like toddlers placed Cheetos puffs into their mouths.

With the ability to continue fighting against the orgasm Hussein sought to give me, I bit my bottom lip. Poorly, I gazed at the man who had been etching his name into my pretty kitty with his dick and fingers since eleven o'clock this morning. It was twelve thirty-five p.m.

"Give me that damn nut, Ava," he sexily growled with a devilish expression on his handsome face.

As my body shook uncontrollably, I moved my head from left to right. I moaned, "Hussein, why are you doing me like this?"

"I didn't get a chance to make love to you when I got off since I was tired. So, I'm makin' up fo' not givin' you yo' nightly dose of yo' lovin'," he genuinely voiced, slowly stroking me and rubbing my face.

And this is how and why I will be in this damn apartment just begging, I thought as he planted his nose on top of mine. Lovingly, he said, "I love you, Ava."

I love you too, I thought, observing his eyes.

I knew Hussein wanted to hear me say that; however, I wasn't quite ready to say those words even though I felt them. I would rather my actions show him than for me to say it.

When he raised an eyebrow, I knew Hussein would Mortal Kombat my pussy. I counted to three, and Hussein flipped me over. Upon being placed into the doggy-style position, Hussein gripped my hair, pushed my back in a little, and smacked my butt. Without further ado, he beautifully slaughtered me.

"You don't love me, do you?" he questioned through clenched teeth, digging deeper.

"I do," I whimpered, flopping against the bed, ass higher than ever.

"Then, why don't you tell me that you love me, Ava?" he probed, spreading my butt cheeks before drilling my pretty pink walls.

As I gripped the sheets, my mouth flopped open. Immediately, I breathed erratically.

"I asked yo' ass a question, Ava," Hussein growled while deep stroking me.

"Hussein! Baby, please," I begged as my body shook uncontrollably.

"Answer me, now, Ava!" he announced, increasing the speed of his thrusts.

"I think I'm afraid to say it, Hussein," I whined as my pussy contracted.

"How in the fuck are you scared to tell me you love me, but you can eat a nigga's ass up?" he barked, sticking his thumb in my butt. "You know what? Don't even worry 'bout answerin'. I'mma take that L fo' a minute, but I ain't gon' keep takin' that shit."

That was the last time I heard his voice for quite some time. It was my voice echoing throughout the room. My pleas, moans, cries, and whimpers loudly sounded as Hussein showed me he was upset by me not telling him that I loved him. Oh, what he did was beyond beautiful. He had me in so many positions until I got dizzy. Every part of my body was in his mouth. My damn eye sockets. My handsome one fucked me into the next galaxy and back. I had never seen so many stars in my life!

After placing me back into the doggy-style position, Hussein inserted his tool into my gushy insides. Then, he slowly spread my butt cheeks before slipping what I assumed was a few anal beads.

"Oou, my fucking goodness," I loudly moaned, flopping on the bed like a fish fresh out of water.

With anal beads fucking my ass and Hussein's dick doing numbers in my coochie, I blissfully hollered, "Solomon Hussein Hamptonnn!"

"What I told you about calling my name like that, Ava?" he inquired, slowing his mushroom-shaped head from banging on my G-Spot

"My God! Oh my God! Hussein, please stop," I begged breathlessly.

"What you callin' His name fo'? He ain't got nothing to do wit' this," he voiced, all the while digging deeper into my goodness—dancing in it.

After long moans and grunts, I smartly cooed, "Well, who else am I supposed to call on … Satan?"

"Yeah, that's the nigga you call on." He wickedly laughed.

Stunned, my eyes grew big as I unintentionally said, "Oh, God."

Smacking my thigh, the handsome being loudly hissed, "Ava, what the fuck did I tell you 'bout callin' that Man's name while I have my dick stuffed deep into yo' guts an' damn near all these anal beads in yo' ass?"

Eyelids rapidly fluttering, I stuttered, "I … I … I'm sorry."

"You have no idea just how sorry you finna be, baby," he sexily replied.

I knew Hussein was flashing his handsomely perfect smile by how he talked. My asshole and anal beads, his dick and hairless monkey, and his fingers and my clit were why I shouted, "I do love you, Hussein. I love you!"

"Nawl, I don't want to hear it now," he chuckled as my body relaxed.

In seconds, my coochie leaked like a busted water pipe. Still, Hussein continued plowing.

Oh my God, I thought as my entire locked body felt as if it was set ablaze again.

With a still body, like an opossum, my pretty lady erupted again.

"Shit, Ava, baby, it's like that?" Hussein hissed in awe.

Yes, it's like that, I thought, unable to speak or move.

After three more eruptions, my eyelids became heavy as hell as I cooed, "I'm sleepy, Hussein."

"I know," he replied, slowly removing the anal beads.

Pumping faster, he placed his lips to mine. Sucking my bottom lip into his mouth, Hussein made my pretty girl throw up some more before he broke the kiss and asked, "You gon' have my baby, Ava?"

Feeling his pulsating dick, I nodded.

"Can I nut in you, Ava?" he quizzed, drilling me.

"Yes, but I want to be on top when you do," I whined as I poorly gazed into his happy-filled eyes.

Smiling, he rolled over, placing me on top of him. With the bit of energy I had left, I kissed my man and rode him while finding the right words to tell him what he needed to know.

As I slowly bounced up and down, I gazed into his medium-beaded peepers, tears filling my eyes. Softly, I genuinely uttered. "Solomon, I love you, and it's not because of how you make me feel sexually. The love has always been there, but I had to be sure it was what it was. I knew five years ago, but I didn't say anything. Hell, I couldn't. I love you because you are my best friend. I can talk to you about anything. You did things, for and to me, I'd never done nor asked for. I never had true happiness until I met you. Honestly, I never knew what romantic love was until I came across you; you dropped it into my lap. Even as a married woman, I longed to be around you. I treasured stepping onto the porch, knowing I would see you before crossing a line that I knew you wouldn't cross with me. I treasured you looking into my eyes. I treasured teasing you, hoping and praying you would touch me, but you wouldn't touch me how I needed you to. You respected me. You respected the vows I took. Even after Jak left me, you took two weeks off from work to stand by me as I buried *our* son. Still, you were the same person you had always been to me. You waited until you felt I was ready to move past my hurts. Solomon Hussein Hampton, I am officially telling you that I am fucking ready to move on with you because I love you and only you. I have to spend the rest of my days with you. I need to create a life with you. I need it all, but I need it with you. I am no longer scared of you hurting me; you are incapable of doing that. I know that now."

Shoving my head towards his, Hussein sucked my bottom lip into his mouth before parting my lips. As we made love, our tongues never ceased clashing against one another. Planting his hands on my waistline, Hussein placed me on my back as his tongue cruised through my mouth. The kiss was broken because I had the worst urge to howl his name. While I did so, Hussein whispered, "Remember one particular night, I told you I had a small problem that I needed yo help wit'? The one where you called my name and waved yo' hands in my face?"

"Yes." I nodded.

Placing his mouth on top of mine, Hussein slowly dug inside of me while observing my eyes. After planting six pecks on my lips, Hussein sincerely said, "Well, that small problem wasn't really small. It was a big problem. It was you, a married woman tied down to someone who didn't deserve you. My problem was the need to spread yo' legs, make love to you wit' my mouth, fingers, followed by gracin' you wit' this dick. On top of the need to satisfy you, I badly wanted you all to myself. At nineteen, I wanted the woman who was made fo' me an' me only. I needed the one woman who caught all of my attention. I patiently waited fo' an exceptional woman to be mine, an' I don't regret a single moment of havin' to wait. Ava Langston, can't a soul fulfill yo' needs like I can. I've centered my entire life 'round you an' Mica as if y'all were mine. Hell, in my eyes, y'all was. You have no idea just how happy I been seein' you in this apartment, turnin' it into a home. You have no idea how elated I am when I come through door an' see you in the kitchen makin' dinner an' to see a rolled blunt in the bathroom. I have every intention to make you my wife. So, know this, Ava Langston, yo' last name finna change fo' the last an' final time. You won't be my girlfriend fo' long; you'll be my wife. I love you too much to have you runnin' 'round this city wit' a girlfriend title. You gotta have the wife title, Ava. I don't see it any other way."

As my body violently shook, tears cascaded down my face. At the same time, I eyed the wonderful being passionately making love to me. Many promises from us, and ten strokes later, we came together, which was beyond beautiful. I felt as if I was floating on the highest cloud. Before the year was over, I was confident I would be carrying Hussein's child, and I wouldn't give a single fuck who didn't like it. My rock deserved a baby popping out of a coochie he couldn't stay out of.

"You want me to bathe you?" he asked, head resting on my shoulders.

Yawning, I replied, "No, I'll take care of it when I wake up."

"Who said you finna go to sleep?" he jokingly asked before kissing my neck.

"My body," I giggled, wrapping my arms around his back.

"Oh, word?"

"Word," I voiced, closing my eyes.

"Well, I guess I'll listen to yo' body fo' a change."

"You should be tired. After all, you have to go to work in a few hours."

"I ain't going in today. Between us breaking in every piece of furniture in this apartment and the first shift not doing an ounce of work over the weekend, I'm exhausted. That job can kiss my ass. I put in a personal day last night before I left. I'll go back tomorrow," he yawned, climbing from between my legs, only to lay in front of me—head on my thigh.

As I rolled over, facing the dresser, my eyes landed on one of my son's pictures as he held tightly to a water gun, clothes drenched in water. I grinned as I thought about that excruciatingly hot day as the sun blasted through the beautiful blue sky. Jak was out of town, as usual. Mica and I were beyond bored. We didn't want to visit a park or a swimming hole. We didn't want to go shopping or to any other amusement place, which was far out.

By the grace of God, there was a knock on the door followed by the doorbell chiming. Once I opened the door, my breath was taken at the sight before me. A smiling, no shirt but swim trunk wearing, super handsome Hussein stood a few feet from the door. He held tightly to three water guns while pointing at three buckets filled with water balloons.

After Mica and I excitedly changed into our swimwear, we fled the house with joy running wildly through our bodies. I had never seen my son so happy and carefree as he flung water balloons at Hussein and me. I'd enjoyed seeing all thirty-two teeth of Hussein's. However, I had never seen him so at peace with himself as we catered to Mica having a great summer day. Once we weren't worn out from the water fight, Hussein offered to take us out to eat. Typically, I would've said no, but that day I didn't. I quickly said yes before my son did. It was all about Mica; it was only right he chose the restaurant or at least what he wanted to eat. Within a matter of seconds, he screamed he wanted pizza. Thus, Hussein took us to a pizza joint in Auburn.

When I asked him why he went so far out, he replied that I was a married woman, and he didn't want any rumors to get started even though we were just friends. At that moment, I fell harder for him. He was more thoughtful than any man I had known.

After the pizza joint, the next stop was the infamous gotdamn Wal-Mart. Everything Mica thought he wanted, his little ass received. Hussein went insane, spoiling Mica as if he was his own. I didn't say anything because Jak never did half of the shit Hussein did for my son. That scorching ass day would always be one of my favorites. It was the last day Hussein and I took him out to eat before allowing him to go crazy at his favorite store.

"I love you, big boy. Always," I voiced before blowing a kiss towards the picture.

Rubbing my butt and looking at me, Hussein softly breathed, "Baby, you okay?"

Looking at him, I smiled. "I'm wonderful."

"You promise?" he inquired, studying my eyes.

Nodding, I rubbed his face and cooed, "Yes."

"You'll tell me if something's wrong, right?" he asked, propping up on his arm.

"Hussein, you'll be the first person I tell if something's wrong. Trust me, I'm fine. I was just thinking about the amazing day before he died. That's all. Like Mo said, I am to think about the good days, not the bad days."

Gently rubbing my face, he smiled. "That you should always do."

While I rested my head on the bed and closed my eyes, I asked, "So, to be clear, we are dating, right?"

"Ava Jane. I understand you have a White woman's middle name an' all, but don't you start actin' like one." He laughed, gently pushing me onto my back and climbing between my legs.

As I giggled, the doorbell chimed, and my cell phone rang. Placing a kiss on my forehead, Hussein grunted as he rolled off me. While I grabbed my cell phone off the nightstand and briefly looked at the screen, Hussein fumbled, putting on a pair of shorts while informing the unknown guest that he was coming.

"Hello," I stated into my phone as Hussein exited the bedroom, closing the door behind him.

"Bitcchhh!" Allie happily hollered.

Giggling, I said, "What girl?"

"Honey, I'm looking at these bloody panties I got on! My lil' freaky ass ain't pregnant! Do you hear me, bitch?"

"Woot! Woot!" I excitedly exclaimed, clapping my hands.

"So, how's the stay at Hussein's place?" she asked as I overheard Hussein's mother's stern and demanding tone.

I whispered, "Hold on for a second, Allie."

"Okay."

"Hussein, I told you to leave Ava alone, and I be doggone if you aren't shacking up with her. She has no reason to be in your apartment. None, son," Pastor Hampton voiced before clearing her throat.

Damn, she's a preacher acting like that. My, my, my, I thought as Hussein spoke, "Pastor Hampton, I pay every bill in this spot, includin' the rent. My name is on everything in here as well. I am grown. Ava is grown. What you call shackin' up, I call growth. She's movin' on as a woman supposed to do after she's lost it all. She's movin' on wit' someone, me, who will never desert or mistreat her. She deserves the world, an' I'mma give it to her. Just as I have been givin' it to her, just not in a way, it disrespected her vows. You've never seen me bring a girl home. You never met Lakin because she was not my girl.

The pregnancy was an accident. You act like I'm the worse nigga roamin' these streets. I'm yo' son, Pastor Hampton. You an' Dad raised me to have morals, standards, an' value marriage. You are so quick to jump down my throat, but you'll worship a nothin' that comes off the street. You've always assumed the worse of me, but praise the ones you know fo' a fact do wrong. If you can't see me fo' who you raised, then I guess you will never see me. If you don't have anything family-related to tell me, then it's time fo' you to leave. I have a lunch date wit' my woman, Ava. Pastor Hampton, be safe on the road. Text me when you make it to wherever you are going when you leave here."

"Son, it's not that I don't see you. She's simply too old for you. Find a woman your age. There are plenty who can ruffle yo—"

Upon respectfully raising his voice, Hussein said, "Pastor Hampton, I don't want anyone but Ava. I surely don't want anyone to ruffle my feathers. I need them suckers set ablaze. Ava does that. You disapprove of our age difference. That's on you, but two monkeys will never stop our show, an' that I can promise you. You can cease talkin' to me if you want. Still, I promise you … that'll be yo' mistake to cease havin' a relationship wit' one of yo' grown sons because of his choice to love who was sent to him. Before you leave, I'm going to be real clear 'bout a few things. One, Ava ain't going nowhere. Two, I ain't going nowhere. Three, she will be my wife … sooner than you think. Four, I'm gon' pop som' babies in her. Five, I'm gon' build *my Ava*, who will be my wife, a house. Six, either you gon' be on board like Jerrard, Gideon, Thaddeus, Dad, Grams, an' Pop Pop, or you will sit on the sidelines an' watch us. You will not make Ava uncomfortable. You know I don't care 'bout makin' you uncomfortable. Accordin' to you, I've been doing that my entire life. At the end of the day, this is my life, an' I'm gon' live it. Now, Pastor Hampton, you have a blessed day. I'll text you nightly like I've been doing since I've had a phone."

"Bitch, why are you gasping?" Allie inquired as the front door closed.

"Hussein and his mother had some words over me," I quickly voiced as I heard his footsteps.

"Bitch, for what?" Allie curiously inquired as Hussein opened the bedroom door.

Seeing the look on his face, I hurriedly said, "Allie, I'll call you back."

"Okay."

Upon ending the call and placing the phone into my lap, I asked, "Are you okay?"

"Yes; however, I'm wonderin', are you okay? Are you going to flee because I know you heard everything?" he questioned, posting up on his six-drawer tall dresser.

With a smirk, I loudly questioned, "Now, Hussein, does it look like I'm trying to flee anywhere?"

Smiling, he replied, "No."

"Well, then, there's your answer. Your mother and mine have opinions about us because of our age difference. Your age doesn't bother me. You are a grown and responsible man. So, never think that our eight-year age difference bothers me. However, I must ask, how long have you and Pastor Hampton been at each other's necks about me?"

"Momma has always been at my neck 'bout you. It's gotten worse now that she knows I be ticklin' that coochie of yours." He laughed, walking towards the foot of the bed.

"Hussein!" I giggled as he snatched the covers and sheets off the bed.

"Yes, ma'am?" he sexily voiced, gripping my ankles.

"I just know damn well Pastor Hampton doesn't know what we've been doing," I voiced while he gently pulled me towards the edge of the bed.

"She heard us a few nights back. Um, I think that was Friday evening or som' like that." He laughed.

Eyes bucked, I hollered, "I know you lying on this good day, Solomon!"

Shaking his head as he lifted me off the bed, he announced, "No, I'm not. That's who was calling my phone repeatedly while the doorbell chimed. When she heard you, the texts started. I think I messed up Pastor Hampton's mind. She can't even look me in the face."

Burrowing my face into his neck, I said, "I'm embarrassed."

As he stepped into the bathroom, he voiced, "You embarrassed. Hell, I was too. It's one thing fo' yo' dad to hear you, but yo' mom. I damned near passed out when I read her texts. I was talkin' dirty ass hell to you while stuffin' you full of dick, Ava. Som' things mommas don't need to hear. Let's not mention when you yelled, 'you just eating my asshole out like it's a pudding cup'. She made sure to put that quote in all caps."

Beyond embarrassed, I clamped my hand around his mouth and said, "Hush up."

While laughing, he removed his shorts before turning on the water knobs. Upon getting the water to my desired temperature, lukewarm, Hussein placed us inside the sparkling white tub. Like the first day I arrived at his apartment, and every day since, he bathed me while we further talked about our future in the desired profession we wanted to be in.

After discussing the weed dispensary, Hussein inquired while washing my back. "So, Ms. Langston, have you thought mo' 'bout what you are going to do wit' yo' career of being a nail technician?"

"I'm letting that shit go. It was something to do to keep my mind sane. It's time for me to get back to the old Ava with a few tweaks and things," I replied, enjoying the exfoliating beads gliding across my skin.

"Do you want me to put in a word when I return to work tomorrow?" he asked, kissing my neck.

"No. I'll be going up there tomorrow morning to speak with Darlene."

"In that case, you got the job. That woman loves you."

"Now, if I get my old job back … we have to be extra discreet, right?" I quizzed, turning to face him.

With a raised eyebrow, Hussein chuckled, "Ava, who do you think I was payin', so no one said a thing 'bout the stuff I had placed on yo' desk?"

"Darlene?" I asked, shocked.

"Yep. Wit' that being said, I will behave at work. I won't bother you. You will be the fine-ass woman in the human resource department niggas will be sliding through with all types of excuses to see. Meanwhile, I'mma be in the bathroom sending you dick pictures and kiss face emojis," he seriously replied as I grabbed his washcloth.

Applying a generous amount of the manly soap to the olive green rag, I giggled, "And once you send me a dick picture, I'm going to politely go to the bathroom and send you a pussy picture."

While I cleaned his body, Hussein's dick grew while he caressed my body. Provocatively, he pressed his succulent lips onto mine before saying, "Oou, you so damn nasty. I love it."

My overly horny ass knew what time it was, and I was all for it. However, my stomach was on the verge of touching my spine. I was beyond hungry.

"Hussein?" I moaned, cleaning his dick.

After pecking my lips four times, he gazed into my eyes and said, "Yes, baby?"

"Um, honey, don't worry about eating your buffet lines because it'll become a two-hour lovemaking session. I need you to go ahead and knock the Super Mario coins out of this coochie because I am starving."

Gripping a handful of my rounded romp, he sensually asked, "Who said we were gon' have sex, Ava?"

Placing my hand on his dick, I raised an eyebrow and broadcasted, "Him. How you look at me right now and groping me tells me so. Plus, my coochie is hungry again."

"Yes, my body an' spirit cravin' you, but I know I need to control it. It's mo' to us than sex, Ava. I'm gon' always be touchy touchy wit' you. I'm always gon' look at you wit' a sex-crazed facial expression. This dick gon' always get hard whenever I see you or hear yo' voice. That don't mean I will slip off in you."

You will wear my ass out every time you see me. I'm going to make sure of that, I thought as I replied, "Okay."

Turning him around, I cleaned his back. Meanwhile, I eyed the one place I wanted to slide my tongue into while jacking his dick and fondling his balls. While thinking of ways to get what I wanted, I bathed him several times while purring and biting my bottom lip. Upon rinsing him off, I turned him to face me.

While we lovingly looked at each other, he quickly said, "I'mma be right back. Gotta get two rags."

"Okay," I voiced as he stepped out of the shower. Just like me, Hussein was a neat freak when it came down to his body. We had to use three rags: one for the body, another for the face, and the third one for the asshole.

"Oou, somebody wants something?" he sang as I grabbed his wrists, pulling him closer to me.

Upon Hussein gazing into my eyes, I wickedly smiled and slowly faced the showerhead. Then, I took my time touching my toes.

"Ooou, my future wife, what you got going on?" he groaned.

Rubbing my clit, I moaned, "Your dick will play a quick game of Hide and Seek in my coochie."

"Oh my God," he moaned, rubbing the head of his dick across my pretty, shaved kitty.

"And what does He have to do with this, Hussein?" I questioned, making my ass clap while he slowly entered me.

"I love you, Ava Langston. Don't you ever forget that," he lovingly voiced while gripping my hair and digging deeper into my honeypot.

"I promise you, I'll never forget it. I could never forget your love, Solomon. Never," I cooed, gripping my ankles and throwing my treasure trove on the only man I would ever be with.

Chapter XV

Hussein

"It is not sex that gives the pleasure, but the lover."- Marge Piercy

The quickie Ava wanted was non-existent the moment she touched her beautiful toes. Her coos were why I kept shoving my dick deeper into her as I gently pressed her against the wet wall tiles. The longing looks in her teary eyes was the reason I slowed my pace as I hit every corner in her leaky core.

My need for our souls to fully merge caused me to pull out of Ava and eat at my favorite buffet lines. Then, the fine woman took the sexual matters into her hands. Oh, Ava became a really freaky woman. She ate a nigga's dick up to a point I was using her favorite line, and I used it well. I couldn't lie as if Ava didn't handle me like I did her—disrespectfully. She gargled, dirt bike, and sloppily sucked my dick before nibbling on my balls. I had never had a female nibble on my shits. It felt amazing.

When she looked up at me with a particular look, I shook my head and said, "Woman, what do you want?"

Sexily, she said, "I wanna eat that dick from the back."

"Mann, no, yo' ass don't. You wanna eat my ass, Ava. Say it fo' what it is?" I sighed, halfway dropping my head and eyeing her.

"I'll be the only one knowing we are doing this freaky stuff. It'll be our little secret, Hussein," she whined, jacking my dick.

"Man, you gon' have to catch me later tonight. I'll be high an' a lil' tipsy by then," I replied, shaking my head.

"Okay," she voiced before sliding my dick down the dark tunnel of her throat.

Ava sucked, kissed, licked, and nibbled on a nigga's dick so intensely that I knew I had to give her fine ass precisely what she wanted. Shaking my head, I looked at the ceiling and pulled back. Removing her mouth off my tool, I eyed her and weakly asked, "What position you want me in?"

"Whatever is comfortable for you," she voiced, eyeing me.

"If I touch my fuckin' ankles, Ava, I swear before God, whenever we leave this damn apartment, I'm going straight to a jewelry store. You will sit yo' fine ass in the car while I purchase my items. When I plop my ass in the seat, you will not ask me what I bought because you will see it soon enough. I swear before the good Lord, you better not say it's too early or none of that shit. You gon' put that gotdamn ring on an' sport the fuck out of it. Within three days after I propose to you, you an' Allie better be plannin' our weddin' an' I mean to the damn T," I fussed, gathering my emotions.

"Yes, sir." She smiled, looking absolutely stunning.

Lord, this woman. This freaky woman, but she mine, though, I thought as I pondered how in the hell I should position my body so Ava could get what her freaky ass wanted.

"Fuck it!" I shouted, shoving my dick between my legs before bending over.

Jesus, I thought as Ava hit that head one good time, resulting in my eyes crossing and my knees buckling.

"Mhm," she moaned, sucking on my pipe like a strawberry Popsicle.

My God!

When the motherfucking rapture came—her gobbling my ass—I saw my soul escape through my nose. I was close to telling her to nut in me. My head began to hurt because I held in my groans. My toes were balled to the point I thought I broke a few. The small of my back was on fire because the arch in that bitch was so deep; it had a curve in it.

I was disappointed but elated when I felt that nut rising. There was no way I could tell Ava I was getting ready to cum. Thus, on wobbly legs, I rose on my tiptoes and rapidly patted the top of her head. Before my shits slung out of me like a rocket shooting into the sky, Ava's mouth swallowed my entire dick just in time to catch the cream filling.

My baby put it down, and I didn't feel anyway! To be honest, I was looking forward to the next time of patting her head, but she would never know it.

After slowly turning to face her nasty ass, I weakly said, "Whew, shit. Whew, shit. Whew!"

"That dick is still hard, Hussein. Sit in the tub and let me deflate his ass," she bossily cooed with her head tilted to the right.

"Avaaa, I'm weak. I know you see it," I fussed, ogling her.

"Yes, I do, but that dick hasn't deflated yet; thus, he's not weak," she responded, pointing at the tub.

As I sat, Ava straddled me and said, "Kiss me, Hussein."

"Lawd, you don' ate my ass, an' now you want to kiss me. Guh, you know you finna get engaged today, right?" I weakly voiced, gripping the back of her neck while pushing her head towards mine.

Licking my lips, she responded, "Oh, I know, and I will proudly say yes."

While I sucked her wet ass lips into my mouth, the fine, freaky broad slid down my pipe. Instead of me knocking the Super Mario coins out of her pretty kitty, she knocked them motherfuckers out of herself and me. I didn't know who moaned the most, but one thing I knew for sure was we were satisfied as my nut and her cum collided, just like our tongues did after we said, I love you.

Three hours and thirty minutes later, we exited my apartment before sliding into her car. Ava hopped in the driver's seat; I climbed my exhausted behind in the passenger seat and closed my eyes. My limbs were weak, as I had a slight headache.

"Are you okay?" she inquired, placing the air conditioner on max.

Looking at the joyful woman, I responded, "I have a slight headache, an' limbs weak than a motherfucka. Other than that, I'm gucci. You?"

"I'm fine," she voiced, reversing from the parking lot.

"Did you feel any type of way this time?"

"No," I honestly voiced.

"So, we will be doing that again?" she probed, dropping the gearshift into the drive position and interlocking our hands.

Hell, fuck yes. As long as you ain't talkin' 'bout stickin' a finger or dildo in my ass, we gucci, baby, I thought as I didn't want to seem too eager or excited to answer. Thus, I coolly responded, "Yes."

"Cool." She smiled as she made a left turn out of my apartment complex. "Um, Hussein?"

"Yes?"

"I want you to fuck me in the ass tonight," she calmly announced.

"Come again?" I stated, sitting upright, eyeing her.

"I want you to slide your dick in my ass tonight. While your dick in that back door, I want you to place some vibrating balls into my coochie," she cooed.

"Ava Jane Langston, head to whatever sto' you want yo' engagement ring from, woman! Then, gon' head to the sex sto', get you a few items up outta there. After that, we gon' go to the grocery sto'; we ain't going out to eat tonight. We gon' prepare our food together at home. Let me be clear, Ava Langston, you ain't stickin' shit in my ass but yo' tongue. Understood?"

"Yes, sir," she moaned, briefly eyeing me.

"A'ight," I stated, not taking my eyes off her. "Ava?"

"Yes?"

Ogling the woman, focused on driving, I kissed her hand. Sincerely, I broadcasted, "I don't want you to clam up on me or let people get into yo' head 'bout us. I don't want you to ever feel that we are movin' too fast. I need you to know, in a way, I'd been courtin' you since the third week of y'all movin' to Grove Land. I need yo—"

"Hussein, I don't give a fuck what people have to say. I used to live for what people thought or said about me. Now, I'm living for me. You will never have to worry about me pulling back from creating a life with you. Yes, I'm older than you. Yes, there will be more than our mothers not liking it. Yes, I know people will whisper behind our backs when they notice our age difference. I'm prepared for Allie's sister, niece, and cousin to cease talking to me. I don't give a damn because all that matters is that *we* are happy. Not anyone else. I saw how hurt you were when I tried to hide you from my mother. Solomon, I never want to see you like that again. So, whenever you pop the question, know I'll never hesitate or recant saying yes. I know exactly what I'm getting into with you. A partner for life, not a sex buddy. A genuinely good-hearted, handsome, bomb sex game-having, protector, and provider of a partner," she humbly voiced.

"Okay," I stated before blowing out air, a little worried.

"Solomon?" Ava softly voiced, pulling into the shopping center of a well-known jewelry store.

"What's up, baby?" I inquired, looking at her.

"You are worried. Don't be. I'm fine. You are fine. We are fine. So, the issue that has you worried should be off your brain by the time I pull up to this jewelry shop," she voiced as my cell phone rang.

"Okay," I stated as I retrieved my device and answered the call from Mo.

"Talk to me," I said as Ava parked before the jewelry store.

"Aye, have you or Ava talked to Allie?" he asked as I kissed Ava's knuckles.

"Nawl. Why?" I stated, opening the car door and stepping into the humid atmosphere.

"Just wonderin'. I've been textin' an' callin' her," he breathed as I pulled up my pants before closing the door.

Furrowing my eyebrows, I said, "Mo, you know y'all dead, right? She doesn't want anything to do wit' you, bruh. She was hurt by what she heard on top of what she saw at the spot. Man, you might as well move on from Allie."

Chuckling, he quizzed, "Since when do you give a fuck 'bout hoes an' there feelin's, my guy?"

Clearing my throat, I responded, "Let's be real motherfuckin' clear, Mo. Ava nor Allie are motherfuckin' hoes. See, I thought you were a real ass nigga. You foul as fuck. Tell me how you leave yo' baby momma to care fo' y'all's sick son while you were out in these streets fuckin' off? How in the fuck you runnin' 'round this bitch wit' me an' the ladies playin' the victim role? You know what, don't even worry 'bout answerin' that shit. My guy, I got som' shit to do. I'mma holla at cha."

Before he could respond, I ended the call before stepping inside the nicely chilled establishment—annoyed at the nigga. I hadn't talked to Mo for a reason; he wasn't on my level and never would be. It was to the point I didn't conduct any illegal business with him. He would lie about anything if he lied about why his son's mother left him. Simply put, the nigga couldn't be trusted; therefore, Nanette would have to hear devastating news soon.

"How may I help you, sir?" a tight, thin-lipped, skinny Caucasian woman with dyed jet-black hair inquired.

"A jaw-dropping gold engagement ring," I told the woman with trembling hands and repeatedly blinking eyelids.

This White bitch scared as shit, I thought, shaking my head.

"Hm," she voiced, eyeing me as she pointed towards the jewelry case inches from the cash register.

While I moved in that direction, two white men came from the other side of the store, talking in a hushed tone. Quickly, I focused my eyes on the men staring at me. I'd been racially profiled before; it was no big deal. However, I always had a point to prove and leave them with a message. Nodding, I dug into my pockets and pulled out four thick wads of cash. Immediately, their eyes bucked.

"Yeah, niggas do it big too. All of us don't jack motherfuckas. Even though we should be jackin' y'all asses since y'all jack these diamonds from the Motherland," I chuckled before slamming the wads on the counter.

Just like all the other fuckers, the woman's attitude changed completely. She showed all her fucking teeth; her hands were no longer shaking. As she showed me several rings, the door opened. The guys greeted whoever stepped across the door's threshold.

"I think your lovely lady will like—"

Upon hearing heels rapidly clinking against the polished tiles and Ava sternly calling my name, I turned and stared into my angry woman's face. Before I could open my mouth to ask what was wrong, she placed her hands on her hips and announced, "You better not buy a ring out of this fucking place. I saw how they looked at you. I saw how your body language changed. I know you don't pull out money like that for any reason before slamming it on the counter. So, this is what we are going to do. We are going to another jewelry store to purchase *my* engagement ring from a company that doesn't side-eye a potential customer because of his skin color."

"Oh no, ma'am, it wasn't li—"

Holding up her right hand, Ava observed the woman and said, "Bitch, shut up! Save that shit. You will not see one damn dollar out of those wads. Now, honey, we have officially finished conducting business here."

Oou, I have never seen her fired up like this before. I love it, I thought, smiling and grabbing my money off the counter before walking away.

As I sauntered towards her, Ava extended her hand and said, "You are driving. To be clear, you don't have to get my engagement ring today. Whenever you get it, just know I will say yes."

I didn't speak until we arrived in front of her car. Cupping her face, I placed my mouth on her and lowly said, "You ate a nigga up today, boff ways. You think I'm comfortable wit' you doing all that, an' you ain't my fiancée? So, yeah, I gotta get that ring today."

After I planted a kiss on her lips, I guided Ava towards the passenger seat. As soon as she had placed the seatbelt over her waist, a familiar black Lincoln sedan pulled beside hers. I could never forget the car or whom it belonged to. While I closed the passenger door, the front doors of the sedan opened. Out stepped Jak Morris and something that resembled a biracial woman. Honestly, I felt like it was a transvestite.

"Ah, look at the young boy fucking around with the desperate divorcee," Jak chuckled as the mixed manly-ish being softly called his name in a shocked and disappointed tone.

Strike one an' final.

Halting, I glared at the nigga. After she rolled the window down, Ava calmly said, "Hussein, get in the car, honey."

"Honey?" Jak laughed. "Really, you are that desper—"

After sliding into his presence, I jacked Jak against his car. Upon rendering him two blows to his nose, blood seeped from his smeller. Meanwhile, the pussy nigga tried to cover his face while hollering, "Ah!"

Shaking his collar as if he was a pup, I shook my head and said, "No, bitch ass nigga, ain't no coverin' yo' face. I want yo' blood to slide into yo' mouth 'til I'm done talkin' to you. This will be my final time sayin' som' shit to you. Also, this will be yo' final time sayin' or even lookin' at Ava. I swore I made myself clear the day *my son* died to never speak or disrespect his mother again. Well, let me speak a lil' louder this fuckin' time. You come at my woman again; I will kill you. I won't care if there is a crowd; I will blow yo' brain out, an' you will not be buried next to *my son*. Know that. I have no idea why you are so nasty towards a woman with a child who looked just like you. You took a good woman down through there for no reason. She didn't deserve that. All you had to do was leave her alone, not destroy her as you did. Do you know how many nights I had the chance to lay wit' yo' then-wife? Do you know how many nights I made sure Mica an' Ava were okay before I went home? Do you know Mica was afraid of the dark an' had to sleep wit' three nightlights in his room? Do you know Mica had night terrors so severely it scared the shit out of Ava? Do you know how thrilled he was to pull out his first loose tooth? Do you know how scared he was when he learned Ava, nor I wasn't behind him when he finally got the hang of ridin' his bike? Do you know *my son's* favorite cartoon, book, or movie? Do you know how many trips I paid fo' so he could experience things outside of Grove Land? Shid, do you know how many of those motherfuckin' trips I was on? All of them, bitch! Oglin' that fine ass woman who was married at the time, wishin' she was fuckin' mine. Do you know how often I was close to blowin' yo' head off? Bitch ass nigga, I can really go on an' on wit' these do you knows, but I won't. You know what? I am gon' say one mo'. Do you know how wet Ava gets when she's overly aroused? Mannn, that bed you bought, my boy, I made her destroy that mattress. Pussy justa leakin', my guy, an' that baby surely told me you ain't never did none of the shit I did. You weren't even close, my guy. I guess only real niggas can do shit like that, huh?"

"Oh my," the manly-ish woman moaned, clutching its throat. I caught a glimpse of its hand and frowned.

In the mood to destroy some shit, I looked at Jak and asked, "Um, yo' lady ain't got no weddin' or engagement ring on her finger. So, I'm going to assume you pullin' the cheatin' shit again on yo' second wife?"

"Jak, what in the hell is this man talking about 'second wife'?" the 'it' stated, stunned.

At the same time, Jak and Shulaine, which he called 'it', argued.

Laughing, I looked back at Ava's car. She had the window down, looking and smiling. "Baby, this nigga here on one, ain't he?"

"He sure is. Poor thing," Ava giggled. "Go ahead and wrap up that conversation. We have things to do."

Nodding, I shut up the bickering couple. With their eyes on me, I calmly spoke to Jak. "Yo' hatred runs deep fo' a woman you kneeled an' asked to be yo' wife, nigga;

that shit doesn't sit well wit' me. However, I can tell you what does sit well wit' me. Me enjoyin' every inch of Ava from the top of her head to the soles of her feet. Me enjoyin' seein' her smile, hear her laugh and call my name, and look at me. Me hearin' her moan a nigga name when I'm makin' love to her. Honestly, my guy, you did the best fuckin' thing fo' her. You left her so a real nigga could aid her in gettin' her life back on track so I could sweep her fine ass off her motherfuckin' sexy ass feet, bitch! You moved on the second Mica died an' never looked back. I had her then. I got her now. Bitch, I'll always have Ava Jane Langston, soon-to-be Ava Jane Hampton. So, Jak Morris, the best thing you can do is act like I'm *AIDS*. Be very afraid to *contract* me; I'm very *deadly!* There is *no survival* rate fuckin' wit' me. Y'all be blessed. Enjoy the rest of yo' day."

Walking off, I blew a kiss to my smiling woman. Upon rendering the same love back, she stuck her hand out of the window and called her ex-husband's name. Instantly, I stopped and looked at them.

"Yes, Ava?" he spoke as the transvestite stared at Ava.

"I forgive you, Jak Morris," my woman calmly stated with much happiness as she rolled up the window.

"She's over the hurt an' the pain. She's really all mine now," I voiced as I skipped towards the driver's door.

When I hopped inside the car, I pulled Ava towards me and sucked her bottom lip into my mouth before I parted her lips. After I blessed her skillful mouth with a kiss like no other, I happily said, "I love you."

Smiling, a tear slipped from her eye as she voiced, "I love you more with your messy ass."

Chuckling, I questioned, "What lie did I tell?"

"Not a single one," she replied, interlocking our fingers after I closed the door and dropped the gearshift into the reverse position.

While we drove off, a tan truck bypassed us. Immediately, Ava sat upright and looked backward. Naturally, I ceased operating the car and asked, "What's up?"

Smiling, she laughed. "Jak's wife, the stewardess, just pulled up. Anywho, on to our destinations. Whew, ain't God good?"

"All the motherfuckin' time," I chuckled, pressing the gas pedal.

Chapter XXVI

Ava

"I love you not because of who you are, but because of who I am when I am with you."- Roy Croft

Three Weeks Later

The past three weeks have been a tremendous eye-opener for me. So much so that I had to discuss it with Hussein. I was so happy. I didn't think I would ever smile like I used to when I was in the eleventh grade. I realized many things about the past situation and myself. Truthfully, I was ashamed of those things.

For starters, I was outgoing and always stood up for myself. Then, I allowed Jak to change me. A motherfucker who wasn't worthy of being in my presence, to begin with. There shouldn't have been a reason I dated him, let alone married him. I guess my naïve ass didn't want to be like my mother and had a point to prove. Instead, I landed into a pile of pig shit that took years for me to climb out of with the help of my male best friend. In addition, I took ownership in understanding and accepting how and why my first marriage nearly destroyed me. I was at fault.

Secondly, I was stuck between June 19, 2017, and July 15, 2017. Literally, I let life bypass me as I was just getting by. I had sunken so low that I couldn't believe Hussein had enough courage and strength to stand by me. I was a fucking disaster, yet, it never ceased Hussein from holding my hands. With every step I took, he told me in due time that I would be somewhat okay.

He was there to breathe a little life into me every turn I made. When the little family I did have kept their backs turned on me by saying that I should get over it, Hussein blew a gasket. Instead of him blowing the gasket, it should've been me. I should've been the one to stand up for myself and how I felt. This issue resulted from being a passive-ass wife to a nothing-ass man.

I was beyond the hurt because a real man loved me daily, showing me what it is like to be loved unconditionally. I had experienced my fair share of pain while shedding numerous tears. I had a month's taste of pure happiness and the best of everything, just as I needed and deserved. Proudly, I let go of my past life and clung to my new one while rocking my badass custom-made gold diamond engagement ring. Still, I kissed my son's pictures every night before snuggling into bed—the one I shared with Hussein at our apartment.

With my past handled accordingly, I restored order to my life. I informed Hussein that I didn't want to live in my house anymore, nor did I want any ties to it. He was beyond elated with the news; he quickly told me I would move in with him until we found the perfect house. I shook my head and reminded him of the cannabis business he wanted in Colorado. I mentioned us living in Alabama for another year, stacking our money. Of course, he asked me a thousand times if I was sure, and every time I nodded while smiling. After he agreed, we placed my house on the real estate market.

A few days ago, my old boss returned my call and happily accepted my request to return. Of course, she had to fire the third human resource manager because she found a lot of weed inside her desk. Stunned, I couldn't say anything; I was thankful the chick messed up. While I had her on the phone, I thought telling her about Hussein and me was wise. Immediately, she summoned me to the job to see my ring and my facial expression—her words.

Once the dark-skinned woman in her fifties saw me, she happily cried. After getting herself together, she told me something that I had already known—Hussein's gifts and the money he paid. I sat in her office for over an hour and talked about everything I had gone through and who was there. Upon leaving her office, I was confident there would be no issues about me marrying an employee. She ensured if Hussein needed any changes made, she would be the person to do them. That way, no one could say he was getting his way because of his wife's position in the human resource department. Just as I was elated about working back at Bigco, so was Hussein.

"Oou, bitch, I can't believe the day has finally fucking arrived for you to be outta here! You have come a long way, Ava!" Allie happily screamed as we packed the last items I wanted to go with me.

Grinning, I responded, "The day is past due, my friend. Past-motherfucking-due."

"Guh, that damn Hussein hasn't stopped smiling since he slipped that engagement ring on your finger," she giggled while snatching a champagne bottle and two wine flutes off the sofa.

"Honestly, I haven't either," I voiced as I heard Charlie Wilson's "Can't Live Without You" bumping from the only car that cruised through this neighborhood, speakers high as they could go.

"He gon' wear that gotdamn song out. I swear!" Allie laughed, pouring the bubbly liquid into the glass.

Giggling, I patiently waited for her to hand me a wineglass. When she did, I sipped from the glass and jigged to the song's beat while walking towards the open door.

"Wait a fuckin' minute? Is that *my Ava*? Like my old Ava before our senior year in high school? I just know my bitch ain't back back?" Allie excitedly screamed from behind me as I danced on the porch.

The moment Hussein parked his car, damned near in front of the door, he hopped out dancing, hands in the air. As I danced to him, his brothers and Jerrard exited his car, smiling and jigging to the beat. While I danced with my fiancé, I didn't see his grandparents sliding onto the property that was soon not to be mine.

At the song's closure, Grams hollered, "Boy, you all excited and stuff. Trust me, Grandma is very happy for y'all, but grandson ... where is my stuff? I have been waiting all damn day for my six grams of weed nih."

As we laughed, Gideon hollered, "Nigga, I just know you ain't selling Grandma weed?"

Before stepping away from me, Hussein kissed my forehead, lightly chuckling. Digging into his front pocket, Hussein replied, "No, nigga, she get free weed."

Messy, goofy-ass Jerrard asked, "So, Pop Pop, you cool with her smoking now?"

Ogling his beautiful wife while licking his lips, Hussein's grandfather groaned, "Now, I am. Oh, my, I am now."

At the same time, the fellas squealed, "That's real nasty, y'all. Real nasty."

"If I wasn't opening these legs, Thaddeus, Gideon, and Hussein, y'all ugly asses wouldn't even be here," she spoke as Hussein placed the bagged weed into her hand.

"An' ladies an' gentleman, the senior Mr. and Mrs. Hampton has shut the crowd down!" Allie announced loudly, causing us to laugh.

After the laughter died, Hussein's grandmother softly asked, "Allie, may I speak to you for a second, sweetheart?"

"Yes, ma'am," my best friend said, descending the steps.

"Ready to break everything down?" Hussein inquired, walking towards me.

Shaking my head, I replied, "Allie and I have packed only the things I want to take. The appliances and furniture can stay. All I need are my son's photos and my clothes. Even the nail kit can stay. Officially, next week, I'll be back to working at Bigco Distribution Center."

Wickedly smiling, he replied, "Oh, I know."

I narrowed my eyes, tilted my head, and asked, "Hussein, what did you do?"

"Oh, nothin'," he said, swindling me into his arms.

He placed his mouth to my ear and whispered, "I just put a few grams of that gas in her desk. You wanted yo' job back, an' I had to get the chick gone so that could happen."

"Solomon Hussein Hampton!" I shrieked, smiling.

"What, woman?" He laughed. "I put just enough in her desk that wouldn't cause her to get a charge. Now, if she used Bigco Distribution as a reference, she stupid as hell."

"You know what, sir?" I giggled, shaking my head.

"What?" he sexily asked.

"You are truly a mess with your handsome self."

"But I'm yo' mess wit' yo' sexy self," he voiced, grinding on me.

As an aching pain cruised through the lower region of my stomach, I frowned while grimacing.

"What's wrong?" Hussein worriedly asked.

"My stomach is a little uncomfortable."

"You gassy?"

"No, more like cramping. It feels like my period is about to start."

"Shit, I got used to not seein' that ugly motherfu—"

My eyes grew big as I realized I hadn't seen that fucker at the beginning of the month like I usually did. Repeatedly and nervously, I lowly chanted, "Ooou. Ooou."

"Why are you ooou'ing Ava?" Hussein inquired with a raised eyebrow and hopeful eyes.

"I don't think we will see it anytime soon, Solomon," I lowly said, eyeing him.

Grinning, he hollered, "Come again?"

"Hush up," I giggled, looking around. "I need you to do me a favor."

"Anything?" he replied, eyeing my stomach.

"I need a pregnancy test."

"Shid, how many?"

"One will be fine, Solomon." I laughed.

"Anything else? Saltine crackers, soup, ginger ale?"

"Sir, I am not sick. I just need that one item. Oh, and for you not to say anything … yet, that is."

"Gotcha." He smiled before doing the beat-it-up dance.

"Stop that with your nasty ass!" Grams yelled at Hussein from her property as Allie stood a few inches away, looking conflicted.

I wonder what Grams telling her, I thought as Hussein kissed me. "I'll be back."

"Okay. Be careful," I replied, giving him my undivided attention.

"Always, baby," he happily stated.

As Jerrard, Gideon, and Thaddeus walked onto their grandmother's porch, chatting with their grandfather, Hussein reversed, speakers bumping as usual. Meanwhile, I ambled towards the porch, intrigued by Grams's deep conversation with my best friend. While my nosey behind tried to read their lips, Hussein's speakers ceased bumping as he approached the stop sign. Within several minutes of not seeing his car move or hearing his speakers, Hussein rapidly reversed, and his name was displayed across my phone's screen. On the second ring, I answered.

"Ava, baby, come to the car real quick," he rushed in an odd tone.

"Okay," I replied, hopping off the porch.

As I walked towards the curb, Allie asked, "Where are you going?"

"Nowhere that I know of. He asked me to come here for a second."

"Okay," she replied as the passenger door opened.

Grabbing the top of the door, I kneeled and asked, "What's up?"

"Sit in the seat an' close the door," he voiced worriedly.

"Hussein, what's wrong?" I inquired after I did what he said.

"Um, Allie needs to have an STD an' an HIV test done real soon," he quickly breathed.

"Whoa. Whoa. Whoa," I loudly voiced, heart racing as I observed him. "You have a lot more explaining to do before I step to her with that type of news, Solomon."

"Mo just reached out to me. He said he'd been tryin' to contact Allie. Accordin' to him, one of the chicks he bussed down raw said she got that pack, an' her pussy broke out. So, Allie needs to get checked. You gon' have to tell her that, an' I promise you, Ava, I can't be 'round when you do."

"Oh my God," I replied as I turned to look towards the Hampton's yard. Allie was walking towards Hussein's car.

"Solomon, she's walking this way. How in the hell do I tell her that shit?" I asked quickly and nervously.

"Just the way I told you, baby," he sighed as Allie knocked on the window.

Rolling down the tinted object, I tried to place a calm expression on my stunned face. It wasn't calm enough because my best friend asked me what was wrong. Instantly and lowly, I told her what Hussein told me.

Laughing, Allie looked toward Hussein's grandmother and yelled, "Grams?"

"Yes, doll face," she replied as I looked at Hussein, confused.

"You called it!"

"She called what?" Hussein and I replied in unison.

"That he was going to call with that bullshit. According to your grandmother, he did his baby's mother the same way. Once she called him, cursing him out, he stated that was the only way to get her to talk to him. With that being said, y'all, I made a horrible mistake of being careless with my body. The next day after Grams aired his bullshit ways, I had the STD and HIV tests done. All tests came back negative. To be sure my private area and mouth were gucci, I went to another clinic and had the same panels done. Clean as a whistle. As far as the HIV tests, I'm staying on top of it to ensure I'm free of that shit. So, Hussein, you tell Mo to kiss my ass. Be sure to tell him I saw my period and stop hounding me."

"How in the fuck does Grams know all of this shit?" Hussein asked Allie.

"She's friends with Mo's baby momma's grandmother and great aunt. Hell, I want to know how you don't know any of this shit about the nigga. You are a street being," Allie giggled.

"No, I'm not a street being. I sell weed. I don't dibble an' dabble wit' the niggas that live that lifestyle. I'm simply a hustler who stays the fuck out of the way an' people's business," Hussein explained.

"Oh. Well, y'all ease y'all's mind because this mouth and coochie is cleaned," she stated before dancing.

While I watched my best friend goofy, reckless behind, I asked Hussein, "What in the fuck is wrong with Mo?"

"Ava?" Hussein called in a stunned manner.

"Yes, baby?" I asked, placing my eyes on him.

"I'm just as mentally fucked up 'bout Mo than you are. I can't begin to understand this nigga's mental. One thing I know, I'm not going to entertain the nigga; he doing too much fo' me. I already cut ties wit' him on that dope tip. Nanette workin' wit' him directly. Let me go to this store because I'm anxious fo' you to piss on this test," he voiced, shaking his head as I kissed his cheek.

"Okay. Be safe," I stated, opening the door.

"Always," he responded as I stepped out of the car.

Upon closing the door, my eyes landed on my best friend. She wasn't okay as she had pretended. While strolling towards the porch, I noticed the worried expression on Allie's face as she stared into the sky. Nightly, I prayed a great man would come into her life. Just like me, she deserved a happy ending as well.

"What are you thinking about, pretty lady?" I inquired, sitting beside Allie.

"Just praying that I'm saved from one of the worst diseases in the world, Ava. I wouldn't forgive myself if I contracted something so horrible all because I was desperate and lonely. I wouldn't be able to look at myself the same if a doctor told me I had HIV. How in the hell would I be able to enjoy life the way I used to, knowing that I put myself at risk? Like how?" she inquired, dropping her head—eyes filled with tears.

Grabbing her hand, I searched her saddened peepers before softly saying, "You will be fine, Allie. All will be well, and you will not have anything wrong with your pussy or mouth other than they haven't seen a dick."

Nodding, she said, "Yeah, we are going to keep thinking and speaking positively, right?"

"Absolutely." I smiled, patting her thigh before interlocking our fingers.

Silence overcame us as we sat on the porch, deeply inhaling before exhaling. The noise around us faded away as I looked up the street, followed by looking down. I observed every house, car, and person within my eyesight. Some people were smiling, while others were zoned out in deep thought. A few people were talking on the phone, as I saw a couple walking their dog. Since living in this neighborhood, I never mingled with any people I saw. I didn't want to be around those with a healthy marriage and family who would come far just to spend time with them. I envied them; many days and nights, I wished I were in their shoes.

Now, I am in their shoes, and it feels incredible. To the point I feel as if I'm dreaming. I'm finally happy, like really happy, I thought as Hussein topped the corner of the street.

After exhaling several times, a grin crept onto my pleased face. Allie stood and said, "I'm really in a sour mood. I'm trying to get out of it, but I can't. I don't want to ruin your day, so Ava, I will leave. I hope you won't be mad at me."

As Hussein pulled into the driveway, I stood, shook my head, and replied, "I could never be mad at you. You are going through something. All I can do is ensure I am there for you so you don't tear yourself down. Just know all will be well. I love you, and I'll check on you later. Cool?"

"Cool," she voiced as I outstretched my arms.

After we embraced in a tight hug, that damn thoughtful man of mine stepped out of his car with two sets of balloons and flowers in the most uniquely designed purple vase.

"Girl, you have found the perfect man," a slightly smiling Allie announced.

"No, the perfect man found me." I praised as Hussein skipped towards the porch, eyeing me.

"I'm glad I caught you before you left, Allie," he sympathetically spoke, extending a set of balloons and flowers to my best friend.

Tears streamed down her face as she hugged him before retrieving her items. Wiping her face, Allie said, "Thank you, Hussein. I swear, the shit that some females say about you, I don't see it. I will never see it; I will always defend you because, shit, you've always been around through all of our shit. You are really a good man. You keep making my best friend happy like you've been doing. She'll never let you down. That I can promise you. Y'all have a good day. Just call me before y'all start gargling each other's bodily fluids."

Laughing, Hussein said, "Gotcha."

As we watched Allie walk to her car, shoulders slumped, I sighed. "She's fucked up right now."

"Who wouldn't be?"

"She learned a valuable lesson from Mo. She better take heed to that shit. Everything that looks good, maybe far from it."

"If I wasn't as close to you as I've been, would you have entertained me?" Hussein questioned as he wrapped his arms around my waist.

Shaking my head, I replied, "Nope."

"Why?"

"Because I would've heard about you and your ways."

"There wouldn't have been anything I could've done to get you to see differently?" he probed as Allie drove away, tooting her horn.

Gazing into his eyes, I shook my head and responded, "Absolutely nothing."

"Damn great thing Grove Land and my grandparents had one thing in common, huh?" he voiced, kissing my neck.

"Yess," I moaned.

"So, do you want to see now if you gon' be a mommy again?" he whispered against my neck as he lifted me off the ground.

"Of course." I smiled as he carried me into the house.

After closing the door with his foot, Hussein sucked on my bottom lip while rubbing on my booty. I loved how he nibbled on my lips while gazing into my eyes lovingly. I adored how his hands clutched my ass while his pinky fingers scribbled the numbers one, four, and three on my thighs. I admired how he smirked when I removed my lip from his mouth before scribbling those numbers back onto his bottom lip.

"You got me floatin' girl," Hussein softly voiced as we entered the bathroom.

"I try. I try," I teased, blushing while gently massaging his neck.

Placing me on the ground, Hussein reached into his back pocket and retrieved the pregnancy test. While he sat on the side of the tub, my shaky hands tore open the box before I ripped the plastic paper covering the desired product.

"Ava?" he lowly announced, looking at me as I unbutton my shorts.

Sliding the denim fabric and panties towards my ankles, I said, "Yes?"

"Are you nervous?"

"Nope. Are you?" I answered, sitting on the toilet as I slid the white stick between my legs.

"Yeah," he chuckled, fumbling with his hands.

"Why?" I probed, urinating on the white strips.

"Because I don't want it to say 'not pregnant'."

Eyeing him, I confidently replied, "I'm very sure it's not going to say that. We are close to another month, and I haven't been stressed. So, it won't say that at all."

"But what if it does?" he questioned as I removed the stick between my legs and placed it on the sink.

"Then, we will keep trying until we have a little Hussein or Ava." I smiled, leaning over to kiss him.

Nodding, he voiced, "Okay. Um, we just wait here until it's done, right?"

Wiping, followed by flushing the toilet, I provocatively said, "Well, I thought we could hop in the shower while we wait on those three minutes or less. Or we could just continue doing the nasty and look at the results after we finish."

Chuckling, he responded, "How 'bout we wait 'til we look at the results first? I tend to do the most wit' you."

"Whatever you want to do, sir, I'm with it," I spoke before nibbling on my bottom lip and removing my shirt and shoes.

While we waited, Hussein and I stared at one another while holding hands. The humble being was afraid; I saw it in his eyes. I wanted to speak on it but couldn't find the right words to start the speech. In time, he would know he would receive everything he'd ever wanted from us.

"Ava, I'm losin' my mind. Please look at that damn thing," he sighed heavily, running his hand down his face.

Grinning, I announced, "As you wish."

Before retrieving it, I looked at the stick. As I had told him, I was very confident that the test wouldn't say I wasn't pregnant; there were two factors against it saying so. I wanted to hold my Poker face just to ruffle his feathers; however, my Solomon was too antsy and damned near ready to lose his mind. Thus, I smiled, faced him, and extended the test.

With a massive grin, Hussein loudly said, "Woman, you pregnant?"

"Look at the test," I told him, cheesing.

After doing so, he lifted me off the toilet and happily announced, "I'm finna be a daddy!"

"Yes, Solomon Hussein, you are going to be a daddy," I happily spoke, tears welling.

"Mannn, I'm finna be yo' fine ass husband an' this lil' one handsome ass daddy," he sang, bouncing.

Busting out laughing, I voiced, "Hussein, really?"

Ceasing his movements, he gazed into my eyes and asked, "What lie did I tell?"

"Not a single one."

"Right, not a fuckin' single one," he voiced, placing me inside the tub. "Start that water fo' us, please."

"My pleasure."

After I did so, Hussein slipped into the shower, gently pulled me towards him, and breathed against my neck, "If you don't know, I'm gon' say it anyway. I'll always cherish you an' our baby, Ava. Always."

I placed my head on his chest and sincerely replied, "Oh, Solomon, I know."

Chapter XVII

Hussein

"True love is rare, and it's the only thing that gives life real meaning."-Nicholas Sparks, Message in a Bottle

Four Months Later

The woman's body and pregnancy were one confusing thing to comprehend. When Ava and I learned we would have a baby, I was under the assumption she was freshly pregnant, like a month. Turned out my baby was further along than I thought. I caught her egg slipping when we returned from Florida.

Thanks to the lovely Coronavirus, I didn't get the chance to physically be present for Ava's prenatal appointments; we had to video chat. The first appointment, I was one pissed-off nigga. I disliked the idea of being unable to shake the doctor's hand or kiss Ava while the physician checked her. Indeed, I was upset that I couldn't hold her hand as she had her first sonogram, which revealed we were having twins and that she was ten weeks pregnant.

She was so excited and happy; my baby cried. I disliked not being in the room with her to wipe her tears, rub her stomach, or kiss her forehead. However, my ill emotions ceased upon hearing our babies' heartbeats. Their beats were the best rhythms I had ever heard. I fell in love with them immediately. Since then, I have been waiting in the car while video chatting. Today was no different, except I wasn't pissed about waiting outside. While Ava checked on our twins, a girl and a boy, I ate my foot-long Club sandwich in peace.

"Oh, so that's how you will do us?" Ava laughed, holding the phone to her face as she leaned back on the examination table.

With a mouthful of food, I chuckled, "Yep. You ate yo' entire sandwich before we got here, damn near in one breath, and didn't offer me a piece of meatball. Sorry, Daddy didn't feel like sharin' wit' y'all greedy asses. I'll make it up to y'all in three hours. Cool?"

Smiling while rubbing on her large belly, she nodded. "Cool."

As I bit into my sandwich and sounded off, Ava squealed, "Hussein, you don't have to do all that, just rubbing it in my face."

"I'm doing you just like you did me last night." I laughed.

She giggled, "Oh, so we are playing that game now?"

"Right now, we are. You ate up all the damn lasagna. I only had a small portion of the container and all the salad. So, I'm hitting you where it hurts," I jokingly voiced.

As I taunted Ava with my noise antics over my thick sandwich, she sweetly asked, "Baby, will you save us a piece?"

Slowly, I said, "Nope."

Howling in laughter, she pointed at the camera and said, "I'm going to remember that when you want to eat at the buffet lines."

"When we leave, I'll buy you a sandwich," I chuckled, grabbing my soda.

"I want your sandwich, just a piece."

"Ava, you rather have a piece of my sandwich than a whole one?" I inquired before taking a large gulp of orange-flavored Fanta.

"Precisely." She smiled as three knocks sounded on the door.

Shaking my head, I exhaled, "A'ight, I'll save yo' beggin' ass a piece. An' it's gon' be just that a piece."

"Hussein," she giggled as the doctor stepped into the room, waving and greeting us.

"Ava, I just know your husband isn't eating without you and the babies," the friendly, Black male doctor in his late fifties asked jokingly.

"Yes, he is. He so mean," she playfully voiced before blowing me a kiss.

"Well, you know how to break that up, right?" Dr. Daniels chuckled.

Spitting out the sandwich, I laughed. "Dr. Daniels, don't start no mess now. I thought you were on my side."

"You know I have to be on Ava's side sometimes. So, what will you do, Hussein, be in the doghouse or save her a piece of that sandwich? You know what the doghouse includes." He laughed heartedly.

Nodding, I laughed. "Oh yeah, I know. In that case, have one of the nurses come get the rest of this sandwich; it's about six inches left."

"Happy babies, happy wife, happy life," he sang, causing me to chuckle.

At the same time, Ava said, "Preach."

"Indeed," I happily announced as Dr. Daniels began examining my fine-ass best friend turned wife.

Most people waited a while before getting married; Ava and I didn't. It wasn't as if we were planning an extravagant wedding or wanted to invite people we didn't deal with. We wanted something small and intimate with our small group. My parents, grandparents, brothers and their wives, and Jerrard and his wife were in attendance. Ava tried to include her mother, but that stubborn woman told her only daughter to kiss her ass. The one person I never thought would turn her cheeks on Ava did so. Allie made every excuse as to why she couldn't be present on our special day. My woman didn't shed one tear at Allie's behavior. Like her past hurts, she let it roll off her shoulders while laughing.

On Ava's birthday, November 8th, my mother officiated our desired wedding on the property my mother and her siblings owned. At four p.m., Ava Jane Langston was no longer; she was Ava Jane Hampton, just the way I needed her to be. At seven p.m., Ava dragged me out of bed while dangling my car keys. Rapidly, she told me to hop in the passenger seat. I didn't ask questions; I did what my wife commanded. I knew she was fuming over Allie's behavior towards her since August. She shut Ava out, which caused her great pain—even though she tried her best not to show it.

When we arrived at a packed Allie's house, Mo in attendance, Ava stormed towards her 'friend' and laid her ass out. Ava gave Allie the business that caused people to gasp and shake their heads. Ava's emotions got the best of her, and there were many times I was afraid she would air some shit out. However, Ava kept it classy in the end as she beat around the bush with what she wanted to say while occasionally looking at Mo. Once she left Allie sitting in the chair, looking dumb, she snatched off the best friend necklace and bracelet they'd had forever and slung it at her.

Her final words hit home: *"Bitch,* I will not beg a fucking soul to be in my or my children's lives. I've done that for so long. That weak-ass bitch in me is dead. Hoe, you stepped like all the other motherfucking ones did. Thus, I will keep you right where you placed yourself! Now, hoe, you can have a wonderful miserable ass life. *Me* and *mines* out this *bitch!"*

I had never heard Ava talk in the manner she did. At that moment, I knew she was over her friendship with Allie. My gut told me not to try to repair their friendship. Allie did the one thing a friend was never supposed to have done: let your friend's good fortune push you away and turn spiteful towards them. To this day, Ava and Allie do not communicate.

"Alright, everything is looking good. The twins' heartbeats are strong, as always. Mr. and Mrs. Hampton, y'all have successfully completed week twenty-four of pregnancy. Enjoy the holidays, and I'll be looking forward to my holiday photos, right?" Dr. Daniels stated calmly, snapping me out of my thoughts.

"Right," Ava and I replied.

"Have a great day, you two."

"You as well," my wife and I responded.

While my lady dressed, she said, "Guess who texted me?"

"Allie?"

"Mhm," Ava voiced, rolling her eyes.

"What she said?"

"That she needs someone to vent to."

"Are you going to talk to her?"

"Nope. I meant what the hell I said on our wedding day, Hussein. That bitch can kiss my motherfucking stretched-marked ass. She broke a promise and left me. So, fuck Allie Jockson." Ava spat, shoving her dress over her head.

"Ava, really?" I stated, shocked.

"Yep. I'm not going to sit down and hear shit a bitch gots to say about a nigga who fucked her cousin in her bed while her pregnant ass was at work. I don't give two fucks! Do you hear me? Not two fucks!"

My mouth hung open as I stared at the phone. I couldn't believe the words escaping from Ava's wet ass mouth. From the time my wife grabbed her bag of a purse off the counter and sauntered towards the front desk, I didn't say a word as she smirked. Upon hearing the receptionist give Ava an appointment date for January, my thrown-off ass exited my whip.

While I continued to stare at my beautiful, glowing wife, Ava laughed. "Close your mouth, Hussein."

"How am I supposed to do that when you dropped that scorchin' ass grease in my lap?" I voiced as I saw her stepping across one of the thresholds of the doors.

Ending the call, as I opened one of the second set of doors, I shoved my phone in my pocket and said, "Ava Hampton, I just know damn well … Allie ain't pregnant by Mo."

"She sure the fuck is. Two months, to be exact," she stated, grabbing my hand.

"So, you ain't gon' call an' get the rest of the tea?" I inquired, really wanting to know. I had to understand why in the fuck Allie placed herself in the hottest chair in the city.

"No, I'm not. It's none of my business. I can't relate to a woman who learned unpleasant things about a man. Left him alone. Alienated me for no reason. Then, turned around and started back messing around with the dude. Moved his ass into her crib, allowing the fraud motherfucker to fuck the same cousin you smashed and dashed. I don't want to hear about the foolishness," she fussed, shaking her head. "Ain't that much good dick and mouth in the world that'll have me acting like I don't have good common sense the Lord gave me. Her pussy can detach from the muscles and tissues holding it together, and I wouldn't give a good gotdamn."

Laughing, I replied, "Woman, get yo' fine ass in the car."

After I ensured Ava comfortably sat in the passenger seat, I closed the door. While moving towards the driver's side, I shook my head and pondered what was wrong with Allie's mind. I didn't want to believe she was slightly mentally challenged when we arrived at her house on our wedding night.

Hearing what she texted Ava, there was no doubt that something wasn't formatted right in her brain. She went above and beyond on some dumb shit. Unlike Ava, I wanted to know what the fuck Allie was thinking about when she decided to have Mo back in her presence. However, getting Ava to get the juicy gossip would be a task—if I pursued to know.

As I opened the door and slid into the driver's seat, Ava dryly said, "Hello."

Placing her phone on speaker, Ava looked at me and shook her head. At the same time, Jamecia, Allie's sister, ranted and raved about her sister's dealings with Mo. My nosey ass was locked in the conversation, so I didn't move my car. Ava pointed towards the gearshift before looking at the road. Chuckling, I nodded; she was ready to go.

"All I'm saying is this, that nigga Mo is going to tear my sister down. If anyone can talk some sense into Allie, it's you, Ava. It's like she's losing her mind. Now, she looks crazy because she's pregnant by the nigga, and Jori hollering she has been fucking Mo. The nigga don't want to pay no bills. Her kids can't stand him. Ava, talk to her. Bring her ass back to the land of common sense, please," Jamecia begged.

As I dropped the gearshift into the reverse position, Ava said, "Well, honey, I don't know what to tell you. Allie's grown. She pays her own bills and cares for her children, so I say do what you do because I am not doing shit. I'm enjoying my nuptials to *my husband* and enjoying *our* greedy ass *twins*. If it's not about Hussein, Solomon Junior, and Avianna, I really don't give a fuck about it. I wish y'all the best to get some common sense back into Allie. I meant every word I said a month ago. With that being said, y'all pray, be blessed, and know Ava has some type of love for y'all. Tell everybody I said Happy Holidays. Have a good one, Jamecia."

The call was clear-cut, and the response from Ava was more evident. She had wiped her hands with Allie.

Sighing deeply, Ava grabbed my sandwich from the bag and said, "Oou, babies, Daddy left us a little treat."

Placing my hand on her thigh, I sexily asked, "Shid, can Daddy get his treat when we get home?"

"I wish Daddy wouldn't get his treat when we get home; I'll just politely take it," she calmly voiced, eyeing me before she bit the sandwich.

"Oh, so you just gon' take it, huh?"

"Yep, it won't be the first, and it surely won't be the last," she spoke between chewing. As I slid my hand up her dress, Ava opened her legs and moaned.

"Don't you choke on that damn food, woman," I sternly voiced, slipping two fingers into the increasingly wet and hot pussy.

"In that case, we don't need a repeat from last night. Let me just put this sandwich up. It ain't all that, no way," she cooed after swallowing. Slowly, I moved my fingers in and out of her juicy treasure trove.

"Oou, my husband," she whimpered, fucking my fingers. I couldn't get enough of her calling me her husband; that shit did something to my soul.

"Yess, my fine ass wife," I groaned as I briefly looked at her.

"You know what today is, don't you?" she moaned, dropping the interior mirror and staring into it.

"I do." I smiled, turned on by her watching me finger fuck her vomiting pussy

"Are you going to hold your legs up for me, Solomon Senior?" she inquired, body trembling.

Immediately, I stopped my fingers from moving inside her thrusting coochie as I bellowed, "Ava Hampton, I ain't finna be in the buck nih. I'mma bend the fuck over an' grip one gotdamn ankle like I been doing. That's gon' have to be good enough."

Pussy going to town on my middle and ring fingers, my pretty wife's gorgeously pregnant body shook uncontrollably as she sexily screamed, "Husseinnn!"

That pussycat on Ava squirted out so much fluid that I mashed on the gas pedal to get her ass to our apartment. With raging hormones surging through me, my dick knocked against my boxers as I shallowly yet erotically called her name.

"I need that dick, now, husband," she cooed, unbuckling my belt and undoing my shorts.

"Ava, we in the middle of rush hour. I ain't able to indulge right now," I explained as I focused on the heavy traffic on the interstate.

"You just sit back and drive. I'll do it," she stated, climbing out of her dress.

"Ava Jane Hampton, the last time I let you get on me while I drove this car, I almost ran into an eighteen-wheeler. I ain't qualified to slide this dick in yo' big belly ass while I'm drivin' in this thick ass traffic. You are not getting on me until I park this car. My fingers will have to do until then. Non-negotiable," I sternly voiced, briefly glancing at her.

"Okay," the freaky being pouted, leaning over.

In one smooth move, Ava inhaled my entire dick into her mouth. One eyelid fluttered, resulting in me pressing the hazard lights button. While zooming off the exit that would lead us to our apartment, I enjoyed the feeling of my woman's mouth and the soft palms of her hands.

"Mhm," she provocatively voiced every time her mouth enveloped the base of my dick.

"Good Jesus," I hissed, massaging the back of her head.

Slowly dragging her mouth off my dick, she asked, "You like that, baby?"

"Like, fuck no. I love that shit," I groaned, turning onto our street.

She continued making me violate traffic rules; I yielded at stop signs when a car wasn't present. When I arrived inside the complex, I moaned, "Get on him, Ava Hampton."

"With pleasure," she spoke after deep-throating him several times.

While driving under the speed limit, I slid the seat back. Patiently, I waited for Ava to climb on her monster. When she did, I moaned, and she gasped. Placing her head on my shoulder, my wife slowly rode me. I felt every clench, every corner, and all the wetness trickling out of her before landing on my body and clothes.

"I ... love ... you," she moaned as I grabbed her romp and dug inside her.

"I love youuu," I sang, feeling her insides contracting.

"Put on that nasty playlist, turn on the speakers, and let's fuck in the parking lot," she sexily whimpered, slowly bouncing before leaning to the right, strategically rolling her hips.

Groaning, I replied, "Yes, ma'am."

Within seconds, I flipped on my amp and speakers before selecting "I Need (Sex)" by Javon Black. Upon the beat dropping, I turned up the volume and parked beside my wife's car. Meanwhile, Ava pussy popped and squirted on the dick. With my tongue deep into her mouth, I gripped her hair and jugged my dick into her clenching pretty kitty. In that damn parking lot, we fucked the shit out of each other. We rocked my whip as if six children were bouncing and moving about.

Ava's high sex drive having ass wanted to be in all sorts of positions inside the vehicle. Being the faithful and honorable husband I was and would always be, I gave her exactly what she asked for but was mindful of our children. She wanted me to dig in that pussy while holding her hand and pulling her hair; I plowed that motherfucker while holding her hand and pulling her hair. She wanted me to place my hand around her neck and spit in her mouth; I cuffed her neck and sloppily kissed her before playing with my spit before sliding it into her waiting mouth.

She asked me to aid her in turning over and slide my dick in her ass. I carefully turned my wife over, sucked on her asshole and pussy. Then, I delicately slid my dick into her ass while tapping her G-Spot with my fingers. She said fuck her; I annihilated her. She said make love to her. Thus, I would pull out of her asshole, grabbed the wet wipes, cleaned my dick, placed my wife on her back, and slowly danced in the pussy.

Once Tank's "Sexy" played, I knew Ava's sexual urges were beyond satisfied. Her once eager and amped body was slowly simmering down. By the closure of the sex jam, Ava and I had made a mess in my car and on my clothes.

After I put her dress on her exhausted body, she sweetly said, "Baby, I'm hungry."

"That ain't nothing new." I laughed. "What do you want to eat?"

"Seafood."

"From where?"

"The usual place."

"Seafood boil?" I inquired as she yawned.

"Yes."

"You wanna ride, or you wanna go in the apartment?"

"I'm riding, but you are driving my car. It's too wet in here," she cooed, eyeing me.

As I fixed my clothes, I chuckled, "I need to tint yo' windows."

"I'll be damned if you do. We are not about to fuck up my car like we be doing yours."

Analyzing her, I slowly and sexily said, "I'm gon' tint yo' windows, an' you gon' fuck the shit out of me in yo' car, my wife."

"Oou, when you say it like that, I guess you can tint them," she purred, weakly smiling.

"Woman, come on here so I can go get y'all food," I voiced, opening the driver's door.

As I exited the car, I stared into my shocked day ones faces. Before I could say anything, Gideon smiled. "Y'all are some nasty motherfuckas. Just out here in broad daylight, justa fucking. Good thang y'all live in the back of the complex, huh?"

"Yep! What *my* wife wants, she gets," I chuckled as Ava shut off the engine before stepping out of the car, smiling and waving.

"Look at her fat belly ass. Don' ate a million times and nutted good." Thaddeus joked.

"An' finna eat again," I replied, glancing at my yawning woman closing the door.

"Where y'all going?" Jerrard asked, rubbing his well-fit stomach, resulting in us laughing. He was greedy, too.

"Ava wants seafood. I have no idea what I'm gon' eat," I responded, lifting her from the ground.

"After y'all get some grub, y'all got any plans?" Gideon asked.

I looked at Ava for the answer. When she shook her head, I replied, "No. What's up?"

"Nigga, we miss yo' yella ass. We wanna hang out wit' you."

"Where y'all tryin' to go?" I asked as we strolled towards the apartment.

"Shoot ball or some."

I ceased walking and said, "Now, y'all know damn well I ain't fit to shoot no ball right nih. I have been in that damn car workin' an' gettin' worked. I don't have that type of energy. Now, we can hop on that game upstairs or pull out the cards an' talk shit."

As they laughed, including Ava, they replied, "That's good enough, brother. That's fucking good enough."

While we ascended the stairs, Gideon sincerely said, "Baby brother, I'm so proud of you. I've always been proud of you, but I am proud of you. Like, you never ceased to amaze me. You may do your thing with that weed shit, but you are solid as fuck. You damn sho' patient as hell. I'm beyond happy for you and Ava."

Turning to look at my only emotionally showing brother, I smiled. "Nigga, don't start all that cryin' an' shit. I'm not up fo' that today, either. On som' real shit, thank you, an' you know I love you too, over-emotional ass nigga."

Resuming the walk towards our destination, I felt slobber trickling down my shoulder. While shaking my head and smiling at my sleeping woman, I noticed my mother pacing back and forth in front of our door. The only time she walked like that was when her mind was heavy.

Worry consumed me as my day ones and I asked, "Momma, you good?"

"No, I'm not," she voiced, shaking her head.

"What's wrong?" we asked as Ava began to lightly snore.

"I haven't been sincere with the love of your life, Son. That's not right. I shouldn't feel negative toward a woman whose life was turned upside down. I shouldn't feel negatively towards a woman who found her way out of the pits of Hell and found the will to love again. To love my son. My handsome, independent, patient, kind, thoughtful, and soon-to-be amazing father. I should have welcomed the two of you with open arms as I did Gideon and Karen. As I did Thaddeus and Lora. Even though Jerrard is like a son, I still welcomed him and Keri. I should've welcomed the one woman I had counseled, sat with, cried with, and held when her world was destroyed. For that, I need to make amends and let the two of y'all in more than I have been. I'm sorry, Solomon. Momma is sorry that her heart wasn't into you and Ava's relationship or marriage. I'm sorry I did the one thing I was never supposed to do as a pastor—pass judgment or act as if Ava wasn't good enough for you. Truthfully, she's as perfect for you as you are for her."

"Thank you, Momma," I replied, heart filled with joy.

Blushing, Momma said, "Solomon Hussein Hampton, out of all my children, you are just like your father."

"What do you mean?" my brothers and I asked curiously.

"Just know you get that sexual nastiness from your father. Anywhere, anytime. Sometimes, I must stop him from trying to have sex in the church," she giggled. As Jesus rose off the cross, a laughing Ava rose off my body.

"Pastor Hampton, how about we dine in for lunch? I was going to eat a seafood boil, but I know a place that serves good seafood on top of other foods Hussein can eat," my wife lovingly voiced as she looked at my mother.

With a raised eyebrow and a genuine smile, Momma commanded sincerely, "One, you are to cease calling me Pastor Hampton. Momma is just fine if you wish to call me that. If not, Mrs. Hampton or Diane is fine. Another thing, I hope y'all are planning on showering and changing clothes because y'all rocked that car for quite some time."

While my day ones and Ava laughed, my face was red. I nodded. "Most definitely."

"Well, it's a date then," Momma replied as I unlocked the door.

Upon stepping across the door's threshold, I placed Ava on her feet. She observed my mother and said, "Momma Hampton, I forgive you. I would hug you, but I don't want you to scream that I'm in labor when I'm not."

I tripped over my feet as I made my way towards the bedroom. Momma gasped as my day ones laughed.

"Oh yeah, you fit in just fine with us, Mrs. Ava Jane Hampton," Momma giggled.

Yes, she does, I thought as I eyed my wobbling wife, blowing kisses to me as she tried to hurry into the bedroom.

Once I closed the bedroom door, I pulled Ava towards me. Pressing my lips against hers, I lovingly said, "Damn, Solomon Junior and Aviana Hampton got one sexy ass, smart, and well-loved momma."

Before she could respond, my mouth covered hers as my hands cruised through her dyed blonde, shoulder-length hair.

"I love you, Ava," I breathed against her lips, searching her peepers.

"I love you, Solomon Senior." She smiled, observing my eyes.

Chapter XVIII

Ava

"When someone loves you, the way they talk about you is different. You feel safe and comfortable."-Jess C. Scott

Six Months Later

My life was beautiful. Everything I prayed for I received, even though it was many years later and not from the people I shared the same DNA code or that I used to call my female best friend. Life did a complete three-sixty, and I accepted it with open arms. I held no malice towards my mother, brothers, or Allie. They had chosen the way it would be with us. I hadn't spoken to my mother since she disrespectfully told me to kiss her ass. I hadn't spoken to my brothers for close to a year. Allie and my friendship died the second she became distant because of my budding relationship with Hussein.

Since Christmas, she tried her best to step back into my life. I rejected her friendship but told her that I still loved her. I couldn't deal with anyone who placed herself into a life I had left. I couldn't be a part of that. I couldn't witness Allie going through the bullshit of marrying a well-known cheater and a non-provider. Allie and I weren't on the same level anymore. It was as if she had lost her mind. I couldn't relate to a woman willing to marry a man who cheated on her with her cousin in her bed. That was too toxic for me.

Sometimes, I thought I was wrong for rejecting her friendship, and other times, I felt it was the right thing to do—all because I sensed envy, hatred, and spite seeping from her pores whenever I saw her in stores. I didn't need that energy around my babies, husband, and self.

Simply put, I left everyone in the past who had left me. They couldn't sit in the limo of my future because God designed it for my real family—The Hamptons and me to ride in. And boy, was it one hell of a future!

As a shirtless, tatted-up, gold grill-wearing, Hussein held onto our two-month-old children while the photographer snapped many pictures. Happily, his brothers cheered, "Show out then, baby brother!"

While I ogled my fine husband, I had to tell myself to cease the urge of wanting to become pregnant so soon.

"Why are you over here moaning?" Keri giggled lowly.

"Honey, I'm on the edge of the cliff of getting pregnant again," I revealed, still eyeing my smoking hot man.

"Well, girl, if you can handle all that pressure from having kids back to back, I say, spit them out. I will still have my schedule clear every other weekend for my niece and nephew," she laughed.

Looking at the short Caucasian woman with freckles on her face, I giggled, "I said I was on the edge of the cliff, not fell off the cliff, Keri. I would lose my mind if I got pregnant within the next six months to a year. Though dear husband hates it, I am taking my birth control pills faithfully."

"Same this way," she stated, looking at Jerrard. "Jess is four years old, and I'm not pressed about having another one right now. Hell, we are dealing with him discovering himself. I can't handle another child and a boy who likes playing with his private part."

Laughing, I responded, "Oh, I've heard all about that. How's it going?"

"I don't check on him when he's bathing; his father does. I've walked in on him one too many times playing with the damn thing while staring into the mirror. He twirls it as if it's a damn baton. He thumps it. Jess abuses the damn thing. He asks questions, and Jerrard looks at me as if I am supposed to know how to answer. I don't say anything; I just stare at my curious son. All I could think was, I'm going to have a lot of grandchildren once he learns what that thing is for besides urinating."

Tears streaming down my face while I laughed, our small group strolled towards us, asking, "What's so funny?"

"I was telling Ava about Jess's discovering himself in depths," Keri's angelic voice announced as Daddy Hampton chuckled.

"Jess is going to be like his Uncle Hussein. He won't stop attacking that thing until he figures it out."

"Darnell!" Momma Hampton hollered, laughing.

"What? It's the truth?" Daddy Hampton voiced as Hussein walked towards us, inquiring about what was funny.

"Yo' daddy said Jess gon' be like you ... won't stop attacking his thang until he figures it out," Jerrard chuckled.

Loudly, my goofy husband grinned. "An' when he do, my nephew gon' be a beast wit' it, just like his uncle."

"And his granddaddy," Daddy Hampton voiced, chuckling.

At the same time, Pop Pop raspy-voiced behind announced, "And like his great-granddaddy."

Whenever Hussein's mouth got the best of him, I was embarrassed for his parents. It didn't take me long to figure out where he had gotten it from. Pop Pop and Daddy Hampton had a mouthpiece on them. They knew how to code their words so the children wouldn't comprehend. After three months of marriage to Hussein, I looked forward to the foolish things the males would say. They never ceased to amaze me. They had a bond like no other, and I loved it.

"Are y'all ready for the family photos to be taken?" the polite, professional, and extremely talented photographer questioned, removing her mask.

"Honey, I'm surprised you ain't been took that damn thing off?" Lora giggled, causing us to laugh.

"Ain't no 'Rona, thissa way!" Hussein, Jerrard, Gideon, and Thaddeus loudly voiced, causing us to laugh.

After the laughter simmered, I looked at Hussein and asked, "We should be ready, right?"

"After I put on my shirt, yes," he replied as Momma and Daddy Hampton grabbed our children while Jerrard, Gideon, and Thaddeus called for their children to come.

Once they were in our presence, the photographer placed us accordingly. We were upfront with our babies since it was Hussein's and my photoshoot. I held Solomon Junior as Hussein held Aviana. Upon the photographer being pleased with everyone in the positions she had placed them, sister girl began commanding us. I had gotten so tired of turning this way and moving that way until I was ready to tell her to chill with all the movements. For the life of me, I couldn't figure out why our photographer had us in many compromising and tiresome poses.

I was close to getting mad. However, when we saw the final products, I was happy, smiling, and crying. That damn husband of mine ensured Mica's photos were near us. Our personal pictures with our twins, two of Mica's photographs, were on the sides of us as we sat on the ground. Throughout several of our photoshoots, I wondered why Thaddeus, Gideon, and Jerrard kept interrupting. They were placing and taking away pictures of my big boy.

"Yes, we visited his grave today an' took pictures there. That wasn't enough fo' me. We needed him here today, also. I promised you that we wasn't gon' forget him, ever. Wherever we go, Mica go too," Hussein lovingly voiced before kissing my neck and wiping my tears. After wrapping my arms around his neck, I kissed him like no one was around us.

"Jess, close yo' eyes, boy!" Jerrard hollered.

Instantly, I broke the kiss and apologized.

"What are you apologizing for?" Jerrard laughed as the others did.

"That was not a kid-friendly kiss. Y'all, I am very sorry," I apologetically stated, looking into the parents' eyes.

"The kiss was not the problem. It's your husband, um … um … the second brain," Gideon voiced, hands clasped over his five-year-old daughter's eyes.

Quickly, Hussein walked towards the apple tree, laughing. Putting his hands on the tree, Hussein hollered, "Whew!"

Momma Hampton loudly spoke, "All right, grandmomma babies, go play or have a small snack. The rest of the family should be arriving soon. Then, we can kick off this family reunion."

"Lord have mercy, a full week of your sister hassling me about finding her a good man. I don't think I'm up for that, baby," Daddy Hampton fussed to his wife as I grabbed Aviana and Solomon Junior from Mommy Hampton, giggling.

"Well, good thing she won't be hassling you. I invited Deacon Smith so she can ruffle his feathers."

"Oou, woman, I thought you were a woman of the cloth?" Daddy Hampton laughed as I strolled away, still giggling at the Christian yet ordinarily loving couple.

"Honey, have you calmed down yet?" I asked, nearing Hussein.

"I'm gettin' there," he voiced, ogling me as he sat on the hammock.

"That kiss did som' to me. You have no idea how close I was to liftin' that dress an' slidin' two fingers in that ass an' two in that fat ass pussy, Ava." He laughed, extending his arms for one of our babies.

As I handed him Solomon Junior, I kissed Aviana's small forehead. I carefully sat on the hammock that had been blessed with my juices. Eyeing Hussein, tears welled as I softly said, "Thank you for thinking when the twins completely consumed my mind. Thank you for keeping every one of your promises. Thank you for being my best friend. Thank you for being my freaky, amazing lover. Thank you for being a wonderful provider and protector to our kids and me. Most importantly, Solomon Hussein Hampton Senior, thank you for being my honorable and faithful husband."

Cupping my face, Hussein kissed my quivering lips as he breathed against them. "Thank you fo' allowin' me to be in yo' world, even when it started fumblin' an' bumblin'. Thank you fo' always being on that damn porch wit' a bottle of wine. Thank you fo' havin' enough faith in me to bring you everything yo' heart desired. Thank you fo' being a true friend to me, Ava. Thank you fo' givin' me the chance to spend those wonderful years wit' Mica. He taught me what being a dad means; I know I will excel at it because of him. Thank you fo' allowin' me to be yo' protector, provider, an' children's father. Finally, Ava Jane Hampton, thank yo' fine ass fo' being the nasty, spoiled freaky woman who rushed those rings yo' finger, just like I hoped you would do."

"Oh, I rushed?" I giggled, tears slipping down my face.

Showing his golden smile, he replied, "Nawl, you didn't, but you did put me in a place to rush it. You wanted to do something, an' in return, I needed some things. Thus, I bent the fuck over because I knew you were on the road to being my wife. I received yo' answer an' one bangin' ass orgasm."

Inhaling his bottom lip into my mouth, I gripped his shirt and climbed on top of him. Breaking the kiss, he groaned, "Oh, you gettin' pretty good at slidin' on top of me while we holdin' the spoiled ones."

"Practice makes perfect," I cooed in his mouth as we heard cars coming up the dirt road.

"So, I think your dick needs to throw up in my mouth. What do you say about us slipping off to a 'store' or something for a bit, husband?" I seductively voiced while wickedly smiling.

"Mann, you wild, but um, I love it." He laughed. "Let's go find Keri an' Jerrard. Now."

"Okay," I replied, slowly climbing off him.

While we walked towards the porch, many of Hussein's male cousins hollered his name while holding up blunts and a doubled Styrofoam cup. After I cleared my throat, I lowly asked, "Hussein, why do I have the feeling that I'm not going to suck an ounce of dick right now?"

"Shiddd, that's a lie. They gon' motherfuckin' wait. Happy wife, happy life, right?" the foolish being earnestly inquired loudly as we neared his weed-smoking grandparents.

"Sure is, grandson, sure is," Grams and Pop Pop announced, eyes glowing at the sight of us.

Stepping onto the porch, we spoke and hugged many of Hussein's maternal family members. He introduced me to them but quickly told them we had to make a store run. Nearby, Keri and Jerrard spit out their drinks before extending their arms while laughing. Apparently, they knew what a quick store run meant, for which I was thankful.

As we descended the stairs, Keri hollered, "Over the cliff?"

Tripping over my feet, I laughed. "Nope, still on the edge of it."

"What does that mean?" Hussein inquired, picking me up as his cousins tried their best to get him to come closer to them.

After he replied he'd be back, I said, "It means I'm thinking about coming off birth control to get pregnant."

"Oh, really?" He smiled, unlocking my car before opening the passenger door.

"I said, I'm thinking about it."

"What can I do to speed up that process an' turn it into a yes?" he questioned, eyeing me.

"Become more concrete by solidifying your cannabis business in Colorado."

"I don't want to move to Colorado."

"We don't have to move there for you to own a business there, Hussein."

"True."

"So, what do you propose we do because, um, I am waiting on som' new—"

"Solomon!" an older lady shouted from behind us.

"Ma'am?" my husband called as we looked towards the direction the woman had called him from.

"Where are you going?" she inquired as his mother and a few more people resembling his mother marched towards us.

"We headed to the sto'," he lied.

"Y'all ain't a bit mo' headed to the sto'. Boy, I see what yo' shorts look like," one of the older men chuckled, which resulted in me turning my head to softly giggle.

"Seems like more babies will arrive from them two, huh, sister?" the oldest woman asked Momma Hampton.

"Could be," she replied happily.

"Well, nephew, before you head onto the sto' yo' wife owns," the man chuckled. "We want to tell you that we've decided that yo' wish is granted."

As I faced them curiously, Hussein excitedly asked, "Fo' real?"

"Yep," the siblings replied in unison.

After he thanked them, one by one, they hugged him before hugging and introducing themselves to me. The last one to leave our presence was the uncle, who knew precisely what Hussein and I were up to. He was sure to tell us not to take too long because they wanted to learn more about 'Mr. and Mrs. Solomon Hussein Hampton Senior and their plans for the future'.

Highly intrigued, I asked Hussein, "What wish has been granted, honey?"

"Me buildin' you a house on this land, just how you want it." He smiled.

Stunned, I sat my ass in the passenger seat with my mouth open. I didn't close it until Hussein started the engine while pushing up my chin.

"So, is that why you have been pussyfooting with the business plans for the cannabis shop?"

As he dropped the gearshift into the reverse position, he nodded. "Yes. I wasn't sure how I would pull it off. I had to take everything into perspective, the house buildin', you, our kids, our workin' hours, an' sitters fo' the kids. I wasn't sure if kickin' off the cannabis business was the best thing right now."

"How about this … you tell me what you want to do, and I'll work around you."

Pressing on the brakes, Hussein shook his head and sternly said, "Oh fuck nawl, that's not how this works between you an' me. You don't work 'round me. I work 'round you. So, I need to ask you: what do you want to do, Ava? Don't say whatever as long as we are together. That's not an answer. What do my wife want besides a healthy an' happy marriage?"

Seeing what was happening, I bit my bottom lip and said, "I'm simple, Solomon, very simple. I want the big house, the kids, the loving husband who knows where home is. I want to cook breakfast before I go to work and have dinner ready for you to take to work before I get off. I want to aid my husband in raising our kids. I want a simple life, Hussein. However, I must also be willing to compromise with your wants. So, no, our marriage isn't solely about what I want. You have wants, too, and you should fulfill them. Wherever we are, we will always be home because we are there together."

Shoving the gearshift into the park position, he eyed me as he sincerely announced, "Ava, believe it or not, I want a simple life, too. Everything you want, I need it. So, baby, please tell me what you need me to do? Either way, I'm gon' be happy as hell because you mine an' always will be."

"Hussein, I will always want to see you win. I will always cheer for you. You've been talking about this dispensary since the first time I had a conversation with you. I am not going to get in the way of your dreams. I will work around you because you are the head of our household. You are my husband. I follow you because you know how to lead, honey. So, this decision is on you, not me, baby. I support you fully," I soothingly voiced, gazing into his eyes.

"If *I* go through wit' ownin' a dispensary, you *ain't stayin' at home wit' our* kids. *We* findin' someone to care fo' them while *we* gone. Let me rephrase it so you know the severity of my statement, Ava Hampton. If *I* have to be in Colorado or any other state, *you* comin' wit' *me*. If *you* get sick an' can't go, guess what? *I'm not leavin' you*. Do *I* make myself clear?" he slowly announced, searching my eyes.

Jesus, this man here. This man here, I thought as tears welled, and I nodded. "Yes."

"Now, that's out of the way; I guess I just decided. I'm gon' start the process of buildin' yo' house. We not movin' out of state unless you want to. If we have to travel, often, then we gon' be eatin' ass an' fuckin' all over the country, often," he seriously said, dropping the gearshift into the drive position, still eyeing me.

"Yes, sir," I humbly voiced, presenting my super attractive, knight-in-shining armor with the Throat-a-lator 5.0.

We didn't make it far before Hussein placed my car in the wooded area. As I hit that head just as he loved, Hussein moaned, "Baby, you know when you turn up, I will be amped than a motherfucka. Now, keep in mind how nasty you want to get because I have plenty of people I must introduce you an' our lil' ones too. So, honey, you know you be dead ass weak by the time I nut in you."

Gazing into his eyes, I sexily said, "I just want to suck an ounce of dick before it throws up in my mouth."

"Ain't no way you tryin' to suck an ounce of dick an' swallow nut, you gobblin' the entire thang. Oh my God, baby, you trynna get fucked in every hole," he groaned, running his hands through my hair.

After slowly sliding my mouth off his delicious dick, I sexily announced, "Oh, honey, this is just the pre-game. Once we leave here and our children are soundly sleeping in their cribs for the night, we will sing way better than those who entertain millions on a Super Bowl game night during halftime."

"Ohh my Goddd," he sang, causing me to laugh. "In that case, you need to come off this dick because it's finna get real nasty in this car."

Nodding, I pouted, "But I don't want to stop sucking, honey."

Sliding me upwards, Hussein gazed into my eyes while lifting my dress. As he slipped two fingers into my wet, pretty kitty, Hussein savagely said, "I know you don't, but if I let you continue, you wasn't gon' be worth a damn. You know I was gon' slide off in that pussy an' long stroke it to the point you would throw yo' birth control pills out of the window. Then, I was gon' cuff yo' neck just the way you like, play wit' my spit, an' let it slide off in yo' mouth. Then, I was gon' beat yo' back loose before I slowly put it back together by dancin' in that juicy, hot baby maker."

"Husseinn!" I hollered before moaning while rocking on my husband's fingers.

Gripping my hair, he pressed his face to mine and asked, "What I told yo' fine ass 'bout hollerin' my name like that, Ava Hampton?"

Heat consumed me from my head to my toes as my body shook uncontrollably. I weakly eyed him and slowly answered, "Oou, you better fuck your wife before we leave this oh-so-secluded spot."

"Is that what you want me to do?" he questioned, handsomely smiling as I grabbed his dick.

"No, that's what I *need* you to do," I whined as he removed his fingers, placing them in between our lips. As we sucked off my juices, I slid down my husband's extraordinary dick.

"Fuck, Ava," Hussein groaned as I slowly bounced while gasping.

"You mine, guh," he voiced, staring into my eyes. "Do you understand?"

Overly aroused, I nodded while hollering, "Yesss, Hussein, I understood! Even way back then!"

Before I knew it, we were in the passenger seat without clothes. Hussein had his face buried between my legs as my feet touched the ceiling of my car. After getting full from his buffet lines, Hussein put that dick to work as my voice box performed well.

"Oh God," I squealed as my pussy leaked massively, as it had always done every time Hussein touched it.

He smiled and pressed his nose to mine, beating up the walnut-sized erogenous spot. "Now, what He got to do wit' this, Ava?"

"Everything!" I loudly moaned as my toes curled. "He gave me you, Solomon Senior. He gave me my walking papers from misery, sadness, loneliness, and pain. He gave me us. He gave me our kids. He gave me a family that loves me, calls me just to say hey, do you want to go out for lunch, or whatever the hell they want to do. He gave me Lora, Keri, and Karen because he knew I needed sincere females who wouldn't hurt me by leaving me for no reason. He gave me overprotective brothers Jerrard, Thaddeus, and Gideon. He finally gave me the life I deserved. The life I love more than anything in this world. The life I adore and would kill a motherfucker over, Solomon Senior. I fucking love youuu. If you haven't noticed or ever paid close attention to the hints I'd been throwing out since the first few weeks we started sleeping together, I've always fucking loved you! This life we have created, I'm in love with it!"

Still driving dick through me like an eighteen-wheeler slamming its front end into the back end of a crazy driver that dared to pull in front of it, Hussein whispered, "Cum on this dick so I can nut in you. Then, we are going to spend two hours here. After that, we will pack up our babies before leaving for Florida. We are going to enjoy our vacation and our children. You gon' nut fo' Daddy, baby, so I can spend som' money on you an' our kids?"

I pulled my hair as I moved my head from side to side. When I came, I screamed, "Yesss!"

"I love you, Ava," he whispered, gazing into my eyes. Meanwhile, my body trembled tremendously before going rigid.

"I love you, Solomon Senior," I breathed, biting my bottom lip.

"Finally, I have you, Ava. I'll always be yours, beautiful one," Hussein voiced as tears slipped down his face. At the same time, my pretty kitty did what it did best—threw up while catching every drop of my husband's protein shake.

"Yes, you finally have me as I have you, Solomon Senior. I'll always be yours, my handsome husband," I softly replied, wiping his tears before kissing his masterful lips.

About the Author
TN Jones

Born and raised in Alabama, TN Jones still lives with her daughter. Growing up, she always had a passion for reading and writing, which led her to create short stories during her teenage years. In 2015, TN Jones began working on her first book, *Disloyal: Revenge of a Broken Heart*, which was previously titled *Passionate Betrayals*.

TN Jones writes in the following Urban/Interracial fictional genres: Women's romance, Street Lit, Mystery/Suspense, Dark Erotica/Erotica, and Paranormal.

Published novels by TN Jones: *Under the Mistletoe: Love from a Hood Pharmacist, If My Walls Could Talk, Her Mattress Buddy, Santa Sauce: A Kinky Christmas Tale, I'm All Yours, Do Me Baby, Tasty Love, Acquainted & Possession, In the Arms of a Devil 1-2, 'Tis the Season: Smitten by an Assassin, 'Tis the Season 2: Loving the Opp, 'Tis The Season 3: Assassin vs Assassin, Thug Passion, Extraordinary Love, Entanglement: Gutta Love Lifestyle, His Little Pussycat, The Opp's Daughter, You Oughta Be with Me, Tainted Love, Enticed by an Alabama Felon, Rehabilitating a Hustler's Shattered Heart 1-2, Dark Tunnel of Pleasure, 13 Days of a Hot Girl Holiday, Deck His Halls, Wet Dreams on Lockdown: The Captain, The Uncircumcised King, Entangled in Toxicity 1-2: The Multi-*

millionaire's Daughter, Courtesy of a Ruffneck Foe I-III: An Arranged Marriage Romance, Call Me Mr. Nasty, & Lemme Feel It.

Novels returning to Amazon: *By Any Means: Going Against the Grain 1-2, The Sins of Love: Finessing the Enemies 1-3, Caught Up In a D-Boy's Illest Love 1-3, *Choosing to Love a Lady Thug 1-4*, Is This Your Man, Sis? Side Piece Chronicles, *Just You and Me: A Magical Love Story*, Yearning for that Young Hood Love 1-2, A Sucka for a Thug's Love, *Chocolate Enchantress*, I Now Pronounce You Mr. and Mrs. Thug 1-3, Disloyal 1-3, The Power of Love: Ecstasy from a Hoodlum, Barcoded Pu**y, Rock Me Tonight: A Nympho's Tale, Impatient, Captivation: In Love with My Destroyer; Captivation 2: My Lover, My Destroyer, In Love with a Zulu Mafia Godfather 1-2, and *Insatiable 1-2*.*

Anthologies: *Big Girls Love Dope Boys Too* (Genesys & Adonis)
Wattpad: *I Hate that I Love You & One Tangled Love*

Collaboration novel: *Dating a Female Goon* with Ms. Biggz

Thank you for reading, *Tasty Love*. Please leave an honest review under the book title on Amazon and Goodreads.

For future book details, please visit any of the links below:
Amazon Author page:
https://www.amazon.com/thetnjones
Bluesky: @udptnjones.bsky.social
Facebook: https://www.facebook.com/udpthetnjones
Goodreads:
https://www.goodreads.com/author/show/14918893.TN_Jon es:
Instagram: @udptnjones
Pinterest: @thetnjones
TikTok: @thetnjones
Wattpad: @taeathewriter4

Made in the USA
Columbia, SC
24 February 2025

54299955R00143